Life's A Bitch

Until You Become One

Joy Lanian

This is a work of fiction. Names and characters are the product of the author's imagination and any resemblance to actual persons, living or dead, is entirely coincidental.

The views expressed in this work are solely those of the author and do not necessarily reflect the views of the publisher, and the publisher hereby disclaims any responsibility for them.

ISBN: 978-0-244-66435-0

PublishNation
www.publishnation.co.uk

Acknowledgements

I'd like to say a massive thank you to Emma and Rebecca, my daughters, and to Paul, my husband.

To Jayne Heyes, Sue Greenwood, and Catherine Greenall for your endless support.

And to Gwen and David Morrison of PublishNation.

Chapter 1

Joanne Harris made her way speedily down an endless stretch of corridors that led to the heavy wooden doors and the street outside. The air felt damp and cold as she stepped out into the daylight. The tears she'd held back until now drifted down her face as she stood shivering uncontrollably.

The last weeks had been fraught and filled with dread of this day arriving. Mr Reed, the family solicitor, had kept her buoyant with some sage words during their brief phone calls. The last time they spoke, he told her to keep her makeup simple, dress well on the day and, above all, make a stab at keeping emotions in check when answering the judge's questions. An easier task, she thought, would have been to go skydiving without a parachute! But at least the degradation of James and his girlfriend being present on the day seemed no longer an issue.

Joanne had rummaged feverishly through her wardrobe on the eve of her ordeal and plucked the black wool two-piece suite from its rail. Bought some weeks back purely as it was classic and well cut, and paired with a crisp white blouse, patent-heeled shoes, her nan's pearls and earrings to match, she almost knew it would be perfect.

She straightened her back, pulled in her tummy and gave one final check in the full-length mirror the following morning when she was ready, then continued to the car where Gill waited. Her scatter-brained flatmate had stated firmly that she would take time off work and accompany Joanne to court. Joanne had argued there was no need but how grateful she was for that act of kindness when they arrived at the grim-looking courthouse in the centre of her home town.

Mr Reed was waiting for them in the marble-floored corridor. He greeted Joanne with an outstretched hand and a smile, then with a heavy sigh he broke the news that the hearing was in an open court, not a private session as he'd been led to believe.

'Not to worry,' he muttered, as he accompanied the girls into the courtroom where they claimed their seats in the crowded, benched area to await the judge's arrival.

All too soon the chattering room fell silent. Everyone stood, as the well-turned-out, tall, rather cross-looking judge majestically made an entrance and took his seat in a raised oak-panelled pulpit.

Joanne and Gill listened to the cases called before hers. It seemed that infidelity, domestic violence and verbal abuse were the most common grounds for divorce. Joanne gained slight relief from the knowledge that she hadn't been alone in all she'd gone through during the four years she'd been married to James.

Joanne's name was called; it was her turn to step into the dock, where she nervously stared at the stern-faced judge who seemed to be glaring at her with judgmental eyes as she stood before him.

Then, with an edge to his voice, his questions and comments came like thunderbolts and were hugely intrusive. She gritted her teeth as her most intimate details were dragged out of her, whilst trying not to lose what little dignity she had left. Wasn't she supposed to be the victim in all this, she thought savagely. The judge obviously didn't see it that way and did his utmost to disprove what she said, provoking her anxiety.

There was a long pause in the interrogation, which left her trembling slightly. White-faced, she stared as the judge peered at her over his half-moon glasses and uttered the words, 'Right … divorce nisi granted on this day.'

Relief left her drained; she slumped into the seat next to her friend after stepping down from the dock.

'You OK?' Gill asked, handing her a tissue from her bag.

'I will be when we get out of here,' Joanne replied weakly, giving a sniffle then a noisy blow of her nose.

After visiting the loo, Gill joined Joanne on the terrace at the top of the steps leading to the street below. Joanne's brief moment of solitude had been welcome and she'd gained some clarity about what this all meant now.

'You OK?'

'A bit shaky, but apart from that, I think so… I'm just glad Mum and Dad didn't come as planned, I had no idea the judge would drag up so much dirt in front of all those people.'

'I must say you managed to stay remarkably in control. I would have gone to pieces as soon as the judge opened his mouth,' Gill said, as they started to descend the slippery, rain-sodden steps.

Joanne attempted a brief smile as they linked arms and supported one another. 'You're a gem for bringing me. I couldn't have done it without you.'

'My pleasure!' Gill grinned then scanned the road ahead. 'Can you remember where I parked my car? I'm buggered if I can.'

Joanne pointed to an adjacent road. 'Mm, I vaguely remember turning down there. Could I ask a huge favour? Could we make a slight detour on the way home? There's a small matter I need to attend to before we head back to Southport.'

'Sure,' Gill nodded, then beamed as she spotted her battered old Vauxhall estate in the distance.

The car headed off after a couple of problems getting it started, 'Damp weather plays havoc with the old girl,' Gill complained, putting her foot down hard on the accelerator, revving the engine noisily until the car shot off at speed.

Joanne gave directions then spilled out all she had in mind causing a frisson of tension to spiralled down Gill's spine and her face paled. But by the time the car took the corner of the cul-de-sac and Joanne's old house came into view at the far end of the street, she'd calmed down.

James had refused to attend the hearing. He'd bellowed the news acidly at her down the phone the night she rang to enquire when she could collect the last of her belongings from the house. 'Ring me at work when it's over, let me know the outcome.' He could barely control his temper. 'I'll tell you when it will be convenient.' Then there was silence. A click and he was gone. His voice had once again ignited fear and tears and left Joanne drained.

Joanne knew full well where he'd be right now – in his office drinking a five-year-old malt, awaiting her call. As for Paula…rumour had it she still worked at the salon where they had both worked until the day Joanne went into hiding.

Joanne had felt sorry for Paula in the early days when they first worked together. Numerous times she had persuaded her to come for tea after a gruelling day of difficult clients. Paula was eighteen years old, on her own, living in a bedsit; it couldn't have been easy. James seemed not to mind Paula arriving unannounced; he even volunteered her a lift home at the end of the night, to which Joanne never attached much significance. In hindsight, she realised his kindness had been stimulated by the possibility of getting his leg over. Paula had been only too willing to comply, it seemed.

What Paula didn't realise was that there'd been numerous other conquests just like her in the time that Joanne had been married to James.

'Mondays were always mayhem at the salon. Pensioners day, so Paula will be knee-deep in curly perms and blue rinses by now,' Joanne said dryly. Both girls' hearts raced as the car halted outside the four-year-old detached house.

The driveway was empty. Joanne leapt from the car, unlatched the ornate iron gates, dragged them open and prompted Gill to drive swiftly down the side of the house until the car was virtually out of sight, avoiding any suspicion from the neighbours.

Joanne assumed that James had changed the locks, so she veered to the rear of the house and grabbed a brick from the pile stacked neatly against the fence. She clambered hastily onto the rickety wooden bench beneath the dining-room window. Adrenalin surging though her veins, she threw the brick and smashed a small window.

'What the fuck!' a shocked Gill shrieked, louder than she'd meant to.

'Shhhhh! Be quiet,' Joanne hissed, whilst placing her hand through the jagged-edged frame and lifting the catch on the larger lower window. Then she clambered into the house.

The air felt stagnant as she made her way across the kitchen to unlock the back door to let in her now-quaking friend. They both stood stock-still and took in the sight of a sink full of unwashed pots, an un-swept floor, overflowing reeking bin and a chopping board covered with toast crumbs – remnants of a hurried breakfast, no doubt .How times had changed, Joanne thought resentfully! Paula's domestic skills left much to be desired – but then a curvaceous eighteen-year-old didn't need domestic skills where James was concerned!

The house appeared soulless as she stood there and she remembered the aromas that had once drifted through it and how orderly it used to be. Joanne had conjured up this moment countless times; she'd planned the whole thing in her mind's eye to the very last detail but hadn't anticipated how chaotic the memories and feelings would be once she was here again. It felt like a freshly-opened wound.

Time was pressing and she could see that Gill was quaking, so she kicked off her high-heeled shoes and began to scan the contents of the kitchen cupboards. She set Gill the task of loading all the decent kitchen equipment and crockery into the car. Most important, she pointed out, were her Denby dinner service, Le Creuset pans and her Kenwood mixer, all bought for her by her parents.

Gill's eyes were like saucers as Joanne continued to delegate, but then she managed a weak smile once she got stuck into the task at hand.

Joanne trod silently through the rest of the house, willing herself to be calm as her heart pounded. Painful memories flooded back: times when James, in a rage, dragged her back down the stairs as she tried to escape his vileness. In an unprovoked attack, he would launch an onslaught of punches and kicks until she fell to the ground. She recalled how she would lie there long after he'd finished, unable to escape.

All that was behind her now, she told herself sternly, and hopefully one day she'd stop remembering altogether.

As she reached the top of the stairs, the master bedroom came into view. Beads of sweat leaked from her brow and her jaw tightened as she turned the handle and the door creaked open.

Inside the room the air felt thick and smelled of stale tobacco and unwashed bedding. It appeared shambolic.

It had taken a mere three days for James to move Paula in after Joanne had left but she knew that it was just a matter of time before he began to tire of her. James was a man of little tolerance and a very short fuse. Right now Paula was exciting eye-candy and gave him back a feeling of youth. But once the honeymoon period began to wane, this slovenliness would not be tolerated.

The bed lay unmade, there was a half-filled ashtray on the bedside table, and Joanne's once orderly dressing table was cluttered with expensive toiletries, hairbrushes and a grubby, well-used makeup bag. The laundry basket overflowed in its new place under the bay window and Joanne noticed the goose-down duvet, pillows and bedding (a wedding gift from her parents which was always kept exclusively for guests) lay in a crumpled heap on the bed.

How clever they must have thought they were, being so self-serving and ruthless, deceiving her those last months, thinking her too weak to wreak any sort of revenge, Joanne cried out in the silence of her old bedroom. But here she was now, doing just that! Seeing all this evoked a toxic anger that suddenly engulfed her, replacing the anxiety and fear that had filled her only moments before. In a moment of madness, she whipped off the Harrods bedding, unplugged the two gold bedside lamps, wrapped them in the duvet, scooped up the parcel and legged it down to the car. Anger was now accelerating inside her like steam in a locomotive, spurring her on.

On her return, she took the stairs two at a time then opened the airing cupboard on the landing and emptied the contents onto the floor. She threw all the expensive towels and bedding over the banister then bundled the inferior ones back into the cupboard.

Not an item of hers was in the wardrobes and drawers. By the looks of things he'd binned the lot – or Paula had in a fit of jealousy.

It wasn't long before Joanne and Gill began to beam at one another, as Gill helped carry out the occasional tables that James insisted Joanne couldn't have. Before long the car was loaded to the hilt.

'Time to make tracks! Start the car, Gill. I have one last thing to do,' Joanne said, surveying the place one more time.

Desperate to get away, Gill bolted from the house and climbed into the car.

Joanne took a pair of scissors from the kitchen drawer and climbed the stairs one last time to the wardrobe where Paula kept her clothes. All those lovely things James had bought her, trying to impress! Designer labels, price tags still intact on some. In a frenzied state, Joanne started to chop and slash at Paula's clothes like some mindless character from a Hitchcock movie. When she stopped she stood back, tearful and breathless, to observe all she'd done. Not one article was left intact. She fled down the stairs, plucked her bag and shoes from the chair and joined Gill.

Both girls' hearts pounded as Gill hit the accelerator and the car roared off the driveway onto the open road. It no longer mattered what the neighbours saw as they watched from behind their net-curtained windows; the deed was done!

'God, that was fucking scary,' Gill roared, banging her hands noisily on the steering wheel as they passed fields filled with cows and sheep. Frustratingly, they were forced to slow down by a tractor chugging along at ten miles an hour on the drive back to Southport. Gill's face suddenly paled. 'What if James phones the police? Can we go to jail for what we've done?'

'"Officer, my wife's broken into her own house and stolen her own belongings." Don't be stupid. I just wish I could be there to see their faces when they arrive home from work. Can you imagine?' Joanne quipped.

'What about what you did to her clothes?' Gill snorts out the words.

'James is all too aware how bloody lightly he's got off today. I could quite easily have claimed half his business as well as half the house, but that would have meant the divorce dragging on for God knows how long. I wanted rid as quickly as possible. So no matter how much Paula throws tantrums or protests, I don't think James will be stupid enough to risk ruffling my feathers more than he has already. Plus you're forgetting one thing: he still has no idea where I live.'

Some time later the car drew onto the hard standing outside the girls' flat and both of them expelled a huge sigh of relief that they were finally home. As they climbed from the car, it struck Joanne that she'd at last managed to cross the bridge between her two worlds and survived.

Chapter 2

The following day, a slow smile developed on Joanne's face as she sat on the couch clutching a much-needed mug of tea and surveyed all her hard work.

She was glad now that she'd taken a few days off work to sort out her rescued belongings and had given the flat a much-needed once-over. How lovely everywhere looked and smelled: the fresh flowers in her nan's glass vase; the smell of *boeuf bourguignon* wafting through as it simmered on the stove; the table laid with decent crockery for a change. This was a far cry from how it was some weeks back when she'd first moved in.

That was two weeks before Christmas, to be precise. How full of guilt Suzy and Gill were, she recalled, leaving her to fend for herself at that time of year but, as Joanne pointed out, families came first at Christmas and they were not to worry about her.

Judging by the silence that filtered through the building after they'd left, she realised most of the tenants in the other flats had taken off somewhere too.

She remembered vividly that snow landing on her bedroom window awakened her on Christmas morning, so early that it was still dark when she opened her eyes. A blizzard must have started and her breath left a trail in the air as she lifted her head to glance round the darkened room. She pulled the covers tightly over her, hoping they might induce more sleep, but they didn't; thoughts of Christmases long gone filled her head as she lay in the stillness of the room.

She was an only child; her grandparents, parents, aunts and uncles had all spoiled her lavishly at that time of year. Her parents' house was usually filled with laughter on Christmas Day. The smell of turkey cooking; people popping in and out like yo-yos as their door was open to everyone. How simple Christmases were back then.

Joanne didn't like uncertainty so she had been straight with the girls about her marital situation from the start when she went to view the shared flat.

'My life's not as straightforward as you might think,' she had said, rubbing her forehead and shuffling nervously in her seat. 'My husband doesn't know where I am – and he can't know! Until the divorce comes through, his threats to harm me physically, should he find, me don't bear thinking about.'

At that point the girls looked quite guarded but Joanne was determined to continue. 'He's violent and volatile at times,' she'd spluttered. 'Four years married… four years of having to cope with his controlling, brutal ways and his faithlessness.' The words fell from her mouth once she'd started. 'To everyone we were the perfect couple but behind closed doors life was a living hell, to be perfectly honest…'

The girls were surprised at how honest she was being. 'I learnt the art of using theatrical makeup, scarves, baggy clothes – anything to disguise the bruising, broken ribs and fat lips so no one would notice. But the art of shutting off when he was abusing me wasn't so easy. I used to cry silently and became a sort of Stepford wife, without the smile. He'd sucked the very being from me at the end.'

'Bloody hell! Couldn't you have gone to the police or your parents? Surely there was someone who could have helped?' Suzy's voice cracked with emotion.

'In the beginning my parents quite liked him. He was older than most men I'd dated; he had all the qualities parents make a mental note about when faced with a prospective son-in-law –smartly turned out, engineering business. But then a sequence of events changed their mood towards him. He brought me home quite late one night, knowing full well my parents had imposed a strict curfew. Another time, when my parents declined permission for me to stay at his house after a party, James flew into a ferocious rage and argued back! There was something about him that Mum didn't like and she told me to be careful.

'How perceptive she was, but I was young, headstrong, and in love. As far as I was concerned, Mum was being overprotective – maybe a little menopausal.

'I stupidly told James, expecting him to laugh it off, but instead he became extremely angry and bellowed that my parents were trying to cause trouble between us. We had to be strong! Stick together! Ignore them. Then the day we married, James made it perfectly clear I was to see my parents as little as possible and they were never to visit our house.'

Tears rolled down Joanne's cheeks at the recollection and the kindness the girls had shown her. Gill even hugged her; a box of Kleenex was pulled from the cupboard, a glass of wine was poured.

'I was fearful of disobeying him,' Joanne continued. 'But being disloyal to parents who had only ever shown me love was the hardest thing I ever had to do. By then, though, I suppose I was beyond redemption.

'In four years there was very little contact with my parents, even though they only lived a stone's throw from the house. Each time they called round, James was insistent that I wanted nothing more to do with them. Then one day they stopped calling altogether,' Joanne said sadly.

'When the abuse began, I was too ashamed to go to them and admit they'd been right and I'd been wrong. I imagined them gloating or saying "made your bed, girl, lie in it." Can you imagine the humiliation?

'There was even a time I mustered up enough courage to tell the police but they were useless… less than useless, to be brutally honest. A stout, bald-headed sergeant with fingers like sausages enlightened me to the fact it was a domestic issue unless there was enough medical proof that James had assaulted me. Meaning I literally had to be a mangled-up mess in an alley before they'd take me serious and do something about it.'

'So, how in the end…How *did you* manage to get away?' Suzy asked.

'It was just another Sunday where James spent the afternoon in the pub with his cronies, drinking heavily and playing pool. As usual he came home worse for wear. I read his expression as soon as he opened the door then, in an unprovoked attack, I bore the brunt of another beating. Much later, as I lay there numb with shame in the darkness of the bedroom, his snores echoing in the room, I couldn't understand how he could sleep so soundly knowing he'd desecrated my body,' she explained to them.

'Thankfully my pillow muffled my sobs on those occasions. His rages were getting far worse, the beatings more severe…I hated and despised him so savagely and at times I envisaged killing him, brutally, in the middle of the night whilst he slept.'

The girls were left speechless by that remark.

'I knew I had to muster the courage from somewhere and get away. I decided that was my last beating! The next morning I heard him wake. He made his way round to my side of the bed. I lay perfectly still. He said nothing, just looked at me then wandered off to the bathroom. I heard him shower, heard him dress in the next bedroom where he kept most of his cloths. The smell of percolating coffee wafted through the house when he was downstairs. I heard him make a brief phone call, then the front door slammed shut forcefully and his car raced off down the road.'

Joanne remembered telling all her darkest thoughts to those two strangers that day when she came to view the flat. She decided instinctively it was where she wanted to live. There'd been a connection between all three of them; she had felt that she was reaching out at long last.

The girls topped up her glass with wine and urged her to continue.

'I became semi-delirious, like I was walking a fine line between bewilderment and heightened consciousness as I lay curled up under the bedclothes. When I was sure he'd gone, I threw back the duvet and peered through the half-drawn curtains to double check. It was then I caught sight of myself in the mirror and recoiled in horror! My face was almost unrecognizable: my eyes were two swollen slits; my lips and nose caked in dried blood, and my jaw felt fragile. I was trembling from head to toe and wondering if anyone really cared anymore.'

The girls' faces paled.

'My instinct was to climb back into bed and regain the foetal position, a thing I seemed to always do when I was filled with that amount of fear and hopelessness. I gasped in disbelief as I looked at my fragile bruised body. What had I done to deserve that?

'The thought of a doctor looking at me filled me with horror. It was far too humiliating but it seemed that was the only option open to women like me if they want to report their abuser.'

The girls stopped her, flung their arms around her and gave her an emotional hug.

At that point Joanne got up and went into the kitchen to stir the *boeuf bourguignon* and make another cup of tea, then continued to reminisce when she sat back on the couch.

'From nowhere a healthy throbbing anger started to gather inside me. I climbed into the shower and let the warm, soothing water ease the parts of my body that were the most painful. My right eye was virtually closed; my jaw was beginning to stiffen, and I seemed to hurt everywhere. After showering I rooted out some painkillers, threw on a loose-fitting track suit, stepped into my loafers and wrapped my duffle coat round me, pulling the hood well down over my face. All the time, I kept checking through the half-drawn curtains that the coast was still clear.

'Eventually I conjured up enough courage to go out into the empty street. I prayed to God that no one was watching as I shuffled the short distance to my parents' house, only stopping briefly a couple of times to reassure myself no one was following me. It was nearly four years since my parents had last set eyes on me.' Joanne struggled to speak as she cleared her throat.

'Imagine the horror on their faces when they opened the door and saw the daughter they thought they'd lost standing there, battered, bruised, a shadow of her former self!'

Joanne blinked back her tears at the recollection of that second when the door opened. 'The look on my dad's face…the anger…the pain as I told them everything and begged their forgiveness. It was a perfect time for "I told you so's" but none ever came, bless them! Instead I felt a huge surge of emotion that overwhelmed me.

'There was an eruption of tears, laughter and emotional hugs – nothing but empathy, kindness and enormous relief. I'd come home at long last.

'"Why didn't you tell us?" my dad asked. "Why didn't you come home before now – we would have helped! We truly thought you hated and despised us for some unknown reason. But we never imagined anything like this was going on."

‘My mother sobbed uncontrollably as I explained how frightened, ashamed and weak I’d become. At that point, she felt she’d heard enough. My father, on the other hand, wanted instant revenge by finding James and killing him but that would have solved nothing.

‘We agreed on one thing at least: I had to get away somewhere safe. Somewhere James couldn’t find me, at least until an injunction could be sought and divorce proceedings got under way. But first my parents insisted I see a doctor.

‘I protested – no police or doctors were going to prod, tut or question… I’d gone through the doctor thing many times before and that’s all they do! I told my parents that bruises heal and so would these in time. This was my one and only chance to escape and nothing was going to stand in my way,’ Joanne recalled, tearfully telling the girls.

‘Being deeply concerned, my mother came up with the plan to get me to Aunt Dorothy’s here in Southport. James has no knowledge of her existence – she’s a distant cousin, not a sibling, so Mum knew I’d be safe with her.’

A phone call later, everything was arranged. Joanne knew James had a meeting with his accountant that morning. She’d heard him talking on the phone before he left. ‘With that knowledge, my parents bundled me into their car and drove me back to the house to collect my clothes. The trauma of seeing the house again left me quaking and blubbering like a frightened child, so they left me in the car, went inside and shovelled whatever they could into a suitcase.

‘Aunt Dorothy welcomed me with open arms. I was always fond of her as a child, but her kindness and patience, putting up with all that crying and self-pity those first weeks… She stopped me falling apart, encouraged me to embrace the future and not look back. So, as soon as my bruises healed, I began to scan the paper with her help and landed a job at the health spa just off Main Street.’

The girls’ faces lit up at the thought of free facials and spa treatments. Joanne broke the news that she was just a hairdresser but that still got smiles.

Joanne was jolted back to reality, remembering she had to turn the dinner down. For a moment she stood outside herself and observed the last months. She was struck by the realisation that the only pressing problem she had in her life now was what she would do when her divorce became final.

She drained the last dregs from her mug, walked through to the kitchen, gave the *boeuf bourguignon* another quick stir and turned the gas down. She was delighted that that day her deeply private self had come tumbling out at last. She'd held nothing back, so the girls knew what they were letting themselves in for if she came to live with them. That was the day Suzy and Gill became her life-long friends.

The day Joanne moved into the flat, Aunt Dorothy put together a huge food parcel, some bedding and a bag full of odds and sods for kitchen use, then ferried her there. Joanne's thoughts trailed back once more as she sat waiting for the girls to come in from work

Joanne saw her aunt's face as the car drew onto the forecourt and they exchanged glances. Two Victorian dwellings had been converted into a labyrinth of flats and bed sits. This flat was in the annexe at the side of the house. Suzy and Gill had greeted her warmly and seated her on the settee and a cork was pulled on a bottle of wine the instant she removed her coat.

And after a while, Joanne no longer really cared what the flat was like; instead, she felt excitement gathering inside her at the prospect of embarking on a new life here with them.

'Would you like to look round the place, seeing you're coming to live here with us?' Gill had grinned at some point after Joanne had revealed all to them.

'As you can see, this is the lounge,' Suzy said mockingly with a long drawn-out sigh, arms and hands outstretched.

Joanne had already noted the large, high-ceilinged room they were in while they'd been chatting, the elegant architraves, the monster of a marble mantle and curtained sash windows, but as she stood up, she was able to scrutinise it all more closely. The flat had been decked out with dated, mismatched furniture and a flowery pub-type carpet. She observed the messy pile of books, records and unopened mail placed haphazardly on the alcove shelving. Jackets were thrown on the back of chairs, shoes and handbags were left where they'd been discarded and the room looked slightly shambolic, but in a way she envied their girly clutter. To her it was evidence of just how footloose and fancy-free they both were.

Joanne had spent the last four years in a house where nothing had to be out of place, meals had to be served punctually and she wasn't allowed to utter a single grievance.

The massive U-turn in James's life now was probably down to the fact he'd started to smoke pot and share his life with a well-stacked, very juvenile eighteen-year-old.

Joanne remembered Suzy telling her the kitchen was at the far end of the room. She popped her head round the door and noted it was the size of a postage stamp; even so, the landlord had managed somehow to cram in a sink, cooker, fridge, and a larder cupboard with a drop-down front.

'I hope cooking's not a hobby of yours,' Gill had mumbled awkwardly when she saw the look on Joanne's face.

'No, not at all – baked beans on toast does me, so no problems there,' she'd joked, then followed them into the hall.

'And this is the bathroom. It's functional,' Gill said with a disagreeable look as she pushed the door open. It took Joanne a moment to take in the sight of the old iron bath with its corroded, mottled taps, large square porcelain wash basin, pull-chained loo; even the tiles looked original. But the girls had managed to brighten it up with splashes of colour by way of towels, mats and toiletries. It was clean and smelt of fragrant bath salts; Joanne rather liked it in a strange sort of way.

'And this is your room!' Suzy said, moving to the next door. Joanne's eyes widened, this time with delight. She was pleasantly surprised that the room was so large and airy. Once again, as with the lounge, it was decked with second-hand furniture and a pub-type carpet but it was spotless. There was a double bed by the wall, 1930s wardrobe and chest of drawers, which met her needs, and a bloody great storage heater resting on a monster of a black marble fireplace.

'Not exactly the Ritz, is it?' Suzy said, rolling her eyes.

'I like it though,' Joanne remembered saying, beaming as she continued to breathe in the atmosphere. 'When can I move in?'

Aunt Dorothy didn't share her enthusiasm as she travelled from room to room. She hadn't gone with the idea that it was the perfect place for Joanne to start her new life, but she saw brightness in Joanne's face for the first time.

Chapter 3

The winter months suddenly seemed to vanish; spring had arrived and Southport was at its prettiest. The trees on the tree-lined boulevard were full of blossom that danced in the breeze as it fell like confetti at a wedding.

There were glass-canopied walkways, Victorian arcades and imposing architectural buildings and all had had a lick of paint. Window boxes were cleverly placed on windowsills; hanging baskets and huge plant pots overflowed with masses of flowers that brightened up the buildings on the boulevard.

The shops of yesteryear had been converted into upmarket bistros and smart, parquet-floored boutiques. There were still miles of golden sandy beach and a Victorian pier, which Joanne loved to walk along and watch the waves come crashing against the pillars on a cold, blustery day.

Joanne's fondness for the place grew rapidly and she'd started to question her plans once her divorce became final. Maybe she'd stay on in Southport a while longer.

She was even making headway at the hair salon where she worked and had her own regular clientele. Then there were her two flatmates who had boundless energy – unlike Joanne! Once she finished work, it was feet up in front of the telly with a glass of wine and a bowl of yesterday's pasta pulled from the fridge and heated up. Gill and Suzy, on the other hand, who were also victims of broken marriages, had turned into party junkies in order to let off steam. They regularly visited the gym after work and went clubbing most weekends, so life was never dull.

Joanne's afternoon of reminiscing was quickly brought to an abrupt end when the girls made a timely entrance. 'Crikey, is that the time?' she shrieked and jumped up from the couch to give them both a hug.

‘Wow, the place looks amazing,’ Suzy said laughing, looking at the changes.

‘There’s a great smell coming from the kitchen, too,’ Gill added, discarding her coat on the arm of the chair.

‘It’s *boeuf bourguignon,’* Joanne told them as she went into the kitchen, hoping it hadn’t been cremated. It was a while since she’d checked it.

Suzy pulled a bottle of Merlot from a carrier bag. ‘Ta dah! Get the glasses out of the sideboard, Gill. I’ll get the opener.’ And they all sat around the dinner table, describing their day and trilling about romances long gone as they ate their meal.

‘Oh, before I forget,’ Suzy said, as she topped up everyone’s glass, ‘the small blonde girl on the top floor is getting married shortly. She was telling me when I saw her in town today she’ll be moving out. Seeing she hasn’t made many friends since she’s been here, I offered to organise a hen night. I thought that nightclub by the beach, Paradise Hall, might be worth using. What do you think?’

‘In all fairness, Suzy, I think that’s a huge task you’re taking on. We hardly know the girl!’ Gill protested.

‘Oh come on, you miserable old trout! What a great excuse to have a night out!’

‘I’m with you on that one,’ Joanne said, clearing the plates in readiness for pudding.

***

Plans developed quickly over the following days and the girls in the other flats responded excitedly. A collection was made for drinks and things on sticks to start the party off in the girls’ flat, and everyone made an effort and dressed stylishly. Most brought bottles of booze.

Christine, the bride-to-be, was a petite little thing, neatly dressed and relatively shy. Joanne had only met her a handful of times, usually at the bus stop; even then she hadn’t really seemed friendly when Joanne tried to engage her in conversation. Joanne had put it down to shyness.

Suzy raced down the hallway to welcome her when Christine rang the doorbell, then thrust a large glass of cava into her hand and told her to take a great gulp before venturing into the main room that was steadily filling up with noise and laughter. She tried to introduce her to everyone as they edged their way round but the poor girl looked bewildered by it all. Truth be known, Christine hadn't really wanted a hen night; Suzy had bulldozed her into doing it. It was only after she'd polished off few more glasses of cava that she looked like she was finally enjoying herself.

As they all piled in, the club appeared to be packed with even more noisy people. After Joanne's eyes adjusted to the dimness of the room, she noticed one of the barmaids was a client at the salon, so threw her a cheery wave. After that their drinks were kept replenished without them having to queue.

The night was themed, Motown music boomed from every speaker in the place. Everyone seemed to be turbo-charged as they hit the dancefloor and danced until they were red-faced and clammy.

At some point Suzy and Joanne felt that they'd had enough, so decided to head to the bar to quench their thirst. En route they were hijacked by two blokes wanting to dance with them.

Under the dim lights, Joanne could only just make out her chap's silhouette, but this cologne was nice and he made her pulse quicken as he snaked his arm around her waist. Their bodies started to move in sync –it was quite a contrast from the gyrating windmills she'd danced with when they first came in.

'Would you like a drink?' he asked. 'Once this record finishes?'

She blushed but nodded gratefully, then followed him through a sea of chattering, inebriated people to the bar.

'Looks like we're in for bit of a wait. I'm David, by the way.'

'I'm Joanne.' They grinned curiously at one another.

The barmaid spotted Joanne and yelled over, 'Hiya, hon, want serving?'

'Please, Jen,' Joanne shouted back.

'Half a lager and a large gin and tonic, please,' David bellowed above the chatter of the other drinkers.

Within a trice two full glasses were placed on the bar. 'Those are on me,' Jen said with a wink.

David thrust a fiver into her hand. 'In that case, that's for you!' He scooped up the glasses and they went into the adjoining room where the lights were brighter and the music much more chilled.

'You don't mind coming in here, do you? It's deafening out there,' David said in softer tone as he placed the drinks on the table in one of the booths. He waited for Joanne to be seated before sliding in beside her.

Joanne put her glass to her lips and took a large gulp, feeling the need of some Dutch courage, then discreetly slipped off her shoes and wiggled her throbbing toes hoping he wouldn't notice.

The lighting being much brighter, she was able to see what he looked like. Normally a guy as good looking as this brought her out in hives or induced her to speak like she'd been sucking a helium balloon but, as the conversation flowed, she felt surprisingly at ease in his company. She listened with genuine interest as he talked enthusiastically about the small steel company he'd just started up with two other guys then went on to explain how it was still only small scale but they seemed to be doing alright.

In return, she told him about her work at the spa. He actually seemed interested in what she was saying. Whilst they exchanged banter, she was half tempted to explain how she came to be in Southport in the first place but thought better of it after realising it was the drink that was encouraging her to offload her life story.

There seemed to be this unstoppable feeling inside her each time his eyes caught hers and they held each other's gaze. She liked the way his hands had a mind of their own when he talked about something he was passionate about.

'Like another drink?' he asked noticing her glass was almost empty. 'Or would you like to dance?'

'I'll chance that dance,' she grinned, cramming her feet quickly back into her shoes, and letting him guide her back onto the dance floor.

Once again their bodies gelled as they danced and she found she was filled with happiness just by being with him. All too soon the final slow record arrived. Joanne nuzzled her cheek into his neck as their bodies swayed together on the dance floor.

'How are you getting home?' he whispered.

Joanne lifted her head reluctantly from his shoulder, scanned the room and noticed the rest of the girls had already left. 'Looks like it's Suzy and me in a cab.'

'No need! We'll give you a lift. And if you're wondering where your friend is – she's over there in that booth with Steven, the guy I'm in business with… having a quiet snog, it seems.'

Joanne grinned. When Suzy eventually came up for air, she beckoned her to follow her to the loo.

'I saw you,' Joanne said impishly, as they replenished their lipstick and brushed their hair.

Suzy giggled in response.

'David mentioned we could have a lift home. What do you think?'

'Great –I'm down to my last quid, not even half the cab fare home.'

'So in other words the cab's my shout,' Joanne grimaced jokingly.

''Fraid so!'

'A lift it is then!'

They waltzed out of the washroom. Joanne's senses immediately heightened when she saw David and Steven waiting for them.

'Car's in the car park, girls.' David smiled, opening the outer door, allowing the girls and his friend to go out first into the cold night air.

Steven was tall and stocky built. Suzy wasn't what you'd call petite either but both managed to squeeze themselves into the back seat of David's weathered old Mini. Joanne flipped back the seat and slid into the passenger seat then the car swung out onto the open road.

Joanne gave directions to the flat but minutes into the drive, she noticed he wasn't taking the route she'd given – nor did she recognise where they were. 'You're going the wrong way, I think,' she cried out, feeling slightly flustered.

'It's alright – just calling at my house first to pick up Steven's car. He left it there before we came out. Don't look so worried.'

Joanne felt her face go red. 'Sorry…'

Moments later the car took the corner of a cul-de sac somewhere on the edge of town and came to a halt in the driveway of a newly built, detached, Georgian-style house.

'Ta dah, we are here!' David grinned, plucking his keys from the ignition. 'Got time for a coffee?'

Joanne nodded without hesitation and clambered from the car, leaving the others to prise themselves out. They trailed behind David as he guided them through the front door to his house.

Suzy and Joanne's eyes widened as they entered the lounge. The room looked large and airy and filtered into a dining area with Georgian windows at both ends. But the room was so sparsely furnished: brown curtains, brown carpet, two deckchairs, stone fireplace and a stereo at the far end of the room. This was a huge contrast from their lounge which always seemed to be full of girly clutter, mismatched furniture and a loud, patterned carpet,

'Is this what they call the minimal look?' Suzy chortled with unmistakable sarcasm. 'And what's with the deckchairs?' she said, planting herself heavily down in one, whilst Steven lowered himself into the other alongside her.

Joanne winced at Suzy's words when she noticed a tense expression appear on David's face. Steven must have noticed it too and got up from his seat to place an arm supportively around his friend's shoulder. 'You'd better tell the girls what's really happened, David.'

David shrugged, narrowing his eyes.

'The reason it's so sparsely furnished,' Steven said, 'is that David got himself into a spot of money problems a short while ago and the bailiffs took everything.'

The girl's jaws slackened, at which David grinned. 'Take no bloody notice! I've only had the place a month – my furniture hasn't arrived yet!'

'You need to get in touch with your feminine side a little more though, mate. Brown is so unimaginative,' Steven continued to joke.

With that, David disappeared into the kitchen to put the kettle on.

'Anything I can do?' Joanne asked, popping her head round the door.

'You could put some music on, if you would.'

Joanne knelt down beside a glass-topped turntable and shuffled through the record collection piled against the wall. There were some old LP sleeves, but mostly CDs: pop, classical, blues, jazz–it was all here. She spied a Van Morrison CD lurking in the pile, pulled it from its case and slipped it on.

Steven gave the thumbs up as she cranked up the volume; he was obviously a huge Morrison fan.

Joanne had considered Steven quite aloof when they were introduced in the car park earlier on. A bit subdued and rather sultry, she thought as they shook hands. But in his company since they'd been at the house, she realised how mistaken she'd been. As she listened to the banter between him and Suzy, she saw there was a ruggedness about him yet he was polite and well spoken. Suzy, she could see, was already smitten.

David appeared in the doorway with four steaming mugs of coffee and some biscuits on a tray. Joanne took a mug and sat on the carpet by the fire. David sat opposite her in a quiet corner, also on the carpet, apologising profusely for lack of chairs.

As the conversation sailed on, mostly with banter and raunchy tales from the boys, she found herself laughing at all they were saying. David had twinkly brown eyes, dark tousled hair, and his fringe kept falling over his eyes so he repeatedly raked it back with his fingers. Her eyes kept being drawn to his almost hypnotically. She was rewarded with a reassuring gaze in return.

She commented on how roomy the house seemed and asked if she could look around.

'Why not?' he asked, clambering to his feet.

She followed him, doe-eyed, as they ambled through each room and listened as he talked about colour schemes and his plans to furnish. She felt quite envious of how excited he was by it all.

The last room he showed her was his bedroom. As he opened the door, the bachelor sparseness was quite noticeable: no carpet, a single unmade bed, a full-length mirror tilted against the wall at the far end of the room. On the floor there was an array of toiletries and a hair dryer that he'd obviously used before leaving. It was hardly the seduction zone she'd imagined him to have, she thought wryly.

She turned to go back onto the landing and he unintentionally blocked her way. As she tried to pass, their faces touched briefly. His mouth descended onto hers in a kiss that took away her breath. The kiss lingered and time stood still as her heart convulsed. She felt dazed as they broke apart – she'd have liked it to continue! Nervously, she backed away. 'It's getting late,' she stuttered. 'I have work in the morning.'

'Well then, we'd better take you home,' he said with a smile.

Suzy agreed to go with Steven in his car and David took Joanne in his Mini. There was a comfortable silence between them on the drive home. As the car came to a halt outside the flat and the engine fell silent, David drew her to him and kissed her fiercely. This time Joanne didn't try to hold back; she devoured his lips, raked his hair with her fingers and allowed his kisses to linger. In those brief moments of passion, she felt that he'd unleashed some sort of sexual hunger within her.

They broke apart and he held her gaze. Then, out of the corner of her eye, she saw Suzy climbing out of Steven's car and heading towards the flat. Reluctantly she knew she should do the same.

'Here… before you go,' David said, taking a pen and pad from the glove compartment. 'Scribble down your phone number. I'd like to see you again, if that's OK.'

'I'd like that.' She beamed with the knowledge that he liked her enough to want to see her again.

She could see that Suzy was getting irritated by the cold night air; she'd obviously forgotten her key. Joanne gave David one last brief kiss, and climbed from his car.

'I'll ring you tomorrow,' he yelled through the open car window.

She nodded and watched as his car roared off and waved until it disappeared out of sight.

Suzy now was stamping her feet and complaining bitterly that she was cold. Joanne wasn't listening as she fished around in her bag and pulled out her keys; she was too absorbed to take Suzy's complaining on board. The two girls tiptoed down the hallway and collapsed in a heap onto the couch in the lounge like giggling teenagers. Their noisy antics woke Gill, which didn't please her; she purposely hadn't gone out with them to the club, due to an early start the following day. Apparently the bigwigs were visiting the office and Gill needed a clear head.

Gill blinked the sleep from her eyes, rubbed them with her knuckles, then Suzy hugged her and began to dance her round the room. 'You're drunk!' Gill snapped, lowering her eyelids in annoyance.

'We're drunk with love, aren't we, Jo?' Suzy teased. 'We met two blokes tonight and we went back to Joanne's bloke's house for coffee and a snog.'

'God, Suze, you make us sound like we were two slappers on a dodgy night out! They were two OK blokes! But there was no trying any –you know. A refreshing change, I must say! We had coffee and a laugh, that's all!'

'Yeah… but they want to see us again. Mine's called Steve and he's David's business partner and I can't remember exactly what they did…' Suzy looked at Joanne for assistance.

'They're taxidermists – they stuff things,' Joanne muttered, straight-faced. They all reeled off great belly laughs when they realised she was taking the piss.

Joanne shook her head. 'They import and export steel, you plonker.'

'Let's have a nightcap to celebrate. There's a smidgen of brandy left in the sideboard,' Suzy shrieked, still dancing solo around the edge of the room.

Gill growled, 'No thanks.' She traipsed off into the kitchen to make a pot of tea.

Joanne yawned. 'And I'll have to say no too. I'm tired. I'll never be up in the morning.' With that, she kicked off her shoes, scooped them up and bade both girls goodnight.

Chapter 4

Three days passed and Joanne heard nothing from David. But that was men for you. Pity – she'd quite liked him!

After a tough day in the salon with her boss Philippa throwing tantrum after tantrum and customers being ill-mannered and difficult to please, to top it all she missed the bus home so had to walk the length of Main Street. What a relief it was to find an empty flat when she let herself in.

There was a notice on the mantelpiece that read: *Gone to the keep fit class at the YMCA. See you later, Gill and Suzy xxxxx*

Joanne couldn't see the point of all that huffing and puffing after a hard day's work – it didn't make any sense to her. But at least she had the place to herself for a while. A large glass of whatever wine was left in the fridge and a Radox bath were on the agenda. She kicked off her shoes, threw her coat on the chair then headed for the kitchen to take the wine from the fridge door. Halfway there, the phone rang and she frowned in annoyance; whoever it was, she was too tired to talk.

She picked up the receiver, 'WHATEVER YOU'RE SELLING, WE DON'T BLOODYWELL WANT ANY SO GO AWAY,' she yelled, thinking it was the girls.

'Oh right then – but what if I'm not selling anything,' a well-spoken man's voice replied.

'Who is this?'

'It's David. We met the other night! Don't say you've forgotten me already?'

Suddenly struck by the realisation of who it was, she felt her face go puce. 'I'm so sorry. We've had a spate of nuisance calls,' she lied. 'I just thought you were one of those... Of course I haven't forgotten you. How are you?' Great, she thought, now he thinks we have all sorts of men calling at all times of day.

'Fine, thanks. And you? I was wondering if you'd like to come out for a drink tomorrow night if you're not doing anything.'

'Er – yes. I don't think I've anything planned for tomorrow,' she lied again. The girls had mentioned something about seeing a movie but only in passing.' I'd love to.' She felt a pang of excitement hit her stomach.

'Shall I pick you up around eight?

'Yeah, that will be great.'

'I'll see you tomorrow then.' With that, there was a click and he was gone.

Joanne put down the receiver and laughed out loud, her tiredness now completely forgotten. She poured some wine into the glass and took a great gulp.

In the months prior to her meeting David, she'd gone through a demeaning process like most people do when they are newly divorced, separated or splitting up with someone, of getting blathered and picking up some random bloke when the girls had dragged her out on a night out.

These guys didn't have to be good looking or have an impressive CV and their names didn't always register; they just had to be someone with a sympathetic ear and a pulse when she felt lonely or unloved. Then the next day was never easy, trying to remember if anything untoward had happened. Happily she recalled that she must have scared them away before they had any sexual interest in her.

Suddenly from nowhere, this lovely man had come into her life and made her feel almost virginal.

That first date flowed into many more in which she found David not only had looks that sent her weak at the knees but he was kind, made her laugh and was the most interesting man she'd encountered in a long time. He listened with genuine interest to all her troubles and she listened to his, not that he had many, and his brightness always seemed to lift her mood.

The passion between them had been wild and intoxicating from the start but there were times she found him gentle, sensual; a man who could dictate the pace until her senses were heightened enough for her to take the initiative herself.

They found themselves doing the usual things people do when newly together: seeing a movie; eating out; going for a quick drink at the pub; spending romantic nights in, and going for long walks. When they were apart, they stayed on the phone for hours on end and talked into the early hours in a quest to absorb each other's thoughts.

They'd only known each other a short while but in that time they started to realise the depth of their feelings, although retaining their own personal space was an important issue, especially for David.

With that in mind, Joanne didn't lose much sleep when at times she only saw him quite randomly and rarely at the weekend.

She recognised his work commitments consumed him a lot of the time. His business was still in its early stages, so he had to buckle down and work every hour God sent in order to generate new business– or so he kept telling her. She too had work commitments, she reminded him firmly when he prattled on one night about how it would be full on in the coming weeks.

She tried to impress on him the importance of her own work, which seemed to have gone unnoticed somewhere down the line. Joanne had studied long and hard to obtain an impressive CV, something she hadn't thought to tell him about until now. But with all the emphasis on him always being busy, it seemed so one-sided at times.

'Just being a qualified hairdresser wasn't enough for me,' she said, trying to reclaim some balance.' I perceived how distressing it was for clients suffering with hair and scalp disorders and there was no simple answer. We were mere hairdressers with limited knowledge, and to train as a trichologist meant years of studying, years which I could ill afford to waste. I'd be nearly thirty by the time I qualified.'

David listened intently, unaware Joanne had any credentials other than hairdressing. 'You've never spoken much about your work, except to complain bitterly about how ungrateful clients are at times and the long hours after a tiring day,' he said thoughtfully.

'As luck had it, 'she continued, 'I was lucky enough to have landed a job in a salon where the owner practiced Triosthetics. In layman's terms, that means the knowledge and use of homeopathic hair treatments. I found the work fascinating and constantly bombarded my boss with questions. I made a point of overseeing every treatment he did, even if that meant staying on long after I'd finished work. My dedication ended up being noted and he encouraged me to attend seminars, which was quite timely as by then my marriage was in tatters. James was faithless and brutal at times, as you know, but his threatening behaviour left me fearful of leaving him.

'Attending seminars opened a whole new pathway for me. It meant I got some respite from James and I was on my way to becoming a consultant. I trained for two years, passed every level I was supposed to, but then sadly I was forced to go into hiding. That's when I came to Southport, but it meant leaving the job I loved! Philippa at the health spa has shown some interest in the work I've done –she even asked me if I could do the same work at the spa. We've talked at length about it over the last few weeks and she sees the potential. So she applied to the Triosthetic Society, explained the situation and has been granted permission with the understanding I'll attend at least four seminars a year just as I did before.'

She could see the wind was taken from David's sails. 'Why have you never mentioned all this before now? I mean… it's amazing!' he said tilting his head in confusion.

Joanne swallowed hard, avoiding his eyes, and let out a long sigh. 'It never seemed important. It was my job, that's all. Our time together is special and it's become quite limited of late. Why would I want to spoil that by talking shop? I left the talking shop to you,' Joanne laughed.

She rooted through her bag, pulled a card from her purse and handed it to him. 'I just got these today.'

Joanne Harris Triosthetic Consultant
Main Street Health Spa
Southport

David sat back in his seat. His eyes lit up with excitement. 'I love you ... my very clever, beautiful, Triosthetic lady.' Then he gathered her to him and sank his lips down onto hers in a lingering kiss.

'You just said you love me.' She lifted her head and looked squarely at him.

With a smile he said it again. 'I love you.'

There it was for the entire world to see; he hadn't even disguised the fact. An unstoppable feeling gathered inside her and she admitted she was in love with him too.

The relationship she had with David now had taken things to another level; it all seemed so idyllic in comparison to the life she'd had with James and fitted in so well with the flat and work.

But as time went by, Joanne became more curious about David's life when he wasn't with her. Who were his friends, what girls had he dated prior to their meeting? He was always so vague when she broached the subject. She'd confided to him in great detail about her failed marriage, and he'd been hugely supportive, but he still didn't divulge much about his own life other than to comment that he had great parents and two brothers: one married with two kids and the other at university.

There was never any indication that other women were on the scene. She'd stayed at his house God knows how many times since they met, so why did her sixth sense tell her all was not as it seemed?

Then one Friday night they'd been out to dinner and as usual ended up listening to music, naked on the rug in front of the fire at David's, only to wake up in the early hours and hop into his bed then spoon and carry on sleeping. Joanne didn't have work the following day, but unfortunately David did - he had an important meeting that was impossible to reschedule.

'No need to get up … you have a lie in. Just pull the door to when you go. I'll ring you later!' he whispered, giving her a parting kiss on her lips before he left.

Bright sunlight filtering through the partly drawn curtains awoke her from a deep sleep much later that morning. She glanced at her watch through her heavy-lidded eyes and noted it was gone eleven. Reluctantly she threw back the duvet, gave her weary limbs a stretch and got out of bed then plucked David's robe from the hook on the back of the bedroom door and wrapped it round her naked body.

She thundered her way down the stairs, wandered into the kitchen, flicked the switch on the kettle and opened the cupboard where he kept his cups. As she did, she caught her hand on a nail that had come adrift. Blood instantly gushed from the cut. Frantically, she started to search through the kitchen drawers for a plaster. It wasn't a plaster she unearthed, though. In one of the drawers she noticed there were some photos of a girl.

Quite a stunner, in her early twenties, with long blonde hair and blue eyes. Joanne suddenly felt numb as mountains of confusion began to cloud her judgment. She wrapped a tea towel round her bloody hand and went in search of more photos. In a chest of drawers in the back bedroom, she found what she was looking for. It was an album crammed with pictures; some were of the girl and David together.

Joanne slumped down on the carpet and began to thumb through each page. Judging by the dates scribbled in pen, it looked like David had known the girl for quite a few years.

She felt nauseated and clammy as she placed the album back in its drawer. She threw on her crumpled clothes and phoned a taxi, feeling that she couldn't get away quickly enough.

With a sense once again of overwhelming, failure, she absorbed the atmosphere of the flat as she let herself in. How relieved she was when she caught sight the girls in their pyjamas on the couch in the lounge. How stunned they were as she told them all she'd unearthed...

'She could just be his sister,' Gill said naively.

'Oh, for fuck's sake, Gill! He wouldn't have photos of his sister and him, arms round each other, kissing and the like unless there's some perverse thing going on between them. In any case, he hasn't got a sister.'

After a while, Joanne erupted at their sage remarks. She knew what they were saying was only out of love for her, they were just being protective, but it was cold comfort to hear their assumptions. When they refused to be quiet, she disappeared into her bedroom, realising it was the only way she was going to calm down. This girl in the photo could well be an ex. Or he could be leading a double life, have a wife and six kids on the other side of town. Either way, the girls sounding off wasn't helping.

David rang much later that day as promised. 'Hi, sleepyhead. Had a nice lie-in?'

She managed, with great difficulty, to force some brightness into her voice. 'I slept until gone eleven! What's your morning been like?'

'Noisy, busy, tense. But never mind me, how would you like to go out to dinner tomorrow night? I thought we'd try the new French restaurant on Main Street.' He babbled on, oblivious to how she was feeling.

Arrangements made for the weekend were rare and tomorrow was Sunday. Dinner sounded nice, plus it would be an ideal opportunity to quiz him about his past, so she took him up on his offer and agreed on an eight-thirty pick up.

***

Joanne classed Sunday as her favourite day of the week since she'd lived with the girls; whether she saw David or not, it always seemed to be a day of undisturbed sleep and respite from work. Usually, if the girls had managed to drag her on a night out, she'd wake up with a tongue twice its normal size due to the vast amount of alcohol she'd consumed.

With that in mind, she declined their invitation to a party on Saturday night. She couldn't face another crazy drunken evening and, judging by the noisy entrance around 4 a.m. when they dragged two random blokes back to their beds, it sounded like it had been just that.

Joanne realised she hadn't exactly been the brightest pebble on the beach when it came to choosing the men in her life but she couldn't cope now with remarks the girls were making about her recent misgivings.

She kept out of their way by taking herself off on a long walk along the sea wall, grabbing a snack whilst she was out, then rifling through her wardrobe for something to wear that night. Whatever she plucked from the rail didn't seem right. Then, lurking under a coat, she noticed the midnight-blue Frank Usher dress bought in a hurry some months back but never worn; it was a timeless classic. As she tried it on, she beamed with the knowledge that it was almost perfect.

So much depended on how she looked that night. This could easily be their last meal together, she realised, feeling decidedly apprehensive.

In the brief time she'd known David, she felt it was the nearest she'd come to being happy in a long time. Love, kindness and sex, she realised, could come in the same package. All she was left with now was a sense of betrayal and a feeling of sadness that she'd allowed herself to be led down the garden path yet again. What was it about her that encouraged men to drain her of love then move on to their next victim?

***

David was punctual and impeccably turned out as always. As she opened the door to him, her heart raced excitedly. He was wearing the grey suit, the suit she always loved him in and encouraged him to wear. God, she loved him. How could she not? But the chain of events leading to this day faced her with the dilemma of whether to confront him full on or bury her head in the sand and say nothing so that he'd still love her, still be there for her. Her optimism had been betrayed

It was a poignant moment as he walked in the door and enveloped her in his warm, strong arms. Her legs went weak.

'You look amazing.' He gave a near-perfect smile.

'Thank you,' she grinned back, feeling her face flush.

David managed to get a parking spot right outside the restaurant. Sunday was always a busy night in Southport, so trying to get into any restaurant at the weekend at short notice was challenging, let alone one that was newly opened. Joanne couldn't believe they'd had such luck.

David gripped her hand and guided her through the elegant, newly refurbished entrance of La Bouillabaisse. The maître d' was a small, pleasant, red-haired chap in a black formal suit and bright red tie. He greeted them warmly as they entered.

'David! Good to see you again. How are you keeping? Your table is ready – unless you'd like a drink in the bar first?'

'No, I think we'll go straight in if that's OK, Stuart.'

First name terms surprised Joanne; they obviously knew each other well. Joanne took a deep breath as Stuart led them through the hustle and bustle of the elegant dining room, where laughter and banter were being exchanged between fellow diners. The aroma from the kitchen reminded her just how hungry she was.

It was incredible what they'd done to the old Victorian drapery store. The work had been extensive but they'd managed to retain most of the fine features of the era in which it was built, which fitted in so well now with the theme of a Parisian bistro.

They arrived at their table at the far end of the room and Joanne beamed. Crystal glasses were placed perfectly on a crisp, white, damask tablecloth alongside silver cutlery that sparkled in the glow of the solitary candle. A tiny bunch of freesias stood in a silver vase; the fragrance instantly brought Joanne's mum to mind, as they were her favourite flowers.

Stuart helped Joanne to sit down then took her napkin, gave it a shake and laid it neatly on her lap. A waitress dressed in a white shirt, bow tie and long black apron materialised from nowhere and waited patiently until David was seated before handing them both huge, leather-bound menus.

'I'll give you a moment to decide what you're having. In the meantime, I'll bring you some drinks.' She smiled politely.

David gave the order, knowing what Joanne's favourite tipple was by now, and then began to scan the vast menu. Joanne felt quite enchanted by the place as she looked round and took in the atmosphere. She also felt overwhelmed that the man she'd fallen hopelessly in love with was sitting across the table facing her. In that split second, she decided to sidestep what she knew she had to do! She needed more time to enjoy the ambiance a little while longer.

'How do you know Stuart?' she asked, peering over the top of her menu.

'His brothers are clients, but I knew all three of them from school. When the other two came in last week, they mentioned Stuart was opening this place. Said he'd look after us if we came and it seems they were right – the food looks amazing.' Looking again at the menu, he said, 'I think I'm going to have *escargots* for starters, then the *bouillabaisse* for my main course. How about you?'

Long French words and exorbitantly priced food made Joanne feel slightly flustered as she tried to decipher what all the fancy words meant.

'I'll have the same as you. Sounds lovely,' she said, widening her eyes.

The waitress brought their drinks: a large gin and tonic in a cut-glass tumbler was placed in front of Joanne, who instantly lifted it to her lips and took a large gulp.

David watched in silence, then reached across the table and took her hand in his. 'Are you OK? You look a little tense.'

She smiled uneasily, trying not to make eye contact. 'I'm fine, just thirsty. This place looks amazing.' Quickly changing the subject, and glancing round to see if she could spot a familiar face, she whispered across the table, 'It's a bit pricey though.'

'Don't worry about that, just enjoy your meal.'

Her face dropped as the waitress placed her starter in front of her – David hadn't mentioned that *escargots* were garden snails. She played her part well, though, didn't flinch and waited and watched to see how he handled his. Once she'd got the hang of the tongs, she closed her eyes and popped the little sucker into her mouth, dreading the taste.

To her amazement, it tasted much like garlicky chicken! She ended up asking for more bread to mop up the savoury butter in her dish. David's mouth softened in amusement as he watched her. 'Anyone would think you've never had snails before,' he said, giving her a crinkly-eyed smile.

Joanne knew she'd been rumbled and started to laugh as she dabbed the corner of her mouth with her napkin.

As the evening sailed on, she could see David was relaxed and in a talkative mood. She bestowed a serene smile on him then manipulated the conversation to past relationships by telling him about the people she'd briefly dated before James.

Her reverse psychology seemed to work as he started to tell her about girls he'd dated; one in particular was someone he'd known for roughly six years. 'We were good together in the beginning,' he said sadly. 'But a couple of years down the line the relationship became quite stagnant. Each time I tried to end it, she became depressed and upset. Cowardice and kindness encouraged me to continue. Pathetic and shallow of me, wasn't it?' he said, looking over to see her response. 'But at least it enabled us to maintain our friendship and that's all it ended up being. We have quite a few mutual friends, you see, who still invite us to dinner or parties at their houses.

'To have severed connections completely with her would have meant split loyalties and the invites, especially for her, would have diminished greatly. But in the end I came to the conclusion that enough was enough and I ended it completely.' His eyes narrowed. 'She just can't seem to move on, though, and now I can't be so cruel as to tell her that even our friendship must end!' He lifted his glass and took a sip of wine, his dark-brown boyish eyes scanned Joanne's face for her reaction.

Joanne felt numb and slightly shell-shocked by his revelation but managed to hide it well by fiddling with her cutlery. She now understood why she rarely saw him at the weekends or hadn't met any of his friends – Sarah had kept tugging at his heartstrings it seemed to keep him in her life.

His fingers briefly touched her hand across the table. 'I've never mentioned it to you before; I didn't think you'd understand.'

Her cheeks felt warm and she took her hand away. 'But we had an understanding from the beginning,' she said calmly. 'We'd give each other space so we could spend time with our own friends. I would have understood. I just wish you'd confided in me sooner, especially as I told you everything I've been through,' she whispered, lowering her eyes in annoyance.

'I know and I'm sorry.'

Thankfully the waiter chose that moment to place two enormous earthenware dishes in front of them, filled to the brim with fish and seafood bubbling in a translucent sauce. The aroma made Joanne's face light up with joy.

She decided not to pursue the subject further. She'd got the answers she needed and nothing was going to spoil the mouth-watering feast she was about to eat. If only she hadn't found those blessed photos, she thought crossly, she'd have been none the wiser and tonight would have been flawless. His guilty secret was out in the open; she had to accept it gracefully and move on.

Joanne chose to ignore her misgivings and enjoyed the rest of the night but the drive home was made in silence. David's car drew to a halt outside the flat. He switched the engine off and slid his arm around the back of her seat. Joanne's silence continued.

'Penny for them?' he said, puzzled by this sudden mood change.

Resisting the urge to tell him how she really felt, she lied and told him she wasn't thinking anything then snuggled into him, hoping a cuddle might dispel the thoughts rambling in her mind.

'I didn't set out to hurt you, Jo,' David said, planting gentle kisses on her neck and around her earlobe.

'I know … but I wish you'd been straight with me, that's all.'

David sat back in his seat abruptly, folded his arms and stared at her blankly. 'I couldn't take that chance. I was too afraid of losing you!'

Joanne frowned. With an element of sternness to her voice, she asked, 'Did you really think I was so shallow?'

'I promise you, Joanne, things will be very different from now on. No more lies.' There was sadness in his eyes as he spoke.

Joanne reached across and drew him to her, trying to dispel any feelings of doubt.

She had an early start the following day, a seminar at the Midland Hotel in Manchester so David knew a nightcap was out of the question. She felt relieved; some space from him was clearly needed in order to gain some clarity!

***

To her surprise, things did change dramatically in the weeks that followed. David telling her about Sarah seemed to have cleared the air. Even weekends were no longer taboo; her gremlins seemed to have gone and the trust and love between them started to flourish at last.

Chapter 5

Joanne mentioned to the girls, when they were all in the kitchen trying to grab a quick breakfast before leaving for work one morning that her birthday was coming up a week on Sunday.

'Great.' Suzy stood back and smiled at her, clearly thrilled. 'Saturday night we can all have a sluttish girly night out. Sunday, David can have you all to himself and indulge you in whatever he has planned for you.'

'I'm up for that,' Gill sang out, spooning peanut butter onto her toast.

The girls' comments seemed to ignite some excitement and plans were in the making even before the Kenco had finished percolating that morning. James had never acknowledged her birthday in the four years that they had been married. Joanne hadn't been used to fuss of any kind let alone on a grand scale like this.

In the days that followed, she managed to throw a few subtle hints David's way in the hope he'd pick up on them. Then, with the thrill of romance in the air, Joanne shopped for outfits for both nights.

Saturday night arrived at last and the flat was thrown into chaos. Joanne didn't think it possible to cram as many girls into the flat as they'd invited. Thank goodness they'd all brought booze. Once that was consumed, they embarked on an outrageous night on the town.

The fact that all three had enormous hangovers the following morning didn't stop Gill and Suzy bursting into Joanne's room around ten o'clock armed with a bottle of champers, three glasses, presents and cards.

'Happy birthday to you, happy birthday to you, happy birthday, dear Joanne, squashed tomatoes and stew,' the two girls croaked noisily at the top of their hoarse voices, as they flung open Joanne's bedroom door.

'Hair of the dog,' Suzy yelled, popping the cork on a bottle of fizz left over from the previous night and just about managing to get it into Joanne's glass before she spilt some over the bed.

Joanne lifted her head from her pillow and gave a swift glance round the room through the narrow slits she'd once called eyes.' Thanks, girls,' she replied, somewhat grizzly, propping herself up on her pillows. She bellowed with laughter when she noticed the state of her two friends, their hair teased and tangled, panda eyes, colourful miss-matched pyjamas.

Squeals of delight followed, as Joanne tore open the wrapping on her presents. 'Perfume...Makeup – awesome… Aw, thanks girls.'

Hugging her two flatmates, who were still pretty inebriated from the previous night, the laughter continued as they started to recall their night out.

'Where's lover boy?' Gill asked, perched on the edge of the bed. 'We thought he might have climbed through your window in the early hours to give you one!'

Joanne didn't disguise the fact that thought had crossed her mind too. 'Under normal circumstanced he would have, I'm sure, but we were on a bender, weren't we? Probably didn't want to spoil our fun! No doubt he'll be waiting for me to sober up before coming round,' she said, trying to hide any signs of disappointment she was harbouring.

'What's he got organised for tonight?" Gill said, taking a sip from her glass then wincing at the acidic liquid.

'Haven't got a clue. I've dropped enough hints though, so it better be somewhere nice.'

From that moment on it was a flurry of excitement, as girls from the other flats called with cards, some with presents, and there was a continuous trail of phone calls from well-wishers and family. But there was no word from David.

Then, around two o'clock, the doorbell rang and with new-found excitement Joanne galloped down the hall to open the door. There he stood, brandishing the most outrageous bunch of cellophane-wrapped stargazer lilies.

'The flowers look amazing,' she said when their lips parted from the kiss he gave her.

'And a card.' He waved a large envelope in the air.

'I'll open it in the lounge. Come on through, the girls are in there.'

Joanne saw that he was making some sort of calculation before he answered. 'Sorry, love, I can't stop. People I need to see! Unavoidable, love, I'm afraid – but I'll pop back later … say around nine-thirtyish? We can celebrate your birthday properly then. I'll bring some champagne.'

She was thrown by his comment and there was something about his expression that told her Sarah had probably stayed at his, truth be known. He'd probably thought that whilst Joanne was otherwise engaged there'd be no threat of her turning up. Sarah would still be at his house – no doubt he'd made the excuse that he was popping out for milk and the Sunday papers.

What was so hurtful was that it was her birthday, she thought sadly. Her special day. How could he be so insensitive, today of all days?

Joanne stared at him in disbelief. Her head was full of angry words she wanted to direct at him. He averted his eyes and made a lightning move towards the door, throwing her a flippant remark, 'See you later, birthday girl.'

Joanne was left standing there in his wake. She looked down at the card in her hand, tore it open and read the lies he'd written: *I love you more than words can say'.*

'PATHETIC!' she almost screamed, binning it along with the flowers as she walked through to the kitchen. Suzy instantly retrieved the flowers, claiming she'd have them for her room if Joanne didn't want them.

The girls didn't comment this time but were as supportive as they could be after hearing every word that had been said.

Joanne settled on the sofa, determined to devise a plan to counter this awful moment. 'I should probably have seen it coming. After all, I went into this relationship with my eyes open wide, didn't I? Knowing full well there was a huge flaw in his character from the word go.' She ran her hands through her unruly hair.

The phone rang. Joanne stared defiantly at the girls. Suzy snatched it up and her face brightened. It was one of the girls from the previous night, calling to enquire how they all were faring after the night they'd had and to wish birthday girl hello! On hearing what had happened, she suggested another night out might help. 'I'm sure everyone would be up for it.'

'The situation does needs dealing with,' Joanne heard Gill say with a heavy sigh.

A few phone calls later, everyone was up for a second innings. Joanne didn't know how they did it in such a short space of time, but all thoughts of David that night were replaced by an incredible amount of flirting, drinking, and shameful behaviour.

The next day, Joanne's hangover was so bad that she couldn't even raise her head from the pillow, so summoned Suzy to call in sick for her. All she wanted was to die peacefully in her own bed. A drum was beating constantly in her head; she felt like something had crawled into her mouth and died, and her tongue felt like a cuttlefish. Every bone in her body ached so badly that no tablet on earth could have repaired what damage the alcohol had caused to her fragile body!

'Never mind a glass of water, Gill. Just attach the hosepipe from the outside tap to my mouth and leave it running,' she whispered gruffly to her flatmate, who also was taking the day off.

Joanne was vaguely aware that the phone in the lounge hadn't stopped ringing all morning. No prizes for guessing who that was! But she was in no fit state to answer it, so she let it ring. Mid-afternoon, when she finally surfaced, she picked it up when it rang next.

'At long bloody last! Where've you been? I came round last night AS WE PLANNED and you weren't there. Where the fuck were you? I brought champagne and chocolates, the works, and today you've not been answering your phone. What's going on, Joanne?' His voice was tinged with aggression.

Joanne paused to collect her thoughts. She'd rehearsed this conversation in her head a hundred times that morning as she'd drifted in and out of sleep, knew word for word what she was going to say when the time came.

'Sorry, David. I went out with the girls… didn't think you'd mind seeing as we weren't doing anything special.' Joanne's tone now matched his in terms of sarcasm.

'Joanne, I'll make it up to you. We'll go out tonight, somewhere nice,' he spat out, now his web of lies and wrong-doing had been sussed.

Joanne was no longer listening. 'Don't think so, sunshine. You've well and truly blotted your copybook, David. You and I are finished.'

He offered no explanation, admission or confession. She knew by his silence that she'd been right – he'd been with Sarah. Her sixth sense had been spot on.

'I'm not feeling too clever, so I'm going… Berrrr... yerrr.... urrrr,' she heaved. She threw down the phone and just about managed to reach the loo before the contents of her stomach hit her throat.

***

She found the weeks that followed difficult, especially as David constantly badgered her with phone calls pleading forgiveness.

But then one morning he caught up with her before she left for work. She was half asleep and in one of her more lenient moods. He stood outside the flat, waiting until she came out, and wouldn't take no for an answer. She agreed to meet him, under duress, but added cautiously, 'Don't put too much hope on it. My mind's made up. I just need to put an end to these nuisance calls, that's all.'

The girls thought her barking mad for even considering seeing him. 'You're pressing a self-destruct button, lady,' Suzy bellowed from the kitchen where she was making a pot of tea.

Their words fell on deaf ears. She had to admit that David had become something of a drug she couldn't bear to give up. She had never anticipated falling in love like she had, and the withdrawal symptoms she was now suffering were far worse than any hangover she'd had in the past.

'Better the devil you know than the devil you don't,' she yelled at them both as she flounced from the room.

Wondering what to wear, Joanne changed her clothes half a dozen times! She redid her hair twice then took time with her makeup – she wanted him to see her at her best. They'd arranged to meet up in a bar both of them had frequented many times in the past.

A bottle of Châteauneuf du Pape and two glasses had already been ordered and were waiting at the table when she arrived. He was immaculately dressed and he threw her an impish grin as she entered the bar. He stood up and gave her a kiss that lingered longer than Joanne would have liked when she reached him.

Seating herself opposite him at the table, promising herself not to engage, be gullible or take in any more lies, she felt confident she could pull this off. But by the time the last dregs of wine were emptied from their glasses, she was once again putty in his hands and she found herself being led to his house for an explosive night of sexual gratification.

It was ludicrous, the chemistry they still shared. They should have parted some months back – he'd been playing her for a fool for the duration of their relationship, it seemed. Even so, she agreed to give it one more try; this time, unknown to him, she'd call the shots. If David wanted to play games, well then, games it would be… but she didn't think he'd appreciate the tricks she now had up her sleeve.

The girls were less than pleased with the outcome. It was her life, she was a big girl and well aware of the potholes. God knows, she'd had her fair share of them in the past.

To the girls' amazement, however, in the weeks that followed their relationship took a new turn. Love blossomed and it seemed that all the mayhem and lies were completely in the past; a new beginning was in the making.

The Friday ritual now usually began with David taking her somewhere grand for dinner then they'd move on to a smart cocktail bar, always ending up at his house. There they'd rekindle the passion they'd put on hold in the time they'd been apart.

Just as a safeguard, though, Joanne left a trail of keepsakes whilst she was there: a note in the tea caddy – 'Thank you for a night of bliss' or 'I love you and miss you', and one he'd find whilst searching for eggs in the fridge. She'd mingle the odd bra amongst his clean linen in the airing cupboard and slotted her empty contraceptive pill carton into his bathroom cabinet. David would just interpret these things as amusing tokens should he stumble on them.

Joanne's hectic schedule in the weeks that followed left David ample opportunity to see Sarah if he was still doing so, but Joanne's antics would certainly cause eruptions if she or any other girl unearthed them. Of that, Joanne had no doubt.

The international seminar in London was the focal point of the Triosthetics practitioners' year. People flew in from all corners of the world to attend and the planned schedule was pretty gruelling, to say the least.

The train journey home was a nightmare, with one delay after another. Joanne felt exhausted when she eventually landed back at the flat. She dumped her bags in the hallway, walked into the living room, kicked off her shoes, threw her coat on the chair and was just about to make herself a much-needed cup of tea, when the phone rang. She lifted it to her ear, 'Hello?'

'Can I speak to Joanne?' a woman asked in a well-spoken voice. It wasn't a voice Joanne recognised.

'Speaking.'

'My name's Sarah. I believe you know David Winston. I'd like to know just how well you know him.'

Joanne cringed as she recognised who it was and suddenly felt herself go cold. It was David's Sarah. She inhaled deeply before answering. 'Yes, I know David well.'

'You mean you've shagged him?' Sarah returned.

Blood surged to Joanne's neck and face. 'Yes, on many occasions,' she replied cockily.

'You fucking condescending bitch! Have you no scruples? Did you not realise he was going out with someone?' Sarah's voice trembled and Joanne detected a slight sob at the end of the sentence.

Joanne's face grew hot! Thoughts of James and Paula flashed in her mind. It seemed she was the other woman now and she didn't like it one little bit.

'Listen! I'm sorry!' Joanne mumbled apologetically. 'I didn't mean it to come out as callously as that! David told me when we first met that he'd had a long-term girlfriend some time ago, but it was over. I had no idea you were still together! He said you still saw each other occasionally at friends' houses or at parties, but were just friends, and I believed him. Had I known you were still together, I would have never continued to see him. And I mean that quite sincerely. There was never any indication you were still around when I stayed at his place these last few weeks.'

'No, there wouldn't be. He was very insistent that I never left any of my things there.'

In between her sobs, Sarah began to tell Joanne how the last nine months had panned out. Her relationship with David had deteriorated. He'd cancelled dates or left earlier than planned, saying he wasn't feeling well.

'That must have been around the time he met me,' Joanne answered awkwardly.

'We quarrelled constantly and saw each other far less; In fact, there were times when I didn't see him for weeks on end. When I did stay at his house the last couple of times, I began to find notes, toiletries, women's clothing, so it wasn't rocket science to know what was going on...' Her voice trailed off to a whisper as she continued. 'One night I took his diary from his briefcase whilst he slept and found your number.'

'Sarah, I'm so sorry. At least we know exactly what a two-timing bastard he really is. In all honesty, I never want to set eyes on him again. I can't believe the deceit and hurt he's caused us both. We deserve better.'

In the brief time they'd talked, Joanne had felt a connection. She felt that Sarah wasn't an over-confident or strong person; she was probably just a normal girl wanting the man she loved to love her back. But Joanne knew David would probably talk her round the moment she confronted him.

Joanne poured herself a large brandy from the bottle in the sideboard then shut herself away for the rest of the night in her bedroom. She couldn't even share this one with the girls. She couldn't tell them what a rat she now knew him to be! Sadly, she'd fallen far more deeply for him than she'd wanted.

Chapter 6

'Morning,' Gill trilled, as Joanne emerged bog-eyed and subdued from her room the following morning.

'Hi,' she muttered back, quickly making her way to the bathroom.

'Didn't hear you come in last night,' Gill said, following her down the hallway after picking up the post from the hall table.

'It was late when I arrived back. I was knackered so I crashed out on the bed.'

'Must have been one hell of a seminar… Want some tea and toast? I'm just going to make some.'

'Lovely. I'm just going to jump in the shower first.'

With that, Joanne escaped the Spanish inquisition by locking herself in the bathroom. She turned on the taps and, as the hot water flowed from the antiquated overhead showerhead on the wall over the bath, she disrobed and looked at herself squarely in the mirror. She expected her reflection to have red-rimmed eyes and a gaunt expression from the amount of crying she'd been doing. Instead, the twenty-six-year-old woman looking back at her was someone she didn't recognise. There stood this bright-eyed, skin-glowing girl whose days of reckoning and shedding tears over men were decidedly over.

The hot, fast-flowing water cascaded onto her body as she stepped into the shower. It felt good. She plucked the loofa from behind the taps, rubbed it against the block of soap and scrubbed her body with determined vigour as if trying to scrub away the debris of the last few years.

A warm towel wrapped round her, she was drying her hair with another towel as she walked back into her bedroom. Waiting for her was a tray with two rounds of toast and a mug of tea on it, a welcome sight as by now hunger pangs were reminding her just how famished she was. Her last meal being breakfast the previous day.

With a final glance in the mirror when she'd finished dressing, she threw on her jacket and emerged into the hallway. 'Bye,' she yelled to the girls then shut the front door noisily behind her. She really couldn't face another onslaught of "I told you so", she thought sombrely.

They were used to her being disgruntled and grumpy in the mornings, so wouldn't think anything was different on this particular one.

As she emerged into the early morning sunshine, she felt the need of some fresh air to jump-start her system before tackling an onslaught of difficult clients. So, instead of catching the bus to work, she decided to walk the half-mile or so instead. It was still only eight thirty and she had plenty of time.

Joanne let the sun's rays warm her face as she walked at a brisk pace. As she turned onto Main Street, she was met by a blaze of colour from the long line of trailing baskets hanging from the wrought-iron canopied walkways.

Vans were parked on double yellows, hazard lights flashing as they unloaded their deliveries. Key holders were unlocking their shops and the waft of freshly percolated coffee reached her nostrils from the open windows of the coffee shops. She'd have missed all these things had she taken the bus. What else had she missed in life by not taking the time to appreciate what was going on around her?

Clients were already queuing in reception, and some were being gowned up as she arrived at the salon. Philippa glanced at the clock and threw her a look of annoyance – she didn't miss a trick! So what if she was a couple of minutes late? Joanne no longer really cared and showed it by cheerily greeting her first client and giving orders for her to be shampooed whilst she slipped into her uniform.

'I need some time off work,' Joanne blurted out when Philippa waltzed into the staffroom, obviously ready to give her a roasting for being late.

Philippa arched her perfectly shaped eyebrows and let out an impatient sigh, hands placed firmly on hips. 'When were you thinking?'

Joanne straightened herself up to her full height, ready for a confrontation. 'Next week, if that's possible.' Under Philippa's gaze Joanne felt flustered but resisted the urge to babble nervously about how she'd never had time off since she'd been there and did she not realise how knackering it was preparing for seminars.

'Sorry it's short notice, but it's been a long, exhausting year. David and I are through and I'm worried at the moment about my parents' health. Dad had another slight stroke a while back. I need to spend time with them, give Mum some respite.'

Philippa held Joanne's gaze, as if trying to decide if this was a fast one she was pulling or her excuse was kosher. 'OK. You can take next week, but only if you can reschedule your bookings …and I need you back for the Birmingham seminar, a week on Monday. I've had a phone call to say they are short of a lecturer. I told them you were more than capable.'

Joanne gave a grateful smile.

'I know sometimes I appear to be something of a tyrant, but keeping you lot in check isn't always easy! That doesn't mean that I don't appreciate all the hard work you do. It can't have been easy with the divorcel.' Philippa smiled then disappeared from the room.

***

An empty flat at the end of the day was always a welcome sight. It had been a difficult day and she'd fought back tears more than once when David came to mind, or when a certain record played on the radio or someone asked how he was, not realising what had happened.

She spotted a note on the mantelpiece: *I'm at evening class. Gill's staying over at a friend's so enjoy the peace and quiet, Love Suze xxx.*

Joanne had managed to grab a burger on her way home. All she wanted to do now was sleep. She didn't even have the energy to undress, she just discarded her shoes and tumbled fully clothed onto the bed, then dragged the duvet over her. She hugged her pillow and allowed herself to drift off into consoling slumber, a slumber that allowed her to forget and maybe just for a short time become someone else.

Ohhhhh, yessss, she heard herself groan as she moved in and out of consciousness when David had materialised more than once in her dreams. Suddenly she was awoken by a door creaking noisily and footsteps in the hallway outside her door. She glanced at her clock through heavy eyelids; daylight had started to filter through her half-drawn curtains. What was meant to be a short nap seemed to have stretched into a full night's kip.

She stretched her weary limbs under the covers, gave her eyes a rub, threw back the duvet, peeled off her crumpled sweaty clothes and replaced them with her towelling robe.

Gingerly, she peered round her door to check the coast was clear. It wasn't unusual these days to see a bollock-scratching, naked bloke disappearing into the loo. The sight of an overnight bag dumped in the hallway indicated Gill had arrived home.

'Hi, you dirty stop-out,' Joanne said quietly as she padded into the kitchen where Gill was making a brew.

'Shit, you gave me a fright!' Gill exhaled noisily, holding her chest.

'Sorry, didn't mean to startle you…I'll have one of those if there's one going. Two sugars,' Joanne grinned.

'Did I wake you?' Gill smiled, reaching for a mug from the cupboard.

'No,' Joanne fibbed. 'I was knackered when I came in from work, so I crawled into bed fully clothed for a nap and I've just woken up.'

'God, I hate when that happens.'

'How did your night go?' Joanne asked, as they sat on the couch in front of the two-bar electric fire.

'Don't ask! Adam was supposedly making a candle-lit dinner and I anticipated dessert would be all-night sex… But he'd forgotten the match was on. His friend Phil turned up so I was sent out to pick up a Chinese and spent the rest of the night watching them shouting at the TV and downing cans of lager. By the time Phil left, Adam was incapable of seeing, let alone giving me an all-night seeing to, so I left him on the couch snoring his head off and went to bed. As soon as it got light, I snuck out and drove home.'

'I don't know why we bother. Drinking pop through a curly straw sometimes seems more exciting than dating men.'

'Tell me about it!' Gill threw Joanne quizzical look.

With some unease, Joanne told her, 'David and I are finished, but don't ask for details – it's still all too raw. I've asked Philippa if I can take next week off, not because of what's happened, but because I need to spend time with my parents. Dad's not been too good.'

'I'm sorry. You OK about what's happened?'

'Yeah, I think so.' Joanne smiled weakly as Gill slid an arm around her in a hug.

Once Joanne was showered and dressed for work, she gave her parents a quick ring to inform them she'd be coming for a visit at the weekend. Predictably that sent her mother into a flurry of excitement and she began stating all the things she needed to do in preparation for Joanne's visit.

'Hang on, Mum – I just need some peace and quiet, that's all... no fuss.'

'Sorry, love, you know what I'm like. I get carried away with the thought of having you home. I know your dad will be thrilled.'

Joanne blew a kiss down the phone. 'I love you, Mum.'

'Love you too, poppet.'

***

It was some time since they'd set eyes on her as James still lived in the village. Knowing how volatile he was, her parents kept in touch with her through phone calls.

Joanne knew she'd caused them a huge amount of crying, anger, heartfelt sadness and worry over the last months but today their eyes were soft and kind. Voices low and soothing, their arms felt hugely protective as they enveloped her in an emotional hug when she arrived at their house late on Friday night.

They had limited knowledge of what their daughter had actually gone through in those four years. Joanne had shielded them from so much, she only told them what she felt they needed to hear, a fraction of what had actually happened. But even that had sucked the very being from them. They delighted now at seeing how she'd blossomed in the time she'd been away.

An only child, although she'd not been spoilt. The shock of these last months had taken its toll on her father's health, but the sight of her now ignited smiles as she started to chatter on about all she'd been up to with those crazy girls, as her mother called Suzy and Gill. She talked about her work and how plans were transpiring, and the men she'd dated. They delighted at seeing she was more of less back to her old self again.

August proved to be a real scorcher, so each day Joanne lifted a deckchair from the outhouse and carried it down to the orchard at the bottom of the garden where the trees would give shelter from the hot sun.

The orchard was relatively small and the grass was soft and delicious; wild flowers grew randomly here, there and everywhere, even at the base of each tree. There were seven trees in all: two pear, a plum, two eating apples and two Bramley apple trees, which her mother bragged were the finest baking apples for miles around. She'd won numerous prizes in the WI bake-off to prove her point.

This part of the garden had been Joanne's secret place since she was a child and now, as she relaxed on the old, rickety, striped deckchair, sipping a cup of tea that her mother had placed on the table beside her, she began to relive old times when she had played there with school friends, and enjoyed rough and tumble antics with the family mongrel, Scamp. How thrilled she'd been when her father made her a swing out of old rope. The seat was some carpet loosely thrown over it once he'd hooked it up between two of the trees. Life was simple and she'd been incredibly happy.

It saddened her how James had forbidden her to see her parents or lend a hand when it was time to harvest the fruit at the end of summer, a ritual she'd been involved in since she was a child. He had also cajoled her into abandoning all her friends. He probably feared that being alone with them would give her the chance to offload how bullied and unhappy she was and he wasn't going to risk that.

She glanced up at the heavily laden trees; their crop this year was quite a bumper.

Her mother answered the phone when it rang then beckoned to Joanne that it was for her. 'Mr Reed would like a word,' she whispered as she passed it to her.

Joanne clenched the receiver. 'Hello.'

'Joanne, I'm the bearer of some good news for a change. The marital home has been sold. It was only on the market a few days when a cash buyer came along and wanted a quick sale, so there's a cheque in my office that has a nice group of noughts at the end of it,' he laughed. 'I could put it straight in your account if that would suit. That way, the cheque will clear within days.'

'Oh yes, please.' She found herself laughing spontaneously when he told her the value.

'I'll send the final paperwork to Southport, shall I?'

'Please... and thank you for everything.'

Financial stability was at last on the cards, bringing some excitement and hope back into her life. At long last she would be able to make plans for the future.

'James is out of my life at last!' Joanne shrieked, as she replaced the receiver. Her mother threw her arms in the air and gave her daughter an emotional hug.

'How about I take my two best girls out to dinner tonight to celebrate?' her dad said, easing himself up from his old familiar armchair.

Helen regarded him and grinned, then went in search of her address book. 'I'll give The Rookery a ring, shall I, love?' she said, throwing Joanne a wink.

Henry was normally quite thrifty and for him to say he was splashing out on a meal at the Rookery was quite a statement.

'Make the reservation for about seven-thirty, will you love? Late eating doesn't agree with me these days.'

Her mum nodded and picked up the phone.

***

Joanne took stock as she realised it was time to sort out the boxes James had dumped on her parents' doorstep when she left.

Her mother's discreetly abstained from her usual habit of hovering and retrieving each item Joanne threw out for the WI's bring and buy sale. Instead, she left her daughter alone to rummage through the remnants of her marriage.

It was quite a journey; at the end of which Joanne decided the WI could have the lot, including her wedding album once she'd burnt the pictures from it. She didn't need any reminders of the biggest mistake of her life.

What a treat to see her parents dressed in their finery! She'd quite forgotten what an attractive pair they were. They were still very much in love, she thought warmly. Why couldn't she find that sort of love?

The Rookery was palatial, an imposing establishment in its own grounds not too far from her parents' home. Joanne had been coming here since she was in her teens, only on the most special occasions though, as her dad always joked that he had to re-mortgage the house to pay the bill each time they came.

All those memories flooded back as they walked through the main entrance: her eighteenth birthday, New Year's Eve parties, her parents' anniversaries. Life was so predictable and uncomplicated back then.

It was four and half years since last she was there but the maître d' welcomed her as if it was yesterday as they claimed their seats in the restaurant.

'To happy new beginnings, love.' Her dad held up his champagne flute.

'I'll second that,' Helen beamed and they sat laughing and joking over an unhurried meal and some exceedingly good wine until it was time to leave.

Helen placed a mug of hot chocolate on Joanne's bedside table before she retired herself.' It'll help you sleep… there's a smidgen of brandy in it too,' she grinned, as she perched on the edge of the bed, just as she'd done on so many other occasions when Joanne lived at home.

The conversation started about how lovely the night had been and then veered to the subject of David .Helen obviously felt she needed to delve whilst she had her daughter's complete attention. She enquired why the relationship had ended so abruptly. 'From your letters, you always seemed so happy with him!'

Her mother listened thoughtfully as Joanne relayed all the comings and goings.

'From what you're saying it doesn't sound like he meant to hurt you, darling, not really. Sounds more like he was trying not to hurt both of you,' Helen said, as she kissed her daughter's forehead and traipsed off to bed.

***

Joanne arrived home from the seminar in Birmingham the following week with renewed enthusiasm when she heard from Philippa that the Triosthetic Society had rung. Praising Joanne for a job well done, Philippa encouraged Joanne to sit the exam and become a full-time lecturer. There was even a promise of some financial support, along with travel expenses.

Joanne knew full well there was no such thing as a free lunch where Philippa was concerned. Financial cogs were turning in Philippa's head; she suspected the salon would reap far more revenue if Joanne became a full-time lecturer, as the fees for her services would be huge.

December was fast approaching and a day hadn't passed when Joanne didn't wonder what was happening in David's life. She'd heard through the grapevine that Sarah had moved in with him. She just hoped at long last they were happy!

Invites began to arrive for festive parties. The girls excitedly sifted through them, deciding which to accept and which not. The night that topped the list was the one where all the girls in the building got together. Suzy, as usual, organised the whole affair. Invitations were sent, stating that the theme this year was upmarket with plenty of bling.

Finding a date though to suit everyone's busy schedule was always going to be difficult but the fifth of December seemed to be agreeable to everyone involved. The piano bar came up as a perfect venue to meet up and begin their night. Suzy agreed.

Everyone arrived in high spirits and squealed in delight as they greeted one another. Happy-hour cocktails followed – lethal but got everyone in the mood incredibly quickly. The bar started to fill up with smartly dressed, undeniably gorgeous men and at some point some serious flirting got underway.

Stupidly, after her second cocktail, Joanne had volunteered to be the kitty keeper. With list in hand and Suzy by her side, they fought their way through the chattering, glass-clinking crowd to the bar and waited patiently to be served. Joanne scanned the room; and her eyes were immediately drawn to a guy standing at the far end of the bar. He looked vaguely familiar then, as she looked closer, her legs suddenly went weak. It was David!

The barmaid approached and asked for their order. Joanne watched her lips move but couldn't seem to decipher what she was saying, her world had gone suddenly numb. She just thrust the list into Suzy's hand in the hope that she'd sort it out.

'David's over there.' Joanne struggled with her words, 'Take over this order, will you? I have to go to the loo.'

Thousands of memories came flooding back as she struggled with her thoughts. With her hair brushed, lipstick replenished, she felt her face burning as she ventured out cautiously into the bar. A swift glance round brought a sigh of relief; there was no sign, so hopefully he'd moved on! But then a tap on her shoulder told her differently and she turned.

'David!' She managed a smile. 'How are you?'

'I'm OK. How about you?'

'Fine, thanks.'

'What's the occasion?' he asked, using the same cocky grin that had always won her over after every row they'd had.

'Early Christmas do with all the other girls from the building,' she said, trying to avoid eye contact.

'Hi David, how are you these days?' Suzy came over boisterously.

'Fine, and you?' His dark eyes still held Joanne's and her heart began to quicken.

'How's Sarah?' she couldn't resist.

He stuffed his hands in his trouser pockets and shuffled uncomfortably from one foot to another – a thing he tended to do when he was nervous.

'It didn't work out with Sarah and me. Trying again only brought more pain. But Sarah, being Sarah, just wouldn't give up.'

There was sadness in his eyes as he made a hopeless gesture, which ignited some weakness in Joanne. Then she remembered what a good storyteller he was.

Gill beckoned from the other side of the room that the taxis had arrived to take them all to the club. She began to press-gang everyone into getting a move on as the meters were already running.

What a bummer, Joanne thought. There he was, right in front of her after all these months, still looking ruggedly handsome, still using the fragrance she remembered gracing her bedclothes...His eyes consumed her but she fought to retain her sanity and left him standing alone. She joined the others in the long line of taxis they'd hailed.

'Bloody hell, Joanne! He's got a bloody nerve coming over like Mr Cool after all he did to you!' Gill shouted from the front.

'Don't go there,' Suzy hollered back and gave Joanne's hand a reassuring squeeze.

Joanne wasn't listening. Her head was still full of memories 'I really need a strong drink now,' she replied slowly.

The nightclub in the centre of town was the bees' knees, according to the girls.

'Easy to stagger home from after a few too many when you haven't managed to cop off,' Suzy muttered with a big grin on her face as they queued to go in.

Joanne wasn't convinced; it had too many flashing lights for her liking and looked like it was overflowing with men. Although that wasn't a bad thing, she supposed, as most of the girls in her crowd were on a mission to get laid!

A short time whooping it up on the dance floor and a couple of powerful cocktails left Joanne feeling like she'd had enough. She'd had months of just eating, sleeping, fulfilling physical functions and work; which hadn't left much margin for a social life, so now she was feeling saturated and somewhat unsociable in this draining atmosphere.

Not wanting to be a party pooper, she took time out and headed to the loo. On the way there, she spied a familiar figure hugging his glass at the bar but resisted the urge to say hello. Instead, when she came back she took her drink to one of the booths where she knew she'd be out of sight but could still watch the girls and the chattering throng without any involvement.

After a while she drained her glass and placed it on the table. A hand reached down and replaced it with a fresh drink. Her eyes narrowed as she followed the contour of the arm, which led to a familiar face.

'Like old times?' David echoed softly.' Can I sit down?' he asked, sliding in beside her. His fragrance once again unlocked familiar feelings.

A song started to play about thwarted love. His eyes settled on hers. 'Want to dance?'

She declined with a shake of her head but he took no notice. Instead he took her hand and guided her onto the dance floor. His arm snaked her waist and she automatically curled up against him as they swayed to the song that was playing. His cheek brushed her hair and suddenly his lips sought hers in a kiss that almost made her breath leave her body. She knew exactly where this was leading and, as the song ended, they made it out of the club without anyone seeing them and went back to the flat.

The minute the bedroom door closed, his kisses suddenly became more urgent.

'God I've missed your body,' he declared, unzipping her dress as they kissed. He skilfully manoeuvred her towards the bed and they began to discard their clothes, whilst their lips were still glued together. He feasted on her naked body and lifted her onto the bed where the passion she'd put on hold for such a long time was unleashed once again. All those empty nights she had longed for him to hold her like this had at last come to fruition. She lay beneath him and they made love-in a way that left her shaking and exhausted.

David was the first to break the silence. 'Can you ever forgive me?'

Tears stopped her answering immediately then she whispered,' I still love you! I never meant to fall in love with you but I did from the very beginning.'

Spooned up against him the following morning when she awoke, she turned over and looked lovingly at his ruffled hair, high cheekbones and unshaven ruggedness as he slept.

His eyelids flickered and, without opening them fully, he reached out and cupped her face in his hands. 'Hi, beautiful.'

His lips, his tongue, sought hers and his stiffness made her gasp. She took advantage of this piece of heaven that was being offered and, as he entered her, they embarked on a passion she'd almost forgotten existed. They ended up exhausted and collapsed in a sweaty heap on top of the crumpled sheets. Their bodies lay entwined and they drifted back to sleep again.

Joanne woke first and edged her way out of bed, trying not to wake him. En route to the loo, she lifted a thong from her drawer; she'd been saving it for a special occasion, an occasion that never came. Now she was desperate for him to see her in something sexier than the Marks and Sparks' passion killers that she wore most days.

Quietly, she took her robe from the hook on the door and shut herself in the bathroom. When she'd showered, cleaned her teeth and brushed her hair, she blasted her body with deodorant and helped herself to Suzy's Chanel from the shelf by the window. Then she scurried into the kitchen to make boiled eggs, tea and toast.

The December sunshine swathed the bedroom in sparkling diamonds as she pulled back the drapes. 'Wake up, sleepyhead! I've made breakfast,' she trilled brightly.

David blinked and tried to adjust to the light as he propped himself up on his pillows. She handed him the tray and slid in beside him.

As they ate, they indulged in touching, teasing and talking about everything that had happened in their lives since they had been apart. The moment was spoilt when he exercised bad judgment by trying to elaborate on why he had never got in touch. 'It was a huge mistake, trying to balance the two of you. What was I thinking? I loved you, but I couldn't hurt her.'

She knew that his feelings were profound but did not want to hear the feeble excuses he was conjuring up!

'I never stopped thinking about you or wanting you. You do know that, don't you?'

Joanne's stomach churned. His words were incredible –but she just could not take this Mills and Boon guff right now. Why couldn't he let sleeping dogs lie?

'Move in with me, Joanne. Let's embark on a life together. I can't lose you again!'

He cupped her face gently with his hands and lowered his lips onto hers. The kiss once again took her breath, but she broke free and stared at him blankly. What he was saying did not sound believable.

'Whoa – hang on there. Let's take one step at a time! Last night we rekindled such a lot and it was amazing, but I need time to let all this sink in. You lied to me once, you could be lying again, for all I know. How do I know it really is over between you and Sarah?'

David threw her a look of disbelief. 'So was it just the booze talking last night? When you told me you'd missed me, your life had been empty without me?' His comment brought about a sharp change of gear.

There was sternness now to his voice as their eyes locked in combat and a vein in his neck seems to double in size.

'Sort out Sarah and we will start from scratch. That's my best offer, David,' Joanne responded with a searching look.

He did a quick turnabout. 'Just listen to us. How many hours have we been together and here we are arguing like an old married couple. Of course you are unsure and you feel I am rushing you. I won't let you down again, I promise. Let me prove it to you.'

The mood was greatly changed between them, as if a great hole in his ego has been punctured by her cutting remarks. Reluctantly he dragged himself out of her bed, climbed into his crumpled clothes then, with a kiss and the promise to see her later that day, he was gone.

This turn of events was something Joanne had not bargained for when she went out the previous night. What would the girls say? What would everyone say when they knew? But who gave a damn – fate had stepped in and banged their heads together. They just weren't meant to be apart so she hustled other people's thoughts to the back of her mind.

She promised herself, though, that she would never get into a situation again where she would have to humble herself for the sake of self-gratification as she had in the past. Nor would she endure torn loyalties any more!

***

David was true to his word. All traces of Sarah seemed to have disappeared from his life in the couple of weeks leading up to Christmas.

They started again to do the usual things couples do like going to restaurants, seeing films and the ritual of David staying at the flat mid-week; in turn she stayed the entire weekend at his. Life could not have been more perfect. So why was she still so indecisive when David would put pressure on her to move in with him? Was paranoia playing such a huge role in that decision? Christmas would be the trial run, she decided. If it felt OK then she'd take that next step in the New Year.

To wake up Christmas morning in the arms of someone you are lucky enough to love was sheer bliss! David was delighted when Joanne introduced him to her child like version of Christmas – opening presents under the tree first thing with all the exuberance of a child, then going back to bed for a more grown-up present.

Showered and dressed, they ate cereal and toast and drank coffee. David gave his parents a quick ring to wish them merry Christmas; they were spending the day at his brother's house in Bath, wanting to be with the grandchildren on Christmas morning. Joanne managed a brief hello to them and exchanged pleasantries but it felt a bit strange not having met them yet.

They drove to Joanne's parents for Christmas lunch and an overnight stay – separate rooms, of course! It would have been disrespectful and embarrassing to suggest otherwise.

Instant warmth was ignited when she introduced David to her parents, and over lunch it just got better.

'I had a feeling you two wouldn't last long apart... he's really nice,' her mother grinned when Joanne helped her load the dishwasher after they'd eaten.

'I remember what you said a few months back, Mum. If it is meant, then it will be. Looks like you were right,' Joanne said, giving her a knowing look.

She glanced through the open door and saw her father and David by the fire exchanging stories, and her heart was filled with an overwhelming love for them both. Most of her mum's friends were widows now, which meant her father no longer had anyone to share his amusing tales with anymore, though David seemed to enjoy listening to them.

Breakfast over the next day, a tearful farewell followed between Joanne and her parents.

'It's been all too brief,' Helen admitted. 'You must come again, David.' She gave them both a parting hug. Joanne agreed to keeping in touch by phone and blew a kiss through the open car window.

The sun shone brightly for the time of year, making the pavements and rooftops glisten as they drove back to David's house. The instant the front door closed, they fumbled and stumbled to discard their clothes as they couldn't wait to make up for their night in separate beds.

Chapter 7

Joanne unlocked the door of the flat and let herself in early one Sunday morning after the New Year was over. It was unusual for her to be there at the weekend but David was motoring down to London with Steven, his partner, for a couple of days. They were going to some sort of export convention so had dropped her off on his way.

The flat was silent as she crept down the hallway to the kitchen to make herself a brew. By the state of the place, it looked like the girls had had a dinner party the previous night. Pots were piled in the sink, the table still had empty wine bottles, half-filled glasses, plates with the remnants of cheese and biscuits on them, and the cushions on the couch were flattened.

Joanne laughed inwardly. Her doubts about moving in with David had been based on the fact that sharing a flat with the girls had been so much fun and, if truth be known, she despaired of losing that freedom. She looked around; this was exactly what she talking about.

David's house was a tightly run ship; no longer would she be able to kick off her shoes after a tough day at work, lower herself onto the couch with a glass of wine then make do with whatever was left in the fridge for dinner. Instead, she envisaged scurrying round the supermarket on her way home, having to crack on with the potato peeler as soon as her coat was thrown off and thumbing her way through Delia to drum up some inspiration about what to serve with the spuds!

No longer would the laundry be allowed to lie in a heap until she was ready to throw it in the wash; nor would she be able to iron on impulse as she had been doing.

It was one thing inviting David into her bed when her bits were de-fuzzed, nails painted, hair and makeup intact! However, to be around him 24/7 – he'd be able to see the *au naturel* Joanne much more than he did now.

Then there were her pre-menstrual days when she tried her best to avoid seeing him because she needed to don her comfortable pyjamas and indulge herself in chocolate, pizza and anything with carbs. The girls understood these things; men did not.

She threw a teabag into the only mug left in the cupboard, poured steaming water from the kettle onto it and gave it a stir.

Suzy's cheery face appeared round the door. 'Oh my goodness!' Suzy let out a shattering shriek when she saw her and enveloped her in a hug. 'To what do we owe the honour?' she grinned, rescuing a dirty mug from the sink and rinsing it under the tap. Without bothering to dry it, she threw an herbal teabag in and made herself a brew.

'David's gone off to London.'

'What? And he's not taken you!'

'He's gone with Steven. You remember the bloke he was with when we first met.'

Suzy's eyebrows lifted and she grinned as she remembered who he was.

'They've gone to some sort of export convention.'

'So you've come home to play with us again, have you?' Suzy laughed. Both bearing steaming mugs, they moved into the lounge and lowered themselves onto the couch.

'Sorry about the state of the place,' Suzy said, scanning the room and lowering her eyes. 'Harry, this guy I work with at occupational therapy– remember me telling you I've been out a couple of times after work for a quick drink with him? Well, I cooked him dinner last night, seeing as I had the place to myself. Gill has gone home to her parents for the weekend. Over dinner we got quietly pissed. I mean, I've fancied him for ages! He's tall, handsome, with a well-toned physique. Over dinner it sort of leaked out how I felt about him.'

Joanne's eyebrows rose.

'It seems he's been feeling the same about me so after we'd emptied a couple of bottles of wine I asked him if he'd like to stay the night.' Suzy cringed.

'Oh Suzy… You did not! What did he say?'

'He looked at me a tad old-fashioned at first and after that he could barely keep his hands off me. I've had the most amazing night.

What a turn of events, eh!' Warmth oozed from her smile the whole time she talked about him.

'He is still fast asleep so I thought I come in here, don my Marigolds and get everything spruced up – you know how anal I get about the place being tidy at the best of times!'

'Look, you go and have a shower, get yourself spruced up instead. Use my room to get ready. I'll see to this lot.'

Suzy threw her arms around her friend and gave her a hug. 'Thanks, Jo, you're an angel.'

Once Joanne saw the place was spic and span, she took herself off for a long walk along the pier to give them more time alone.

***

The decision to move in with David was taken out of Joanne's hands. The landlord decided he was doing a major revamp to the whole building! The tight old bugger was turning all the flats into bed-sits, which would no doubt double his revenue.

He informed his tenants formally that they had just a month to find somewhere else to live. Gill and Suzy knew instinctively where Joanne would be going and were OK with her decision.

Their new flat was in a block of flats overlooking the sea wall. It ticked all the boxes, plus it was cheap, but it was on the third floor with no lift. Joanne did not share their enthusiasm when she went to visit; she felt the whole place smelt of damp. A guilt pang gripped her. Had she stayed with them, maybe the extra rent would have merited something better.

Valentine's Day fast approached so, masking her uncertainty, Joanne saw it as a good time to make the sacrificial move.

She could sense David watching carefully as each box, ornament and suitcase came through the front door and was shocked by how cluttered the house appeared once all her things had arrived. Then, in the grand scheme of life, they began to embrace their life together with some gusto.

He bought her flowers, they shared chores and he even found her morning confusion quite engaging at times. Their friends called them sex junkies but they called themselves happy and in love.

Each night after the dinner, when the plates were tidied away, they'd listen to warbling love lyrics and drink good red wine from large glasses as they lay entwined on the rug in front of the fire. Chatting until the early hours to find out more about each other, Joanne couldn't understand why she'd been so apprehensive and wished she'd moved in sooner.

Past relationships for them both had proved to be suffocating and repressive but, instead of casting off those thoughts, they let them dwell in the midst of any dramas that seemed to surface, which led to cracks appearing in their newly entwined lives.

The green-eyed monster also appeared more frequently; in those cases anger was propelled by jealousy. David seemed to feel it more than Joanne did and would fly into a rage as his imagination ran wild when other men flirted with her when they were out.

Resentment soon began to gather. Arguments erupted, usually for the stupidest of reason. David constantly left the toilet seat up, or left his unwashed clothes strewn across the bedroom floor where he discarded them before going to bed. His snoring left her furious as it echoed round the room, especially when he'd had a skin-full.

In return, he'd go ballistic that she felt the need to use every pot, pan and plate in the kitchen when cooking even the simplest meals; lights would be left burning unnecessarily and the top being left off the toothpaste caused constant mayhem!

Even their foreplay seemed to be turning into the marital kind, Joanne began to realise. She should have read the small print when she moved in with him, she thought after a heated row one day. It probably would have read: 'In return for bed and board, you have to give blowjobs on demand and speak only when spoken to!'

David started meeting up with his single friends again whenever possible and usually did not come home until the early hours. In return, Joanne asked Philippa if there were any seminars coming up that she could attend.

'I need some time away on my own. I feel a bit hemmed in at the moment,' she told Philippa candidly.

Philippa checked her inbox. 'A lecturer in Leeds is needed in two weeks' time,' she said, giving Joanne a hard stare. 'I didn't think you'd be interested, that's why I didn't mention it. Appointments would have to be juggled, but I suppose it's doable,' she said, checking the diary.

***

The traffic was fierce on the drive to Leeds, leaving Joanne feeling wilted as her car purred into the hotel car park half an hour later than she was supposed to arrive.

With no time to grab a quick coffee, she dumped her bags after checking into her room, replenished her lipstick, had a quick wee, plucked the appropriate paperwork from her briefcase then ran at speed down the corridor to catch the lift that had just pinged its arrival.

Jonathan Miles, the head of the firm, a smallish chap with receding hair and a sallow complexion, was standing in the lift when she stepped in. Joanne felt the blood drain from her whole being when she saw a flash of recognition on his face. She must have looked very unprofessional staring back at him, breathless and open-mouthed.

He held out his hand. 'It's Joanne, isn't it?'

'Yes,' she managed to squeak.

'I was hoping to catch you at some point. I need to speak to you,' he said, straight-faced. 'But I see you're busy right now.' He eyed the mound of paperwork wedged under her arm. 'How about you join me for dinner in the dining room, say around seven?' His face was set with a permanent sneer as he spoke.

Joanne had never met the chap before but she had seen photos. Everyone knew him as a patronising, limp-wristed little twerp. Joanne thought they were spot on as he grizzled his orders at her. She really was in no mood for this after the start she'd had that morning.

Instinctively she threw him a smile and nodded. She let out a sigh of relief as the lift doors opened. 'See you at seven then,' she said brightly, making an exit.

The day had gone relatively well seeing it started so disastrously, Joanne thought as she got ready to go down to dinner. Perhaps Mr Miles wasn't that bad a person after all; she'd probably caught him out of sorts, that was all.

Her composure was lost as she entered the dramatically lit, newly refurbished dining room and saw Jonathan Miles and his entourage seated round the large table at the far end of the room.

She felt confused at how she had been drawn into this little soirée; she had assumed it was going to be a one-on-one meal and a chat.

Jonathan spotted her and instantly beckoned her to the empty chair beside him; a glass of champagne was already waiting next to her place setting. Determined not to drink too much and make a fool of herself, she sipped her drink with some decorum.

No expense was spared that night on the food they were served and the bottles of wine placed randomly along the table. She felt it served no purpose her being there as there was just a flow of pleasantries amongst people she hardly knew, plus Jonathan Miles hardly said a word to her all night. He just watched her when she joined in the conversation, which she purposely kept to light social chit-chat. That unnerved her slightly, as at times she didn't have a clue what she was talking about.

There was a highly charged silence as the meal ended. Jonathan Miles stood up and gave a brief thank-you speech to everyone involved in the seminar, after which they all start to leave, eager to get to the bar – and who could blame them? The others were probably summoned here just like her to act subserviently around his table. At least she'd had a first-class meal and more to drink than she'd meant to.

Joanne considered bolting too and was just about to stand up. Then she felt some degree of annoyance as Jonathan turned to her and said, 'Joanne, could you stay a moment longer, please? There's a small matter I need to discuss with you.'

His manner was stomach-churning. He turned to give orders to his chauffeur who was waiting behind him. Whilst he wasn't looking Joanne emptied the content of her wine glass down her throat, hoping it would inject some Dutch courage. As she did, her eyes locked with Jonathan Miles who was now glaring at her.

'How would you like to work in Singapore for six months, all expenses paid?' His eyebrows rose dramatically as he spoke.

Joanne gasped in response.

'Triosthetics, as you well know, went global some years ago,' he said, sitting down again next to her. 'I need a temporary lecturer, consultant and area manager at the Orchard Road salon in Singapore whilst we set up a support group centre there. You'll be expected to do tutorials, earmark salons where the Triosthetic standards have dropped below par. You know the score – pretty much what you've been teaching here.'

Joanne stared at him unblinkingly. What he was telling her did not sound believable. 'Why me?'

'I have watched your progress over the years with some interest. Even when you worked for Leon, your old boss on the Fylde – who, by the way, sent us an outstanding reference in your favour after I talked over the phone to him and told him what had in mind. You're more than qualified, you have good people skills, no ties as such. I'd cover it with Philippa, so don't worry on that score. She'll be reimbursed and a temporary stand-in will be found whilst you're away. Come on, Joanne, it is a chance of a lifetime. Think about it at least,' he said, holding her gaze coldly.

He reached into his pocket. 'Here's my card with my personal details. Ring me when you've made your decision, but don't take too long!' With that, he stood up, drained his coffee cup then strolled over to join his long-suffering chauffeur who no doubt would be expected to drive him speedily back to London.

She understood now why people feared him at times; he obviously had nerves of steel. No social skills, probably never married, he demanded instead of asking! And if anyone dared object they were ousted, so she'd heard.

The wind was taken from her sails; under normal circumstances she would have jumped at the chance but these weren't normal circumstances. She and David had embarked on something she hoped would develop into a lifelong expedition.

Joanne took a great gulp of wine from a half-filled glass one of her fellow diners had left behind then ordered a double brandy from a passing waiter. She sat there long after the dining room had finished serving, pondering, digesting, trying to answer her own questions.

Work had always been a welcome distraction. Even now, when she was trying to avoid facing up to the fact things at home weren't going as well as she'd hoped, maybe a six-month break wouldn't be such a bad idea. She ordered another double brandy to go on Jonathan Miles' bill.

Joanne climbed into bed and telephoned home, feeling she needed a friendly voice to talk to, but David wasn't there. She remembered he had mentioned something about going somewhere with the lads. All these anxious thoughts and feelings of uncertainty left her uneasy so she got very little sleep that night.

Before going down for breakfast, she picked up the phone and dialled Jonathan's number; the elation in his voice was noticeable as she accepted the offer of a job. She felt now that she was doing the right thing.

He told her that a visa and details of her apartment and flight would be forwarded to her in due course, then finished the call with a curt goodbye.

Two weeks passed and Joanne heard nothing in the way of confirmation. She decided not to say anything to David about the job just yet; no point in causing concern. It might never happen, knowing Jonathan Miles.

***

Joanne pulled onto the driveway and climbed from her car after a gruelling Friday in the salon. She entered the house and was met by a full-on kiss from David that was quite a contrast from the harsh words they'd exchanged before she'd left that morning.

Flickering candles in the hearth and around the room cast a romantic haze and there was a lingering smell of bath salts denoting that a bath had been run for her … sex was on the cards, it seemed. It had been a while since they had been civil enough to get close, so she had been rather relieved about the lack of pressure on the seduction front in the last few weeks.

She took off her coat and threw it on the chair. David passed her a glass of wine. Feeling slightly puzzled, she asked, 'What's all this about?'

'Can't I do something nice without there being a reason?'

Joanne felt her face reddening.

He held her gaze and smiled briefly. 'Let's stop all this squabbling. Aren't you sick of it? I know I am.'

She agreed wholeheartedly but she knew that within a short space of time some issue would erupt and he would end up storming off to the pub like he always did.

'You've got exactly half an hour to spruce yourself up,' he said, looking at the clock on the mantelpiece. 'I've booked us dinner at the Crab and Lobster. Maybe we'll be able rekindle some of that romance you keep reminding me is missing.'

His eyes were soft, his words kind and pleasing. 'On the other hand we could cancel dinner. Maybe have a spot of duvet action instead. It's been a while,' he grinned.

Joanne burst out laughing. 'No chance, Bonzo. Tonight it's going to cost you plenty.'

What to wear! What to bloody wear, she muttered continuously under her breath as she discarded one dress after another before settling for her faithful black little number that never failed to impress. She rifled through her drawer for the expensive underwear bought some weeks back, and plucked her highest-heeled, suede shoes from the wardrobe in a desperate gamble to inject some passion back into their lives and eclipse whatever problems they'd been having.

David looked smart in his charcoal-grey suit, white shirt and red tie. His hair was longer than normal and slightly tousled, but it suited him.

Joanne slid onto the bar stool beside him after her visit to the ladies room and smiled tentatively as he settled his eyes on her. 'If you're trying to pick me up, madam, you're out of luck. I'm with my wife.'

She giggled and sipped the gin and tonic that was waiting for her on the bar. 'Why can't you be like this all the time?' she teased.

'Because I like to save this mood for special occasions,' he said with a pleasant smile, placing his hand on top of hers.

The waiter interrupted them by telling them that their table was ready. He guided them through to a marine-themed dining room, settling them into a booth facing one another. Low lighting, the muttering of fellow diners, then the wonderful smells that were wafting in from the kitchen left her feeing incredibly hungry. She'd not eaten all day; the salon had been far too busy to even grab a snack.

'Try the lobster. It looks amazing,' David said, scanning the menu.

But images of shell flying across the table as she tussled with it didn't really appeal so she opted for the crab-stuffed lemon sole.

Feelings began to gather inside her as they sipped expensive wine, played footsie under the table, and exchanged forkfuls of food over dinner. The evening went from good to wonderful and, in a moment of madness, he drew her to him and gently kissed her on her lips before they climbed back into the car at the end of the night. She wondered if there really was a chance of survival after all.

'One last surprise,' he whispered, starting the engine up.

David took the coastal road and veered off onto the beach. He came to a halt in a totally deserted spot. The engine went quiet; there was just the radio left on low.

David beckoned - he wanted her to move into the back of the car. There they nuzzled, kissed and recklessly fondled and he ended up making love to her.

With an uneasy feeling in the aftermath that someone might come along, Joanne suggested they go. David started to laugh, seeing how deeply embarrassed she was at what they'd just done.

'If the police catch us you won't be grinning!' she teased and handed him his shirt.

He laughed again and kissed her softly on the cheek. 'Well, you did say you needed more romance in your life.'

The next day was Saturday. Neither of them was working, a rare event. David slipped quietly out of bed and made his way downstairs to sort breakfast, leaving Joanne to catch up on her sleep. Half an hour later, he breezed back into the bedroom brandishing a loaded tray with tea, toast, boiled eggs and the post.

'Letter for you Jo, postmarked London. Who do you know in London?' he asked.

He handed her the letter and she felt the blood drain from her face. She knew exactly who the letter was from; she has been waiting long enough for its arrival.

Joanne tore at the envelope and unfolded the letter. It was handwritten on expensive-looking paper.

Hello Joanne,

Everything is now arranged for you. Your visa, apartment, and flight ticket details will be forwarded to you in a week's time. I have been in touch with Philippa and a replacement will visit her at the salon. She'll work three days a week for the next six months.

Raymond Hogarth is the salon owner in Singapore where you will be based, on Orchard Road. He will guide you through everything once you arrive.

You'll be leaving 24th May from Manchester Airport, flying with Singapore Airlines. That gives you two weeks to sort out your affairs. Good luck. I'll be in touch on a weekly basis so you can keep me updated.

Regards
Jonathan Miles

'Well, who's it from?' David asked, dipping a sliver of toast into his softly boiled egg then taking a bite.

Not knowing how to answer, she handed him the letter in a vain effort to make light of the situation. As he read it, his face drained. There was sadness now in his eyes, which was not nice to watch. He looked up and glared blankly at her.

'When did all this come about? Were you going to tell me? Or were you going to disappear one day, leaving me a Dear John letter on the mantelpiece?'

Joanne reached for his hand. He snatched it away. 'David, I didn't think anything would come of it.' She could see coldness now in his eyes; his world was falling apart and she was responsible.

'Do you remember the time I went to Leeds some weeks back? Remember me telling you I had dinner with the bigwigs?' Her eyes became tearful as she spoke. 'Well, over dinner Jonathan Miles offered me the job.'

David's eyes narrowed in disbelief.

Joanne rubbed her fingers forcibly against her forehead as she tried desperately to explain. 'You and I weren't getting on…we were arguing all the time. A six-month break seemed the answer. I didn't mention it because there wasn't much point until I had had confirmation from head office.'

David sat on the edge of the bed and lowered his head into his hands; he was on the brink of tears and his silence was unnerving. 'Joanne, why didn't you talk to me about this? I know us living together has not been anything like we imagined. Maybe it was too soon. Maybe commitment was not for us – well, not just yet.'

He moved closer and took her hands in his. 'I understand you've missed out on so much and your aim was always to travel, wasn't it, once you were free? I have thwarted those plans, haven't I?' There was no malice in his voice.

'In a way, I can see how the prospect of a job like this must have seemed a rare opportunity… too good to miss, especially when it was offered to you on a plate. Maybe you should take it. Maybe you should release that travel bug from inside you. Fulfil that dream, if that is what you want. You will regret it if you don't … but at least let's talk about it.'

Joanne felt like a child being chastised for a wrong-doing. It took her breath away, though, how understanding and controlled he was being.

The following few days were tough. David kept blowing hot and cold about the whole thing - he made her feel like she was having some sort of mid-life crisis rather than taking time out to further her career. The plain fact was they were not getting on; the whole process of living together had been draining.

He loved her, though. Always would. He assured her he would wait, however long it took.

Chapter 8

Joanne's feelings ran far deeper than she dared express as David led her through the airport to the check-in desk the day she left for Singapore. Why was she doing this? What had seemed such a good idea at the time, she was now not so sure about.

With her luggage checked in, it was time for them to say goodbye. A lurching sensation hit the pit of Joanne's stomach as they clung to one another; neither one wanted to be the first to let go. She caught her breath as David stroked her hair. The memory of his tear-stained face as she left him standing there would stay with her for a long time to come.

The flight seemed endless. Joanne hated flying, but at least it gave her time to reflect. Finally the pilot announced they were approaching the runway. Joanne's stomach churned.

She hadn't been prepared for the enormity and drama of Changi airport as she followed the steady flow of people making their way through passport control. She was excited but at the same time fearful of what lay ahead, if this was an indication of how it was going to be.

Joanne followed faces she recognised from her flight on the moving walkway, knowing that in all probability they would lead her to the baggage carousel.

Raymond Hogarth, her new boss, was waving frantically as she pushed her loaded trolley through the arrival doors. He introduced himself and she shook his hand warmly before he led her to his chauffeur-driven car. On the drive to her apartment he said very little apart from asking about the flight, and was she was looking forward to working here. Joanne began to feel strangely vulnerable and overwhelmed as she took in the view of this chaotic, futuristic-looking city.

'I hope this meets with your approval,' Raymond said, unlocking the door of the marble-floored apartment on the tenth floor of a high-rise block of flats right in the centre of Singapore.

Joanne gave an audible intake of breath as she entered and saw the view from the lounge window. The breath-taking city stretched out before her like a massive designer theme park. Hundreds of bright lights flashed, beamed and twinkled against the backdrop of a darkened sky.

'You see that building down there, the one that looks like it's made completely from glass?' Raymond pointed to a building to the right of them.

Joanne nodded.

'That is the salon. As you can see, it's just a short walk.' He noticed how stunned she was and grinned. 'You'll soon get used to it.'

Raymond Hogarth was exquisitely dressed, with perfect teeth, well-groomed hair, perfect eyebrows and just a hint of jewellery by way of a Rolex watch. Joanne sensed that underneath his pleasing disposition he was not someone to be toyed with. It was the way he explained what she'd be expected to do and how she should behave now she was here in Singapore.

'I'll leave you to unpack. I'll see you first thing at the salon. We start at eight sharp. By the way, the fridge is full of food. No need to go out to eat.' He pointed to the welcome pack on the worktop. 'Your keys and all your instructions are all in there.' With that, he bade her goodnight and let himself out.

This was certainly an eye-opener. She could hardly contain herself as she wandered through each room, opening and closing cupboards and drawers, turning taps on and off, sitting on couches and chairs. Everywhere was tastefully furnished with gadgets throughout – in the kitchen, bathroom, bedroom, lounge. She could control the lights, curtains, and music from just one remote. The fridge looked huge and lit up the whole kitchen as she opened the door to check what was in there.

Once she'd unpacked, she made herself a meal, showered then climbed into bed where slumber instantly claimed her.

***

Joanne's fast-paced life in Singapore left her with little margin for a social life, once she started to make her way through the huge list of salons she was expected to visit. At least Felix, her driver, spoke good English. He was also bestowed with a wacky sense of humour and showed her some incredible eating-houses, most of them run by lady boys of whom one was his cousin. He pointed out the best places to shop, too, when she had time.

It was the humility of the people she worked with and the salon owners she visited and the ambiance of the place that made her love it all. In her letters to David and her parents, she tried to encapsulate everything but it was too overwhelming to get across.

To her delight, all her letters were answered almost by return of post.

David allowed his feelings, thoughts and fears to come tumbling out! In addition, he surprised her by telling her he had been staying with her parents most weekends since she'd left. He explained that he'd not really had time to get to know them properly and knew they were concerned about her. With the aid of an audio recorder, he recorded their voices and sent her a tape showing how proud they were that she had followed the dream to travel she had been harbouring for such a long time.

It was David's letter in mid-August that sent excitement charging through her veins. He had booked to come out and see her; it was only for four days, but would give them chance to spend some time together.

Joanne was up at dawn, anxiously awaiting his arrival at the airport. Raymond had generously granted her some time off and even put Felix at their disposal should they need to go anywhere,

She took her time to dress with care and tend to her makeup and hair. The figure-hugging, white linen dress she'd bought specially showed off her tan as she checked herself out in the bedroom mirror before she left.

In his letters, David had said so much! However, it was such a long time since they had shared the intimacy of being in the same room together.

Emotions ran high as they ran into each other's arms and hugged when she met him at the airport. A brief guided tour of the city followed as Felix ferried them back to her apartment.

David's face was a picture as he took it all in. He stood stock still when she led him through the apartment door; at last he was able to see the grandeur in which she'd lived for the last four months.

Their words drizzled into silence as nerves got the better of them. Joanne busied herself making a pot of tea and David began to update her about all that had gone on back home and how the business was doing. By the time they'd drained the last dregs from their cups, they seemed to be more like their old selves again.

'Joanne, before you left,' he said taking her hand in his, 'we both promised that if ever one of us felt differently towards the other we'd be brutally honest and say so.'

Joanne's stomach churned; she had a feeling something very unpleasant was about to occur. Had he come all this way to tell her he had met someone else? Was this visit his way of letting her down slowly? Oh God! She couldn't bear it. Tears pricked her eyes as she looked at him.

'Joanne, just tell me … do you still love me?' She could feel his hands trembling as he held onto hers.

Her hands were trembling, too, in anticipation of what he was about to say. She nodded. 'Of course. I think I love you more now than ever.'

'Then will you marry me?'

Joanne let out a loud shriek. Shock, disbelief, a feeling of bafflement at what she'd just heard him say overwhelmed her. She threw her arms around him and drew him to her. 'Oh yes! I'd love to marry you.'

Relief etched itself on David's face and he breathed a sigh of relief. He looked exhausted and elated. They kissed.

They spent the next four days rekindling their passion. They made the most of Felix's knowledge as they sampled all Singapore had to offer in the way of beauty spots, street food, shopping malls, temples and culture. They managed to cram so much into those four short days and promised to revisit some day and cram in the things they never got chance to see.

'It's only six weeks,' Joanne reminded David tearfully at the airport as they held on to each other before she waved him on his way.

Chapter 9

Raymond threw Joanne a huge leaving party at the salon on the eve of her departure back to the UK .All the people she had struck up a friendship with turned up.

Even Raymond, with his stiff manner and no-nonsense attitude, surprised her by shedding a few tears the next day when the time came to say their goodbyes.

The last six months had stripped away several layers of Joanne's naivety; she had become much more streetwise.

Everywhere was blanketed in December snow as the plane touched down. Joanne trudged through passport control and had an endless wait for her luggage to turn up on the carousel. Finally she pushed her loaded trolley through the swing doors and saw David galloping towards her with outstretched arms.

Then clung to one another as they kissed, eventually pulling apart like two deflecting magnets, leaving her feeling her life at long last had fallen back in place.

David managed to cram the huge amount of luggage into the boot and onto the back seat of his car before climbing in next to her. He sat perfectly still, scrutinising her face as he told her they were driving over to her parents first before going home. That seemed a bit strange; she had anticipated making up for lost time back at his house.

'Why?' she asked.

He broke the news: her father had had another stroke a couple of weeks after she left for the Far East. 'Your mother swore me to secrecy and made me promise not to breathe a word until you came home, which I found a massive strain to be completely honest. I'm so sorry. That is the reason I stayed most weekends at your parents, to help where I could.'

Tears streamed down Joanne's face and she could not speak for her sobs.

When they eventually arrived, she could see at a glance that the stroke had taken its toll. Henry broke down in tears as soon as he set eyes on her …his little girl had come home, home where she belonged. Joanne read his thoughts.

How pale and gaunt he was. The right side of his face had collapsed slightly, noticeable mostly when he spoke. His right arm and leg seem to have a mind of their own too, he told her jovially.' So I can no longer chase your mother round the house like I used to.'

Her mother's eyes brimmed as she tearfully watched her daughter cradle her father in her arms. Helen had been so brave coping alone. David sat quietly through it all, smiling supportively, saying very little. Her mother pointed out that David had phoned her most nights for a brief chat, which had kept her focused, and he stayed most weekends so there'd been a fair amount of support from him and from her friends in the WI.

Helen gave Joanne a motherly smile as she wrapped her arms around her, admitting how relieved she was that her daughter was home. 'We have been so proud of you, love! Pursuing your dream – not everyone gets the chance to do that. I didn't want to spoil things and Dr Wyley pointed out that Dad wasn't in any danger.'

It was upsetting being here under these circumstances and Joanne felt ashamed she had not come home sooner.' If I had only known!' she responded tearfully.' But I'm here now! That's all that matters, to give you respite and support when you need it most.'

She realised that David had displayed an abundance of tenderness and love for her in those months they were apart. How unselfish he'd been, coming here to support her mother. It didn't seem enough now just to say she loved him!

Over dinner, Joanne relayed stories of her time in the Far East and about the moment David asked her to marry him. Henry joked about how nervous David was when he asked their permission. 'Oh, I told him, "Have, her lad – we're glad to get rid of her."' It was lovely to see him so jovial.

Joanne pulled presents from her case and the laughs continued until her father felt tired and needed to retire. David volunteered to help him up the stairs, a slow process, but David had the patience of

Job where her dad was concerned. He helped him undress then stayed and chatted for a while, knowing Joanne needed time alone with her mother.

Helen was quite insistent they get themselves off the next day. 'It's not fair being around old fogies when you have so much to catch up on. Your dad's been reassured that your OK, he's seen how happy you both are.' She admitted to Joanne that they loved David like their own son and couldn't be more pleased they were getting married.

It felt strange walking through the familiar doorway of David's house again. Joanne stood quite still by the window at the far end of the sitting room whilst David unloaded the luggage from the car. This had not been the homecoming she had imagined. She sighed inwardly.

'You OK?' David asked as he walked back into the room.

Joanne continued to watch the winter wind toss the rust-coloured leaves on the back lawn like mini-tornadoes. 'I guess… I just need time to absorb everything that has happened,' she said, turning to give him a faint smile.

'Glad you came back?' he asked with some caution.

'Oh God, yes! I have never been as sure of anything in my entire life as I am about us. It's just Dad and everything…bit of a shock.'

He walked over and cradled her in his arms as she began to weep. Her tears intensified but through it all she felt a deep love for the man who was holding her.

David ran Joanne a hot bath and handed her a glass of chilled wine, which led to a couple of hours of sexual gratification between crisp white sheets.

'I haven't had time to stock the fridge, I'm afraid,' David muttered much later as they lay beneath the duvet. 'So unless you want a mouldy tomato and some rock-hard cheese for dinner, I'm going to have to tear myself away and nip to the Spar for some milk, eggs, bread and whatever else we need to tide us over until we can do a shop.'

'Get whatever you think. I will eat anything.' Joanne yawned and rubbed her eyes.

David slipped out of bed, climbed into his jeans and pulled a black wool sweater over his head.' Are you sure there is nothing you fancy?' he asked, scanning the floor for his discarded socks.

'A kiss would be nice,' she grinned back at him.

His soft lips descended on hers in a kiss that lingered. 'I'm going,' he said, breaking away from her,' before you persuade me to give the shops a miss.'

She listened as his car purr away from the drive and stroked the side of the bed where he had been only moments before. She could still smell his cologne on the sheets. Then she reached for the phone on the bedside table and punched in Gill and Suzy's number.

Suzy answered almost immediately, sounding half asleep. 'Hello?'

'Helloweee...It's me. I'm home!'

Suzy let out an ear-piercing shriek as she heard her friend's voice, then continued in a flurry of excitement. 'When did you get home? How is David? Has he done anything to the house whilst you have been away? When are you getting married?'

Joanne responded, 'Hang on, will you? This is just a call to say I'm home. David has nipped to the shop for some food, so I will have to be quick. I'll give you a proper update when I've unpacked and spent some quality time with my husband-to-be!' They descended into giggles at his new title. Then, on a more serious note, Joanne relayed the news about her dad.

'I'm so sorry...' Suzy empathised. 'He is such a lovely man. I hope he makes a speedy recovery. I bet they have missed you!'

'Yes, but Mum hid Dad's illness from me until now. She even swore David to secrecy so it's been a huge shock. I've missed you lot so much; your letters kept me sane at times when I needed it the most.'

'David really must love you, kiddo, to have gone to this trouble to get you back. It's going to be so much better this time, you'll see... Speak soon!'

The girls' letters had kept her updated with all the hot gossip – who had dumped whom, in addition to who was up the duff. Joanne had missed their wackiness, their hugs and their laughter, and looked forward to catching up.

She replaced the receiver, threw back the duvet, paid the loo a quick visit and then ransacked her case for clean pants and a tracksuit.

'I'm back,' David shouted up the stairs.

'I'm coming down …just getting dressed.'

'Don't bother getting dressed on my account,' she heard him say, which made her smile.

After devouring a full English fry-up and a decent pot of tea, which David made, Joanne gave a satisfied grin. 'There's something about sausage, egg and bacon and fried tomatoes! I've really missed all this,' she explained as she cleared the table and slotted the dishes into the dishwasher.

'And I've missed you,' he said, drawing her to him.

Neither of them was under any illusions about the pitfalls of living together. They were well aware of each other's faults. They were not juveniles as they had been before, so this had to be a grown-up version.

Joanne rang her mother umpteen times a day to keep tabs on her parents and visited regularly. She felt happy knowing she was just a stone's throw away should her dad be ill again.

***

Christmas loomed and, under sufferance, Joanne managed to drag David around the shops for presents and the biggest Christmas tree they could find.

They'd already met up with Peter and the gang for a Sunday afternoon piss-up at the pub by the canal; it was nice to see them all again and catch up. Joanne had still not met David's parents because they had only just returned home from an extended holiday to the Far East. Joanne realised Sarah had taken up a huge chunk of David's life and they had probably become quite attached to her but she hoped they'd like her too, once they got to know her.

Joanne started to embrace her new life by getting into some sort of routine whilst David was at work. Saturdays was usually spent food shopping, a pub lunch then an afternoon romp in the sack...

David had been in a work-related bad mood all day so, instead of their usual Saturday-afternoon romp, he slumped on the couch to watch a news item. Joanne took herself off to the bedroom to read a book, feeling that some space was clearly needed, but she fell asleep after reading only two pages. She was woken by the doorbell ringing noisily.

She heard David answer it then a male voice greeted him loudly. Eager to know who the voice belonged to, she dragged a brush through her hair, straightened her jumper, tugged at her jeans and made her way down the stairs. Halfway down, she felt her face redden. It was David's parents.

Jessica was petite and tanned; her highlighted hair was pinned into a pleat and under her camel cashmere coat she wore navy tailored trousers, a navy twin-set and a single row of pearls that made her appear to be a woman of some standing. She greeted Joanne with a peck on the cheek.

Oliver, David's dad, introduced himself and Joanne could see where David got his looks. Oliver was quite a handsome chap – he'd probably been a heartbreaker in his time and still was, by the twinkle in his eye. Tall, tanned, well turned out, under his sheepskin coat, he wore a cashmere golfing jumper and check pants. He was an architect – Joanne remembered David had mentioned his dad had retired after a slight heart attack. He now lived off the rich pickings from property he had acquired and rented out.

Being retired did not mean they sat around all day and vegetated, like their peers. 'Far from it,' Oliver almost bellowed. 'We love to travel and when were home, I have my golf.'

They sat on the couch as soon as their coats were taken and Jess relayed how happy she and Oliver were that David and Joanne were getting married. At that point, Joanne's stomach somersaulted. Somewhere down the line, surely there must have been some reservations or concerns? Their son had declared that he was getting married to someone they had not even met.

Oliver changed the subject, anticipating that his wife would start delving into Joanne's background seeing that they had no knowledge of where she came from or who her parents were. He wanted to keep their first meeting light-hearted.

Not being prepared for their visit, Joanne hadn't bothered with makeup and wore her oldest faded jeans, not an outfit to make a good first impression on future in-laws, she thought. She scurried off into the kitchen to make some tea. Jess joined her the moment after David carried a loaded tray through to the lounge.

'Can I help?'

'No, it's all done, thanks, Jess. I'm just going to take some hot mince pies out of the oven.'

Jess touched Joanne's arm with some tenderness.' Joanne, it's only a flying visit, love. No need to make a fuss. We've really called to invite you both to dinner next Tuesday night so we can welcome you into the family properly before the mayhem of Christmas begins.'

Joanne felt thrilled. 'Jess, we would love to come!'

***

David's parents lived in a converted farmhouse in the small leafy village of Aughton, not half an hour's drive from Southport. The security lights flooded the gravel driveway as David's car crunched to a halt.

'What a lovely old house,' Joanne whispered before climbing from the car. She took in the manicured lawns and walled gardens. There were leaded windows with stone sills, and a large porch with a studded oak front door, which opened almost immediately and David's parents came out to greet them.

Joanne's eyes danced round enthusiastically as they entered. It was a house straight out of *House and Gardens*. They followed Oliver down an oak-panelled hallway into the sitting room where he took their coats. Jess scurried off into the kitchen.

A log fire crackled in an impressive stone fireplace, above which hung an enormous gold-framed mirror. Opposite that were three huge cream sofas around a large, square, black-lacquered coffee table on which bowls of crisps, nuts and dips had been already placed. The windows were dressed impressively in cream brocade, gold piping and tassels. Joanne's parents' home was humble compared to all this, she mused.

Oliver opened the doors of a huge cupboard against the far wall. The interior light came on, making the shelved crystal glasses glisten like jewels. 'What's your tipple, Joanne?' he smiled over.

She perched on the edge of the sofa, too afraid to sit back and crease the brocade cushions neatly placed in a row behind her. David's dark eyes twinkled as he watched in amusement at how nervous she was. He came to her rescue. 'She'll have one of your specials, Dad,' he said. He and Oliver smiled in unison.

Oliver filled the cocktail shaker and shouted for Jess to bring in some fresh orange juice and more ice. He poured the concoction from the shaker into two glasses and handed one to Joanne.

She was intrigued as she sipped her drink. An orangey, liquorish-tasting liquid filled her mouth, which was really quite pleasant.' It is lovely … does this drink have a name?' she enquired.

'It's a Harvey Wallbanger, one of my favourites,' Jess answered, seating herself next to Joanne.

'Jess and I would like to welcome you to the family, Joanne,' Oliver said, raising his glass.

Joanne felt her face redden and smiled. She made sure she expressed interest in the issues they talked about, not wanting them to think her boring or unintelligent. She had not been prepared for how grand it all was.

Over dinner, Jess put Joanne at ease by chatting about Joanne's job in Singapore and about her own travels there. Then she went on to talk about her two other sons and her grandchildren.' You'll be able to meet them all. I know they're dying to meet you. Oliver and I alternate Christmases with Jonathan and Abby at their house in Bath. I love being with Amber and Lily on Christmas morning, seeing their little faces when they open their presents. I have been stockpiling presents for them since summer; they are wrapped in the loft. I hope the snow keeps off before they get here,' she said, frowning.

'The house comes alive when all the family is home,' she continued. 'Oliver has so many relatives on his side of the family,' her eyes rose heavenward.

Joanne helped Jess clear the table and loaded the dishwasher whilst Jess served dessert.' What a great kitchen,' she commented.

Before her stood a huge Agar above which copper-bottomed pans hung from an overhead rail. Granite worktops ran the length of the kitchen, a fridge-freezer the size of a double wardrobe and state-of-the-art equipment were installed behind handmade cupboard doors. Joanne had only seen a kitchen like this in magazines before.

'It's German,' Jess commented light-heartedly. 'The kitchen was all made in Germany.'

'Oh? It's amazing.'

'Yes, it is nice, isn't it? Oliver always has to have the best but I'm afraid it's not always easy living with someone with such high expectations.'

The men took their coffee and brandy into the sitting room after they had finished eating. Jess asked if Joanne would like to see her special room whilst the men talked shop. David had already mentioned this room. It was one which Jess had designed herself, a room where she found peace when the family got too much. Somewhere she could read, write letters or just listen to music uninterrupted.

'You almost need a letter from God to get be invited in there,' David had said mockingly on the drive over, so Joanne felt privileged to be asked.

An arched oak door creaked open and, as they entered, Joanne felt like she'd been transported back in time. It was quite a large, airy room, with shelved alcoves each side of the chimney breast, which were crammed with books of every shape, size and description. Old books, new ones, leather-bound ones all seemed to have found a home there. A wood burner was fitted into an open hearth and crackled away merrily. The walls were a light willowy green; rich burgundy-velvet curtains with tasselled tiebacks hung from huge wooden poles in the two windows overlooking the garden. To one side of the fireplace was a burgundy buttoned-back nursing chair with a matching footstool, next to which was an antique wine table. On it lay a solitary book – a first edition, no doubt – and a pair of gold-rimmed specs.

Joanne lowered herself onto the chaise lounge opposite the fireplace as her eyes danced excitedly round the room, taking in all it had to offer .The feeling of tranquillity and peace enchanted her.

'Would you like a glass of port or maybe a brandy?' Jess smiled.

'A brandy would be lovely, thanks,' Joanne grinned back.

Jess walked over to the leather-topped desk in front of one of the windows. Amongst the pile of books, paperweights and silver trinkets was a silver tray. On it sat three cut-glass decanters and two crystal glasses. Jess lifted the top off one of the decanters and half-filled two glasses with amber liquid, then handed one to Joanne. She lowered her onto the button-back chair and raised her glass. 'Cheers.'

'Cheers.'

'I bet you think I'm an eccentric old fool, don't you? Having a room like this, when the rest of the house is so stylish,' she said.

'Not at all – I love it! It is very different from the rest of the house but that's what I like about it,' Joanne said, beaming from ear to ear.

'Being an architect, Oliver took complete control when we bought the house… it's his way or no way! He planned everything, down to the colour schemes and doorknobs,' she said with a frown.' But when it came to this room, which originally was a children's play room, he said I could do what I wanted with it, so I designed it round the furniture my mother left me.

'When I was a little girl I was something of a dreamer. I adored old movies and books, classics like *Jayne Eyre* and *Wuthering Heights*. God! I'd have loved to have been born in that era.' Her face lit up as she spoke.' When I suggested to Oliver that I would like my room themed on that era, I thought he was going to blow a gasket. But he didn't, he just said, "If that's what you want, go ahead and do it!" And this is the result,' Jess said, eyeing the room fondly.

'This is the place, I come when things get a little too much…You will probably understand that a lot more when you have a family of your own. Always make sure you have a place to escape to, dear, and find yourself again.' She took a sip from her glass. 'Sometimes men can be a bit much,' she said and grinned.

There was a gentle knock then David's head appeared round the door. 'Well, what do you think? Dad and I have concluded Mum's a white witch and this is where she keeps her cauldron,' he mocked affectionately, pecking his mum on the cheek as he spoke.

'Often a true word spoken in jest, son,' Jess smiled back.

'We'll have to be going soon, it's getting late.'

Joanne glanced at the chiming clock on the mantelpiece and saw it was nearly midnight. 'Oh blimey, so it is… I hope we haven't outstayed our welcome.'

'You certainly have not. We have enjoyed your company immensely,' Jess said, getting up from her chair.

***

‘Your mum and dad are lovely and the house is amazing. Why didn’t you warn me?’ Joanne sighed on the drive home. ‘I feel like we are the prince and the pauper now. I didn’t realise you were posh.’

‘Would it have made any difference?’

‘Definitely – I wouldn’t have waited so long to bed you!’ she teased.

Chapter 10

Joanne imagined Christmas in the Winston household probably verged on being amazing, still she found some comfort in the fact that she had prearranged Christmas dinner at her own parents' house. It would have been chaotic and slightly intimidating for her first meeting with David's clan. The Boxing Day invitation sounded far more relaxed; she would be able to mingle inconspicuously and adjust to everyone.

Christmas morning finally arrived. Both she and David ran excitedly downstairs in towelling robes, eager to open the mound of presents waiting under the tree. The biggest surprise of all was the little box David had placed inconspicuously amongst the others; Joanne had not even noticed it was there!

He handed the present to her and his face lit up in anticipation as Joanne tore at its wrapping then opened the small leather box inside. Her eyes widened in disbelief as she saw what it was! It was a seven stone diamond-cluster engagement ring; the one she had admired in the jeweller's window the day they went Christmas shopping.

She was speechless as she sat on the floor staring at it for what seemed an age. She glanced up and saw David watching her nervously. 'Aren't you going to try it on?' he said softly.

A lump appeared in her throat as she slipped it on the third finger of her left hand. It was a perfect fit. 'It's amazing,' she cried out, tearfully admiring her outstretched hand.

She jumped on David, hugging him, kissing and struggling to think straight.' This makes the briefcase, jumper, socks and bottle of smelly I bought you look sad,' she jested.

'I just wanted to make it official. You really do belong to me now.'

'How did you know it would fit?' she beamed.

'I took one of your rings from your jewellery box and got them to size it for me.'

The security of knowing how much he loved her brought tears to her eyes but laughter took over as they continued to open the rest of the presents.

The drive to Joanne's parents was serene; the fields were white with frost and the sun shone, making everywhere glisten and look cheerful and Christmassy. She had never been so happy.

Helen and Henry's faces lit up when they arrived an hour late due to some intimate moments before they left. 'Merry Christmas,' they all chorused.

Joanne flashed her hand under their noses. 'We're engaged!'

'Blimey, lad! Have you won the pools or something?' her dad retorted dryly, examining the ring closely.

Joanne brimmed with pride as she showed it off.' We have also set a date for the wedding – June fourth if we can get the church and a venue for the reception. We decided on that date on the way here. You are the first to know.' She glanced at David for moral support.

'Better start shopping for a new hat, Helen,' Henry teased, giving his daughter a wink.

'And I don't want you two to worrying about money. Joanne and I are footing the bill for this wedding; you have done it once, can't expect you to do it again,' David proclaimed.

Joanne's parents looked at one another in a stunned silence.

'Seems like you've got it all worked out lad,' her dad said, lowering himself into his favourite chair.

Helen emerged from the kitchen armed with four champagne flutes and a tray of canapés, which they consumed whilst they exchanged presents.

It was heart-warming to see how mobile her father had become in such a short space of time; he'd even taken to helping in the kitchen, wiping the pots. Nothing major but it kept up his morale knowing he was being useful.

Jess was not the only one whose Christmas dinner was exceptional, it seemed. Her own mother was a stickler for detail when it came to setting the table: best china, silver candelabra and Waterford crystal all got an airing on that day.

Celia and Arthur, her parents' friends from down the road, joined them. Arthur had been tremendously helpful when Helen needed a hand. This was her way of thanking them.

Arthur turned out to be a character and had them all laughing throughout the meal with his offbeat stories, whilst Celia pretended to be entertained by his antics. They all sat there long after the meal ended surrounded by silly hats, toys from pulled crackers, half-filled wine glasses and half-eaten mince pies, telling more tales of days long gone.

Joanne helped her mother clear the dishes once their friends had left. Her mum whispered that she'd put them both in the guest room, if that was alright. 'Well, it seems silly you two living together and sleeping apart when you come here.'

Joanne grinned.' Thanks, Mum –but what did Dad say?'

'He agreed. We were young once you know… '

'Dad looks smashing, doesn't he?' Joanne said. 'I was quite surprised when I saw him.'

'His blood pressure's relatively stable and Dr Wyley reckons he's got seventy percent of the use back in his arm and leg. Hopefully by summer he'll be walking you down the aisle, as proud as punch.'

Joanne was filled with relief as they set off home the following day after Helen prepared them a king-sized breakfast. David apologised profusely for having to leave so early but explained that it was his parents' party, which started promptly at seven.

Helen hugged him. 'It's lovely you were able to come yesterday. We've had the best Christmas because of that. Just enjoy yourselves at your parents.' With that, they waved them both off.

***

Jess and Oliver's gravel driveway was crammed with parked cars when they arrived half an hour late. Luckily David managed to secure a spot at the edge of the lawn. Joanne's usual slowness in getting ready had delayed them.

The house was already packed with people drinking, laughing and chattering noisily as they let themselves in. They managed to edge their way towards the kitchen where Jess spotted them and gave them both a hug.

‘Merry Christmas, you two! Let me see that beautiful ring,’ she said excitedly, reaching for Joanne’s left hand. ‘Oh Joanne, it is gorgeous,’ she gasped.

‘Bloody hell, Mother. You have invited enough people! Sorry we’re late, by the way.’

‘It’s OK, love. And as for all these people–well, you know your dad. He had a few too many at the golf-club dinner dance and it seems everyone got an invite.’

‘Where is Dad?’

‘Last time I saw him, he was at the far end of the sitting room deep in conversation with your brothers.’ With that, she thrust two full champagne flutes into their hands and disappeared into the dining room.

‘Are you ready to face the onslaught?’ David grinned, giving Joanne’s hand a quick squeeze.

She nodded and smiled back then they shuffled through the assortment of relatives and golf-club friends, all beaming, eager to congratulate them on their engagement. David was on a mission to find his father and introduce Joanne to his siblings first, so didn’t stop to chat.

The sitting room was unrecognizable. The furniture had gone, as well as the cream carpet, leaving the highly polished floorboards exposed. Joanne noticed the tasselled curtains at the far end of the room were drawn back and the French doors flung open. Beyond them she had assumed there was a patio and garden but instead they led to an enormous orangery where the DJ had set up his station and was hammering out tunes from bygone days. David spotted his father and brothers and shunted Joanne in their direction.

David was the elder of the three sons. Jonathan, who was two years his junior was twenty-five, then there was Philip, the baby at just twenty.

‘Hi, guys. Let me introduce you to your new sister-in-law-to-be,’ David beamed. There came a hug from Jonathan, which nearly sucked the breath from her.

Joanne marvelled at how alike they all were. The same dark hair, chocolate-coloured eyes, the same mannerisms –now as they stood together she could see they were all clones of their father.

Her introduction was met with affection. Joanne was overwhelmed by two attractive girls standing nearby who excitably rushed over, eager to see the sparkler on her hand. Their eyes widened and they beamed as Joanne showed off her ring. They introduced themselves.

'I'm Abby, Jonathan's wife ...lovely to meet you at long last.' The woman's bright blue eyes twinkled and her infectious giggle made Joanne grin; she knew in an instant they'd get on.

Joanne saw that Jonathan was besotted with his wife by the way he clung to her every word and snaked his arm around her waist as she stood beside him. Her stance was proud, her dress was timeless, the classic velvet type, her blonde wavy hair cascaded softly onto her bare shoulders, giving her a look of youthfulness.

Kristy, Philip's girlfriend of three years, introduced herself next. Both she and Philip were in their last year at Loughborough University; both had bodies that were toned and lean. Her sequinned cat suit, which must have been all of a size eight, made Joanne feel like a bag of spuds as she stood alongside her.

'These two are keep-fit fanatics; they run in marathons and climb mountains for fun. Training to be PE teachers,' Jonathan mocked.

'You'll have to give me some tips,' Joanne urged.

Kristy seemed much shyer than Abby and didn't say much; she just nodded, smiled sweetly and stuck by Philip as if she'd been glued to him.

Abby, on the other hand, continued to chatter excitably, telling Joanne how upset her two girls were that they hadn't been allowed to come down to the party, as they were dying to meet their new aunt-to-be!

'Oliver promised them a day at the park in the morning to compensate. Amber's five and Lily's three,' she said warmly.

David thought it was time Joanne had a guided tour of his relatives now that she was acquainted with his siblings. Her glass was replenished a couple of times on the way round, so remembering people's names was nearly impossible. At some point, the fizz from bubbles and the pastry from a canapé caught the back of her throat and sent her into a coughing fit.

'You OK?' Joanne was still gasping for breath so she couldn't answer. Her eyes watered, her face reddened, her mascara ran; she knew by people staring that she must resemble a panda. They'd only been there an hour and already she felt like the village idiot. She screamed inwardly.

David pushed her into the downstairs loo, where she tried to repair the damage by rubbing her eye makeup with loo paper and tap water. That just made matters worse. 'Oh for God's sake,' she shrieked to herself. Now someone was knocking at the door, obviously bursting for a pee. She took a sharp intake of breath and opened the door slowly. To her relief, she saw it was Jess.

'Are you OK, sweetie?' Jess asked with concern.

Joanne burst into tears. Jess grabbed her hand and told her to keep her head down as she guided her up to her bedroom where she could freshen up properly.

They entered the master bedroom. Joanne's eyes widened as she feasted on the decor. The windows were flamboyantly dressed in taupe and cream silk; the material continued in the canopy over the French four-poster bed and bedding. There were huge gold lamps on the tables each side of the bed, and the only other piece of furniture in the room was a large ivory damask chaise-longue. There was no wardrobe, no dressing table, just carpet you could sink in up to your knees.

Jess walked over to the wood-panelled wall opposite the bed, pressed a button and a panel opened. She beckoned Joanne to follow her as she headed towards the dressing room at the far end of the corridor. It was an Alice in Wonderland moment and Joanne's jaw dropped as they entered a room decked floor to ceiling with rails of clothes, racks stacked with neatly placed shoes and a dressing table crammed with creams, perfumes and cosmetics. What wall space was left was cleverly mirrored so that you could see yourself from every possible angle.

'Just help yourself, love. Use whatever you want and when you've finished, switch the light off and come back and join us.'

Joanne was stunned. The rails were colour coordinated and the shelves pristinely packed. She thought about her own dishevelled, unruly wardrobe at home and how David had picked items of clothing from the bed after she'd discarded them. Her face reddened.

The dressing table appeared theatrical in every sense of the word. She sat on the gold-leather studded chair in front of the light-framed mirror, which showed up every blemish as she proceeded to tissue off every scrap of makeup and start from scratch. Her eyes travelled along the row of bottles and jars in front of her: Dior, Chanel, YSL, Cartier. How could you not look good using all this stuff?

Once she'd finished, she stood up to admire herself in the full-length mirror. 'Yes!' she said, raking her hands through her hair, giving it some volume, then made her way back along the passageway towards the master bedroom. She couldn't resist a quick peek into the his-and-her bathroom as she passed. It was surreal. She switched off the lights, closed the concealed door and almost skipped her way down the galleried staircase to let David see the finished result.

She caught Jess's eye as she passed the kitchen. Jess gave her the thumbs-up and mouthed, 'You look fab.'

'Thank you,' she mouthed back.

The dining-room doors were open and caterers were starting to plate up food. There was no sign of David though, and she knew he would be feeling peckish.

Guests were already gyrating like windmills in the lounge to some dated record, someone's favourite no doubt. Joanne shuffled past as she tried to reach the orangery. At the doorway, she spotted David near the back wall talking to an attractive, heavily tanned, dark-haired girl wearing a dress that clung to every inch of her hour-glass figure like a second skin. Their faces were close as they spoke; Joanne noticed a fair amount of flirting taking place as the girl fed off David's attention.

It disconcerted her slightly as she watched the girl toss her hair with her hand, pout, then touch David's arm with her long manicured fingers. It was as if they were harbouring some sort of secret. She continued to watch from the doorway as a cat watches a mouse and felt slightly threatened by the way they looked at each other.

Joanne managed to control her feelings after a short while and walked over to them. David spotted her and smiled. She noticed an imprint of red lipstick on his cheek and swallowed back the lump that appeared in her throat.

'Joanne, come and meet Octavia – she's a sort of step-cousin.' They both laughed at the title. 'Uncle George married Octavia's mother so this is Uncle George's stepdaughter.' David's speech was dissolving into some sort of babble, which Joanne had only seen when he was nervous or drunk.

Octavia offered Joanne her cheek for a kiss that Joanne felt reluctant to accept. By now, her hackles had risen and instead she offered her hand to shake. David sensed the tension between the girls and shoved both hands deep in his pockets whilst shuffling awkwardly. That was another thing he did when he was nervous.

Octavia told Joanne that she had just arrived back from Barbados; her parents had a holiday home there. Then, annoyingly, she smiled at David, flicked her hair from her face with her bright red talons and fluttered her eyelashes at him

'Really,' Joanne said sarcastically. 'Which part?'

'Oh, I don't know … the north side of the island somewhere!'

Joanne was completely dismissed at that point when Octavia turned to face David.' David, would you be an angel and get me a refill?' she said, holding out her glass.' It's so tiresome trying to fight my way through that lot. Your mum knows which champagne I like!'

David took her glass, gave a juvenile laugh then headed for the kitchen, not even considering if Joanne needed a refill too.

'David mentioned you come from a small village oop *north*,' Octavia said, mocking Joanne's Lancashire accent.

Did he now? The fuck-face twat! Joanne seethed silently.

'It's a place called Thornton, on the Fylde coast. Have you ever been that way?'

'Goodness, no! I prefer not to venture any further than Cheshire if I can help it.'

Joanne dignity stopped her from being drawn into anymore conversation with this willowy, Tangoed witch from hell, and she clenched her teeth. She wished to God someone would rescue her; she only had a certain degree of tolerance.

Philip must have noticed something was not right. 'You OK?'

'Yes thanks, Philip,' Joanne said tensely.

'David's just gone to get me another glass of champers,' Octavia butted in, noticing that Philip had not acknowledged her.

'Oh, hi, Ocky. I didn't see you there. How are things?'

'Fine – and I wish you wouldn't call me Ocky.'

Philip's sarcasm told Joanne that he was not a fan of the bitch from hell. 'What do you think of my new sister-in-law to be then?'

Octavia's smile was noncommittal. 'We've only just met, so I haven't had time to make any judgment,' she sneered.

'Has she shown you the ring David bought her? It's an absolute dazzler.' Philip grinned, guiding Joanne's hand towards Octavia's face, knowing it would infuriate the hell out of her. Joanne could have kissed him.

'I hadn't noticed it,' Octavia grimaced. 'Oh, it's lovely.' She hardly glanced at it. 'I hope you'll both be very happy,' she said with not a morsel of sincerity.

Her expression suddenly changed from the lemon-sucking killjoy to the cat that got the cream as David entered the room again. He handed her a glass; he had brought one for Joanne too. 'I wasn't sure if you were ready for a refill, love, but Mum sent you one of her specials.'

Joanne took the crystal tumbler and recognised the drink as a Harvey Wallbanger. A look of annoyance crossed Octavia's face as she glared at the chilled white wine he handed her.

'David, I would have preferred one of those, too, if there was not any champers.' Her voice now sounded like she'd been sucking at a helium balloon.

'Sorry, Ocky,' Philip smirked. 'Harvey Wallbangers are Mum and Joanne's special drink exclusively.'

It was obvious the rust-coloured drama-queen's ego had been dented by his words. She flounced off to have words with Jess.

'Could we please have hush?' Oliver's voice echoed from the speakers. 'I would like to make an announcement. Would Joanne and David kindly make their way over and join me in the lounge?'

Blood surged to Joanne's cheeks as David guided her through the crowd to where Oliver stood facing everyone, microphone in hand. All eyes were now on them.

'In case you haven't had the chance to meet Joanne yet, I would like you all to meet her now,' Oliver continued. 'You're probably all aware of the romantic way my son chased this young lady half the way round the world to ask her to marry him – and the darling girl accepted.'

An 'Ahhhh!' and clapping erupted; the noise filled the room.

'And after meeting her, I can now see why he went to all that trouble! Well, Christmas Day they got engaged and a little bird tells me they have set the date for their wedding for June the fourth next year, so pencil this date into your diary everyone – and ladies, start looking for new hats!'

The cheering and clapping continued from everyone except Octavia. She stood stone-faced by the French windows. Each time Joanne glanced over, their eyes locked in combat. Joanne sensed something probably had gone on between the two of them at some stage but it was her that David wanted to marry, she assured herself.

Oliver continued, 'I'd like you all to raise your glasses. To the happy couple.'

'To the happy couple,' the room chorused then more clapping erupted.

The next half hour was a flurry of pats on the back, congratulations and hugs. Octavia, it seemed, had made a hasty exit for some unknown reason: a sudden migraine, so someone said. Jess reminded everyone there was still plenty of food in the dining room before they started to leave.

It had been an eventful night and Joanne adored David's family, even though Cruella de Ville had done her best to put the dampers on things

'Looks like the wedding is going to be one hell of a do if tonight was anything to go by,' she said excitedly when they got home.

Chapter 11

Joanne and David had not thought to make plans for New Year's Eve. Jess did try to cajole them into going to the golf club but David thwarted that idea the minute it was mentioned. One night with the Winston family was more than he could handle in a week.

He suggested they join the gang at the pub by the canal and go back to Peter and Claire's afterwards to welcome in the New Year. It turned out to be a great night to end a tremendous year.

New Year's Day had no sooner begun than Jess rang to wish them both a happy new year, then the conversation veered towards their forthcoming nuptials.

'In theory, planning a wedding is a pretty simple affair, Joanne, as long as you have a well-planned strategy. The sooner you get cracking the better, love,' she said.' How about I do dinner tomorrow night and we can have an informal chat.' That was her way of saying that she was itching to take total control of the whole affair. Joanne knew that going to dinner at theirs would narrow her chances of having any say in the matter.

She stared long and hard at David when she came off the phone; she could feel her face burning.' If you think for one minute your mother is going to plan our wedding, forget it. This is our wedding, David.'

'She just wants to help, that's all. I won't let her do anything you don't want her to.'

He was staring at her now as if she were someone who struggled with joined-up writing, someone totally incompetent, naïvely thrown in at the deep end. He obviously saw his mother as the guru she needed.

'You already knew about this though, didn't you?' Her question didn't need an answer; she could see by the look on his face that she was right.

‘Well, Mum did mention something about it the other day. She thought as your own mother wasn’t on hand to help, she’d help you organise everything instead…’ He raked his hands through his hair in an agitated way.

‘My mother wouldn’t make those sort of demands on me so I’m damn well not letting your mother do so.’ Joanne stared at him long and hard, barely keeping control. ‘And unless you’ve forgotten, I’ve already done it once so I know the ropes.’

A full-bodied Kenco was what she needed at that moment, none of this decaf crap everyone seemed to be urging her to drink. She banged around in the kitchen, slamming doors and sloshing pots around in the sink as she waited for the coffee to percolate.

That night was the first in a long time that they went to sleep back to back without uttering a single word to one another.

The following morning David was up and out at the crack of dawn. He did not give her a second glance or the usual peck on her cheek, which left her tearful. The day dragged on but then David rang and her face lit up. She thought he’d rung to apologise but he spoke hurriedly down the phone, telling her he’d be home early and to be ready when he got there.

The dispassionate look he gave her when he came in let her know he was sticking to his guns and that Jess should definitely be allowed a hand in the wedding arrangements. Joanne was also sticking to hers.

Joanne’s good humour when they arrived at his parents’ house stemmed from the large glass of wine she’d had before they left, and the fact that Oliver cracked opened a bottle of champers on their arrival. Maybe he also realised this could be quite a challenging night.

The meal Jess laid on was exceptional. It wasn’t until the last morsels of pudding were being eaten that Jess began the conversation Joanne had been dreading all night.

Joanne’s drink was once again replenished by Oliver. She felt her head spinning but even so she took a large gulp from her glass. She decided she wasn’t going to utter a word. What was the point? It was three against one, as far as she could see. She would listen, nod her head in agreement then, when she got home, ring up Jess and tell her to go screw herself.

The strategy Jess endlessly went on about would have only ended up with lots of people clamouring about flowers, dresses, venues, invitations, and cars, and have left Joanne screaming inwardly.

The golf club was mentioned as the perfect venue. 'And as I'm Lady Captain, strings could well be pulled,' Jess bragged. 'Amber and Lily obviously will be flower girls,' she went on, reading from her notes.

Joanne gave her response defiantly. 'In that case Gill and Suzy will be chief bridesmaids.'

David stared at her in disbelief. Jess was about to come out with a huge 'BUT' and now had a brittle look on her face.

At last David managed to grow a pair of balls and spoke out in Joanne's defence. 'Mum, I don't mean to offend you but I think the organisation of our wedding is down to Joanne. I know you're only trying to be helpful but you seem to be completely taking over. You've hardly allowed Joanne to utter a word since we got here.' He glanced at his mother's notebook. 'That's probably because you've already got everything sewn up.'

The look on Jess's face was priceless; her composure was completely lost. She rolled her eyes and threw her hands in the air dramatically. 'I'm sorry if you think I'm being presumptuous, but I'm only trying to help. This is my son's wedding, after all,' she almost bellowed at Joanne.

Jess rose from her seat and irritably started to clear the plates from the table. Everyone fell silent at that point except for Joanne, who hiccupped noisily. How grateful everyone was that dinner had ended before all this erupted.

Joanne didn't feel any need to pussyfoot around Jess now by helping clear the table – not that she felt capable. Jess had created this drama. Joanne just wanted to bolt from the house; words were flaring in her head that she would have liked to say but it was best that she didn't.

Oliver looked saddened and apologised for Jess's behaviour once she was out of earshot.' I'm so sorry, Joanne. I'm afraid Jess has a bad habit of going headlong into things, totally unaware she's upsetting anyone. She does it all the time at the golf club but she means well.'

‘It OK, Oliver. I understand where she’s coming from but, as David said, it’s our wedding and we should be the ones to organise it. Thank her for a lovely meal – hic!’ Joanne’s eyes felt they were about to close.

‘I think it’s time I got Joanne home. Thanks for everything,’ David said, frowning and shaking his head as he got up from his chair whilst urging Joanne to follow suit.

With no sign of Jess in the kitchen or in any of the downstairs rooms, it was obvious she’d stormed off to bed in a huff. Oliver saw them out and waved them off.

At least David and Joanne were now talking and starting to laugh again, her sense of humour fuelled by the wine she had drunk.

The next day a huge bouquet of flowers arrived at the house from Jess, apologising for the misunderstanding the previous night. Joanne knew it was Oliver who’d instigated their delivery.

She had woken that morning with an alcohol-induced headache and felt deeply embarrassed at her own behaviour. Why had she drunk so much? But then it was Oliver who kept plying her with drinks; they had been the only two drinking. So it wasn’t all her fault. As for an apology from Jess, Joanne knew that would never happen. Joanne’s broom was already in place to sweep everything under the carpet and forget it ever happened.

***

How difficult can it be in the grand scheme of life to organise a simple wedding? Joanne asked herself as she settled down on the sofa one Monday morning with a clipboard, pen and a freshly made mug of tea. She was ready to make some calls after David went to work.

She knew her day wasn’t going too well when she found not a vicar or priest who was prepared to marry them. David came from a long line of devout Catholics; Joanne was a high-days-and-holiday church goer verging on Methodist. In addition to her long list of mortal sins, she was also a divorcee.

In the end, a lovely Methodist minister came to their rescue on hearing their plight so the wedding was booked for June 4th, at two o’clock. Now all she had to find was a venue and, at the rate to which Jess kept adding to the guest list, it had to be somewhere huge!

Joanne remembered reading an article in the local paper about a stately home, which had just been completely refurbished, not a stone's throw from Southport. They were doing a huge promotion to generate business. She rooted out the paper from the pile by the side of the settee then thumbed her way through the pages.

'Ah here it is – thirty per cent discount on all weddings booked before July.' There was a picture too, which looked quite impressive. This would still enable them to afford the wedding breakfast they had hoped for, even though they were now feeding half Jess and Oliver's golf club as well as relatives and friends. Joanne did not waste any time; she rang them to secure the date and book a viewing.

Oliver generously chipped in with a handsome cheque to compensate for the extra people they had invited and Joanne allowed Jess to get involved after all by asking her to write and send out all the invitations, seeing that most of them were in Jess's address book.

The months of tantrums, tears and preparations finally came to fruition.

Jess, not wanting to be outdone, threw an elaborate dinner party on the eve of the wedding for David, his siblings and some close friends. Joanne and her parents met up for a simple meal in town with Suzy, Gill and the handful of family members that had travelled up for the wedding.

The following morning, Helen crept into Joanne's bedroom bearing two mugs of tea.' You awake?' she asked.

'Mmm…what time is it?' Joanne groaned.

'Just gone seven. The forecast's good – the sun's out already.' Helen drew back the curtains with a whoosh, allowing the sun's rays to fill the room.

Joanne rubbed the sleep from her eyes and scanned the chaos of her room. Excitement crept through her veins at the realisation that her big day had finally arrived.

'Today you become Mrs Winston,' Helen said, perching on the edge of the bed.

'I know…'

'Any doubts?'

'Not a single one,' Joanne admitted with a smile.

'Good… I could not go through all this a third time,' Helen said, glancing around at the clutter then starting to laugh.' Hope our lot found their way back to their hotels last night. They had drunk a fair amount with that meal. There'll be a few bad heads this morning.'

'I bet Suzy and Gill will be reaching for the Alka-Seltzer too. I know for a fact they'll have gone on somewhere after they left us,' Joanne chuckled.

'You're going to have to get your skates on, lady.' Helen eyed her watch. 'The bathroom's free and Suzy mentioned last night that they were picking you up around nine to take you to the salon to get your hair and makeup done. You can comb mine out when you get back and arrange my hat too, if you would. Want a bacon butty before you leave?' she trilled as she headed for the door.

'Thanks, that'll be nice.' Joanne smiled, flipping back the sheets and dangling her legs over the side of the bed. She walked over to the window, closed her eyes and soaked up some of the early morning sunshine through the glass.

There were no regrets, no nerves. Mrs Joanne Winston… well, it just rolled off the tongue, she couldn't help thinking.

The calmness within the house was short-lived when they arrived back from being beautified. According to her mum, the phone had rung constantly; the flowers had arrived and she still hadn't been able to get into the bathroom to get herself ready.

Abby and the girls turned up, all looking as pretty as a picture.' Don't you look lovely?' Joanne squealed excitedly as soon as she saw them.

'Yes, don't they?' Abby laughed, looking radiant in her cream floral floaty dress and big floppy hat. 'Jess took them with her this morning when she went to get her hair done.'

'How's David?'

'Like a caged lion and as jittery as hell,' she laughed.

Joanne made her way up to her room. Abby followed, armed with two glasses of Buck's Fizz, which Henry thrust into her hand as she passed him.

'Well… how did last night go? Did Jess put on a scrummy dinner?'

Abby's eyes shot up into her forehead and she pouted. 'As always, Jess did an amazing meal. Lobster starter and a rib of beef for roughly twenty people. Oliver cracked open some bottles of Crystal. We all were high in spirits. Then guess who decided to gate-crash and descend on us?'

'Don't tell me …Octavia.'

'You should have bloody heard her. "Oh, I had no idea you were having a family dinner!" The lying cow – of course she bloody well knew! Uncle George called in at lunchtime to drop off some presents and saw Jess preparing the food, even joked about getting an invite.'

'"I only called to drop off your present, David,"' Abby said, mimicking Octavia's squeaky voice to a tee. 'Jess was then obliged to ask her to stay and a place was laid at the table for her.'

Abby noticed some displeasure on Joanne's face, so quickly changed the subject. But Joanne was no longer listening. All she could think of was Octavia cooing over David and him wallowing in the attention she was paying him. Then she realised he couldn't have been that taken up with her; he'd bombarded her with phone calls into the early hours, drunkenly telling her how much he loved her.

Joanne stepped into her dress, at which point everyone became tearful. Lily and Amber twirled in their dresses and Gill and Suzy looked incredibly grown up in theirs. Helen appeared, looking much younger than her years. They all made their way down the stairs

Joanne eyes instantly sought out her father's; his face at that moment, shone with pride and his eyes filled with tears as he looked at her. How incredibly handsome he was in his morning suit. She had thanked God a zillion times for allowing him to be here on this day. Fighting back tears and the giant lump in her throat, she made her way over to give him a hug. 'You look stunning love,' he whispered, trying to fight back tears himself, as they shared a private moment.

Joanne noticed people were gathering in the street outside so she made her way to the window to see what was happening. She stood riveted to the spot as she spotted a landau and four dappled grey horses with a chap decked in full regalia sitting proudly in the driver's seat. She gasped with excitement, realising this was the surprise David had spoken of before he left. She'd assumed it would be flowers.

Everyone in the room was becoming more excitable than ever as they began to leave and make their way to the church.

Then the moment Joanne dreaded most arrived; her father and she were alone. She felt the lump in her throat return but this time tears surfaced and rolled down her face.

Her dad put his arm around her shoulders and held her. 'I am so proud of you, pet lamb,' he croaked. 'I just want you to be happy.'

'I am, Dad,' she whispered back reassuringly.

They walked out to applause from the onlookers in the street. Once they were settled in the landau, they shared a glass of champagne as the carriage glided towards the town. Well-wishers waved along the way as it swept into the grounds of the church and came to a halt outside the huge, open, studded doors where her bridesmaids were lined up, faces beaming.

Joanne clung to her dad's arm as they made their way down the aisle. Heads turned and David beamed, leaving her in no doubt whatsoever –this time it was for keeps.

It was funny how everyone cried at weddings, in that frantic hour of clicking cameras after the two of them emerged as husband and wife. The ride to the venue in the landau gave David time to tell his new bride just how unbelievably beautiful she looked and how much he loved her.

Jess greatly approved the venue; she admitted it had slightly knocked the golf club off its perch.

The next couple of hours were a haze of champagne, expensive canapés, sugared-almond parcels, plates of perfectly prepared food, a three-tier wedding cake and a sea of drunken well-dressed guests.

Jonathan's speech highlighted some parts in David's past that he would rather have forgotten but it seemed to amuse everyone.

Joanne managed to grab a solitary moment in the sunshine whilst tables were being cleared and the room was prepared for the evening entertainment.

She emptied the last dregs of champagne from her glass and enjoyed the fresh warm breeze as it rushed by her face. She closed her eyes and tried to recapture the day again. It all had gone all so quickly.

'Having a quiet moment on your own?' A sultry female voice brought her back to reality.

Joanne could not make out who it was as the sun blurred her vision. Then she saw the outline of Octavia standing next to her.

'It all seems to have gone well,' Octavia said curtly, tossing her long hair back with her talons. 'Such a pity it could not have been at the Catholic church…' Her eyes narrowed. 'I know Aunt Jess was gutted when she found out you weren't Catholic and a divorcee. Then, when she heard you were getting married in the Methodist church, I think that's when she started to take her Prozac again. That's one thing they liked about Sarah – she was a good Catholic girl.' She paused and sneered. 'When Sarah stayed over at their place, which was most weekends before David got his own house, she always went to Sunday Mass with Oliver and Jess. They were very fond of her, you know.' There was menace in her words.

Joanne had vowed nothing was going to spoil today and so far it had been perfect in every way – but she'd forgotten that Octavia had been invited.

'Octavia, get over yourself. Today must have been a huge disappointment to you. I mean, you really did think you would be the one to marry him, didn't you? Wait until he hears what a sad spiteful bitch you really are.'

With hatred in her eyes Octavia told her that Jess had often harped on to the family how flawless Sarah was whereas she always thought of Joanne as flawed. She stopped in her tracks as she spotted David heading their way and instantly brought on the waterworks.

'Octavia …what's up?' David said with some concern.

'Joanne's being mean. I was just congratulating her on how lovely she looks and she called me a sad, spiteful bitch.'

'Is this true?'

'Well yes, but—'

'I am sorry, Octavia, she did not mean it. She's not usually so outspoken.' He looked at Joanne without a trace of a smile. 'She's had a long day and a few too many glasses of bubbly by the sound of it,' he said, trying to console Octavia.

Joanne couldn't believe her ears and became outraged.' I have not! And as for being outspoken, this sad bitch has a master's degree in being outspoken! Get your facts straight, David, will you? Wake up and smell the bloody coffee for once!'

Joanne stormed off to the loo, passing Abby on the way, who noticed her eyes were filled with tears. 'Hey, what's up Mrs Winston?' she asked. Joanne cleared her throat, grabbed some loo roll and gave her nose a noisy blow then told Abby what had happened.

'Ah, the viper has struck at last, has she? That was quick; we were married a whole month before she accosted me. She's a witch – take no notice.'

'Yes, but what she said about Jess being upset because I'm not Catholic – do you think there's any truth in that? She said Jess is always commenting to the family how Sarah was flawless and I am flawed.'

'That's all bollocks. Jess is thrilled to bits with the wedding, you – even the Church. And the part about Saint Sarah going to church with them – that happened once and that was just to get into their good books because Oliver caught them at it. I never did like the girl myself.' She handed Joanne more loo paper and gave her an affectionate hug. 'Now get your newly married arse out there. You have a husband to take care of. I'll take care of Octavia.' With that, she stormed off.

David was waiting patiently outside when Joanne finally came out. As soon as he saw her, he swept her up into his arms. 'Jo, I'm sorry… I didn't give you a chance to tell me your account of what happened.'

'Shush.' Her finger was on his lips halting his words. She could hear the band starting up and a guy on the mic asking them both to make their way to the dance floor. Evergreen' started to play as they stepped out and everyone applauded.

Octavia was not seen again; Joanne realised that was all down to Abby.

***

The wedding had consumed most of their savings, so a four-poster bed in the bridal suite and a few days in the Cotswolds was all their budget ran to, but those few days were memorable.

The excitement of opening all the presents on their return made coming home worthwhile as everyone had been exceptionally generous.

A couple weeks after the wedding, David suggested they have a run over to her parents at the weekend to give them a chance to look at the wedding album. Joanne nodded enthusiastically and rang her mum immediately.

Over dinner, Helen mentioned that Joanne looked a little peaky. 'Not been overdoing things, have you, love?' she asked as she spooned roast potatoes onto her plate.

'She certainly has, Helen,' David said, grinning as he helped himself to some more roast beef. 'She's been decorating and moving the furniture around. I never know if I'm in the right house when I come home.'

'Well I have to do something – I can't sit around reading *Woman's Own* all day.' Joanne's voice sounded a little ungracious. 'The days are so long after David's gone to work, so I thought I'd do a re-vamp.'

David gave a faint snigger at that remark.

'Make sure you don't do too much, pet lamb,' her dad uttered softly.

'I won't.'

'I would ask the doctor for a tonic if I were you. It has all been hectic with the wedding and all.'

'I have been telling her the very same thing but she takes no notice,' David said, siding with her mother.

Bullied into submission, Joanne went along to the surgery the following week. 'All they did was take blood and tell me to call in for the results in a week's time. I hope that then they give me that prescription for a pick-me-up,' she told her mum over the phone when she rang that night.

However, when she called the following week to get her results, her doctor sat opposite her stern faced as he told her, 'You're roughly two and a half months pregnant, judging from your dates, Mrs Winston.'

'But I have suffered for some years with endometriosis! Could it be that?'

'No, young lady, you're definitely pregnant!' he said jovially and asked her to make a further appointment for about a month's time.

'Fuck...bollocks ...shit! David will have an epi!' she muttered under her breath as she slumped down in the chair in their lounge after she arrived back home. She was numb and slightly stunned.

If she had not been up the duff, she would have chucked a large brandy down her throat to help get over the shock. She and David had never really discussed kids, only that it might be problematic if they wanted them. She'd put her missed period down to the stress of the wedding. Now she had a dilemma on her hands. Should she pick up the phone and tell him or cook him a special dinner to prime him before she dropped the bombshell? She'd opt for the latter.

She climbed the stairs and at the top she paused to look out of the landing window. Brenda next door was on her hands and knees digging at the weeds. A house martin swept down from its nest in the gable end and sat patiently near her, hoping a fat juicy worm would surface. As one did, the bird whisked it up as quick as a flash and flew back to her nest to feed it to her babies.

Joanne hardly knew how to look after herself, let alone a baby.

Would it hurt? Would she be able to cope? Would she look grotesque when she was pregnant?

She could not bear to think about it; the thought scared her witless. She slumped down on the bed, pulled the duvet over her head, and blubbered until she fell asleep.

It was gone three by the time she awoke so she was instantly thrown into panic. She had a meal to prepare. She discarded her crumpled clothes, threw on her towelling robe and thundered down the stairs.

Thank God she had stockpiled the freezer the previous week: langoustines, Dover sole, summer pud, all bought with their three-month anniversary dinner in mind. She rooted them out then went ahead with defrosting and prepping. She gave one final check before she went up to get ready.

Damask tablecloth on the table … check.

Best china and crystal …check.

Candles ready to light…check.

Langoustines marinating …check.

Dover sole stuffed, ready to pop in oven …check.

Vegetables in the steamer…check.

Summer pud turned out …check.

The wine chilling …check.

She showered and went through the ritual of carefully applying makeup, putting on some decent underwear before zipping herself into his favourite dress and spraying on some Chanel.

Her heart nearly stopped as she heard David's car pull onto the drive and his key turn in the lock. 'Helloweee,' he trilled as he came through the door. He stopped dead in his tracks as he saw the table. Two place settings; at least no one was coming. Joanne walked out from the kitchen.

'OK Joanne… is there something I've forgotten? You know I'm hopeless at remembering dates but whatever it is, I'm sorry and I'll make it up to you, I promise,' he said with some concern.

His eyes travelled over her clothes. 'Oh mother of heaven – what have I done to deserve this?' He grinned.

'Nothing,' she said, blushing. 'I just thought it would be a nice change.' She walked over to kiss him.

'Sounds good to me.' He took off his jacket, placing it on the back of one of the dining chairs, then loosened his tie and undid his top shirt button. Joanne handed him a class of chilled wine when he joined her in the kitchen.

'Mmmm that's nice,' he said, taking a large gulp.

'It's the last of the bottles your dad gave us.'

'You're not having one?'

'No, I'll have mine with dinner,' she lied.

She continued to chatter as she chopped feverishly at the tomatoes for the tossed salad. He watched her as she jabbered on about Brenda and her gardening, about the fact that the window cleaner hadn't been and about how he'd have to have squirty cream as she'd not got the pour-on type. She sensed his eyes were continuously upon her as he continued to sip his wine, which unnerved her slightly.

'Are you going to tell me now what this is really about?' His voice was soft and undemanding.

She looked down at the massacred tomatoes and placed the knife on the chopping board, fighting hard to find the right words without bursting into tears. 'I'm pregnant, David,' she said almost in a whisper. She avoided his eyes.

His silence continued. She glanced at his face – his eyes were bulging in disbelief. He took another large gulp of wine, then his face lit up and their eyes locked as he opened his arms. Joanne walked into them and nuzzled her face into his neck. A huge sense of relief washed over her and she felt almost drunk with happiness.

He lifted her face, lowered his lips and gave her a kiss that told her everything was going to be OK.

'Are you pleased?' she asked.

'Pleased– are you kidding? I'm over the moon,' he said, running his hands through her hair. 'When did you find out …and why the hell didn't you ring me? I would have come home. Did you not suspect anything? I mean, women are supposed to know, aren't they?' Words spiralled from his mouth like a whirlwind.

'I only found out this morning. I suppose I was shocked. I had to get used to the idea,' she smiled. 'I just thought my non-existent periods the last two months were down to fatigue from the wedding.'

'Jo, we're going to make amazing parents,' he laughed.

'I know!' she grinned back.

Chapter 12

Joanne woke the following morning to see David standing by the side of the bed grinning like a Cheshire cat. He had brought her up a mug of coffee and was just about to leave for work.' Take things easy today. I will ring you later. Try and make a few calls if you can.' Then he bent, kissed her and left.

Joanne still felt incredibly numb about the whole thing. She was bringing new life into the world in roughly six months' time. No more provocative lingerie, no boozy nights out with the girls – and she would probably be the size of a beached whale within a couple of months!

She scooped up her mug and placed it to her lips. The smell from the coffee instantly brought on a wave of nausea and seconds later the contents of her stomach were down the loo. She slumped to the floor beside the washbasin, feeling exhausted, clammy and tearful. It was not supposed to be like this, she sobbed resentfully. They had not even discussed having children!

By now David would probably be brimming over with pride, telling all his staff he was going to be a dad, which she imagined would bring numerous pats on the back and chants of 'Well done'. Life for him would go on virtually unchanged.

Unlike her life… Hormones would probably cause carnage: her boobs would grow to the size of melons; varicose veins, piles and heartburn would appear from nowhere, and she'd have to swallow iron pills daily. Shellfish, eggs and coffee would have to be avoided and instead of drinking her usual vat full of white wine on their Sunday afternoon jaunts to the pub with the gang, she'd have to drink Perrier water instead. She'd be crunching pickled onions instead of humbugs; baby manuals would clutter the living room instead of *Homes and* fucking *Gardens* and to top it all, she'd end up being one of those tedious people who go on mercilessly about every stage of their pregnancy.

'Aaaghhhhh!' she screeched, feeling herself hyperventilating.

There was no way David would fancy her when she waddled instead of sashayed in. And how could anyone appear remotely sexy in a bra that resembled a hammock? 'Aaaghhhhh! I'm not grown up enough to be a mum, I can hardly look after myself, let alone a baby,' she screamed at the top of her voice.

David had been so elated when she told him. How could she possibly let him know the news was freaking her out so much! Gill and Suzy would probably tell her she was a basket case too, when she confided how she really felt.

Number one item on their wish list had always been to find a husband, lasso him, reel him in, marry him and have half a dozen kids. To them, she was living the dream.

She dragged herself off the floor and gave her face a cold swill. As she surfaced from the fluffy white towel, she took a long hard look at herself in the mirror: ghoulish white, with dark circles under her eyes. Wasn't she supposed to bloom or something?

Only two days ago she'd put these symptoms down to a virus or wedding fatigue. How simple life would have been if it were true! A quick vitamin B12 jab would have probably sorted out everything.

She'd promised David she would make some phone calls and 'spread the good news' as he put it but she was in no mood to put on her happy-clappy mum-to-be face yet.

Judging by her dates, she must have conceived sometime in April, around David's birthday to be precise – that romantic weekend away, a pre-wedding gift. A suite at the Midland Hotel in Manchester, a mixture of business and pleasure for David. Whilst Joanne had shopped, he drummed up business.

'Getting away will give us some us time!' he had said jovially.

'Well, it's ended up as the three of us now!' she thought dryly.

That would make her roughly three months pregnant; somewhere down the line she'd either skipped a pill or she'd puked it up after one too many cocktails.

She flopped back down on the bed until the nausea subsided. Blimey! What if it didn't, she thought miserably, gulping back her tears. What if this continued for the duration of her pregnancy? Tears started to trickle down her cheeks and she wiped them away with the sleeve of her nightie. She felt badly in need of a hug so she hugged her pillow; it was better than hugging nothing at all!

It was gone ten and she still felt drained and out of synch. She propped herself up on the pillows, lifted the receiver from the phone beside the bed and, with some trepidation, punched in her parents' number.

Her mother answered almost instantly but hearing her voice encouraged another lump to appear in Joanne's throat.

'Hi Mum…' she said then paused briefly, unsure how to start this difficult conversation. 'Mum, I'm going to have a baby,' she blurted out.

'Oh sweetie, that's wonderful news – but why are you getting upset?'

'I don't know…I don't know how I feel…' she sobbed. 'I mean… We've only just got married … it might spoil things. I'm going to be fat! And mumsy! And David is bound to go off me because I'll constantly smell of baby puke instead of Chanel.'

'Oh Joanne, David's not going to go off you. He loves you and I bet he's over the moon about the baby. All this you are feeling right now… it's natural, love. It's your hormones, that's all. In another month or so, you will feel wonderful, you'll see. Go and make yourself a cup of tea. Ring me back when you've stopped crying. Just enjoy being pregnant, Joanne; it's the most natural thing in the world. Nothing to get upset about. I'm going to break the news to your dad as soon as he wakes from his nap. He'll be thrilled.'

'Thanks, Mum… sorry I'm being pathetic. I'll ring you back later.' The receiver replaced, Joanne gave her nose a noisy blow on a crumpled bit of tissue. Then she pulled out more tissues from the box by the bed and dried her eyes.

Her mother's sage words already had a calming effect. At least she was thrilled by the news, she thought wistfully. If she could just stop this pathetic blubbering, she'd be able to make one more call.

Joanne inhaled deeply through her nose, sat rigidly up on the bed and tapped Jess and Oliver's number into the phone. It took forever for them to answer; maybe they'd gone away. Then Jess said breathlessly, 'Hello?'

'Jess, it's Joanne… Am I calling at a bad time?'

'No, love, I was just out in the garage. Oliver's off to play golf and my car was blocking his.'

'It's just I have some news.' Joanne paused for an intake of breath.

'What's that, love?'

'I'm pregnant, Jess... David and I are going to have a baby. I'm nearly three months.'

There's a slight pause before Jess spoke and when she did there was not a shred of elation in her voice. 'Oh... lovely news. But I thought you and David would have wanted to wait a while. Get on your feet a bit before starting a family. I mean, the wedding must have cost a packet besides the money we gave you towards it. It would have been far better if you could have gone back to work for a while, don't you think? Oh well! It will be nice to have another grandchild running around the place...But, dear –and I do hope you don't take this the wrong way – I hope the baby's going to be brought up Catholic. I know you got married in your church but David was brought up with the faith and I think he'd want his children to be too.'

Jess's abrasive comment shook Joanna ridged, and Octavia's words at the wedding came flooding back about how disappointed Jess was that they'd not married in the Catholic church. At the time, Joanne put it down to Octavia being vile, but now it seemed it had been an issue after all. The wind momentarily was knocked from her sails, Joanne quickly recovered.

'Well, things happen, Jess... True, the baby wasn't planned but David and I are thrilled,' she said curtly, then bit her lip to stop her chin quivering.

There was tension between the two women and Joanne wasn't quite sure how to continue the conversation without ruing the consequences of saying something she shouldn't. Her parting words to Jess were that someone was at the door and she'd have to go .Joanne replaced the receiver, and felt a muscle in her neck pulse.

If hormones were preventing Joanne from being happy, what was Jess's bloody excuse for acting like a constipated wasp? This was a side of Jess that she really didn't like.

Joanne tried to brush away her grievances with little success, so she rang David at the office to offload a barrage of venom at him about his mother's attitude to him putting her up the duff. Unfortunately he was in the middle of an important meeting and quickly dismissed her ranting by saying he'd ring her later, which sent her flying into a rage, which encouraged another bout of nausea.

She just about made the loo before she retched and retched until she could retch no more. Then she slumped on the bathroom floor for what seemed an age until eventually she managed to get up and shuffle barefoot down the stairs to the kitchen. She flicked the switch on the kettle and reached for the coffee but remembered her bad reaction to coffee that morning, so she thrust a teabag into a mug instead, nostrils still in full flare at Jess's comment.

The clock on the kitchen wall stated it had just gone eleven. Joanne wondered if Gill would be at her desk .She carried her tea through to the lounge, drew back the curtains and allowed the sunshine into the room. The sun made her screw up her face and narrow her eyes; it showed up the layers of dust which had descended on the furniture but she dismissed it all, flopped down onto the couch and took a sip from her mug.

Thankfully the tea didn't have the same reaction as the coffee. Joanne picked up the phone and punched in Gill's office number.

'Hi, kiddo, what's it like to be a lady of leisure?' Gill said, hearing Joanne's voice at the end of the line. Joanne relayed the news that she was pregnant and there was a glass-breaking shriek from the end of the line, followed by, 'You lucky, fucking bitch! It's not good enough you're married to a hunk– and a not-too-badly-off hunk at that – but for him to get you up the duff as well... Well, that's fucked my day up, I can tell you! Brian and I are still only at the getting-to-know-each-other stage, which means we don't yet fart in front of one another and I still wear makeup to bed. Sometimes I wonder is it bloody worth it? Five minutes after we've both jumped in the sack he's usually snoring his head off. Anyway, enough of me and my boring life, when did you find out... tell all!'

Joanne explained everything that had happened, including how wretched she felt and what her mother-in-law had just said.

'It's fucking mother-in-law syndrome, that's all,' Gill said sympathetically. 'They're all alike. My last mother-in-law was a nightmare and I don't think Brian's is going to be any different. Don't put up with it, kiddo. Don't let her intimidate you. She's probably menopausal; her looks will be failing, hips widening and she'll be jealous of your youth. She knows you aren't going to answer her back because if you do she'll tell her precious son and then there'll be a row. Been there, worn the fucking T-shirt. You have to set a precedent, stand your ground and to hell with what David thinks.' Her friend sounded angry on Joanne's behalf as she continued to rant.

'I know …I know, I know what you're saying, but it's difficult to be rude and offhand. Jess is the sort of person you can't argue with, she'll feel it's disrespectful.'

'You don't need to be rude or offhand just be a bit cannier. If she gets away with insulting you once, she'll know she can do it again. Tell David yourself. Hiding what she said will only breed more insults.'

It wasn't like Gill to be such a straight talker but what she said made sense. Jess and Oliver had taken over Jonathan and Abby's life: they went on holidays with them; organised their Christmases, never taking into account that they might want one on their own for a change. They'd even paid for the girls' schooling, which gave them the right to choose what school they went to. It hadn't hit Joanne until now just how controlling the pair were.

She understood now why David declined numerous offers of dinner, holidays and gifts. He was nipping things in the bud before they took over his life too.

She'd only just put the phone down when David rang her back. 'Joanne! I'm so sorry, love, if I sounded abrupt before. We had the accountants in. Gerry wants us to buy him out. He's getting a divorce from Anne and he wants to make a new start over in Canada where his brother lives. So we've been seeing if it's feasible to pay him off and for Steven and I to carry on with the business. It's going be a bit of a struggle at first; we'll have to get a bank loan, but I think once the loan's paid off, we'll be fine.'

He paused for a moment. 'Now, about my mother! I've just rung her and given her a roasting. She said she didn't realise she had upset you. The thing is, Jo, her and Dad have had a bit of a fall out and you phoned right in the middle of it, so maybe you got the backlash. Dad has had, shall we call it, a few indiscretions with women over the years. You know what he's like, Joanne, a real charmer at times.

Mum always turned a blind eye; they've been flings, nothing serious. She'd send him to Coventry for a while, disappear into her little room and he, in turn, would buy her an expensive piece of jewellery, take her on holiday and all would be forgiven. But his indiscretion this time was with someone at the golf club, someone Mum knows quite well, and now it's public knowledge. Mum feels humiliated, hurt and angry. When you called, they were in the middle of one humdinger of a row. She said she's sorry if she upset you – she didn't mean to.'

Joanne felt ashamed, even embarrassed. She'd made such a fuss, 'Oh! I'm such a klutz! She must have been going through hell and I phoned up to tell her we're having a baby and expected her to be bursting with bloody happiness. I'll ring her …see if there's anything I can do.'

'No,' David said sharply. 'No, don't do that, Jo. I think she needs to be left alone to sort things out herself. She'll only feel more embarrassed if you ring and start talking about it…' He paused realising his voice was louder then he'd meant it to be. 'I'll try and get home early tonight. We'll go round to Peter and Claire's, break the news and have a few drinks with them – if you think you're up to it.'

'Yes, that'll be nice.'

Joanne felt awful now. She'd misjudged Jess. Even so, Jess's words still stuck like glue.

Chapter 13

Having a baby meant Joanne and David were catapulted into a new period of their lives. Hormones were causing havoc, leaving her high on life one moment and the next in a heap, whingeing and wailing about some trivial matter.

David was kind and supportive, but wasn't too good at tea and sympathy, or tolerance with women throwing tantrums on a whim, or slopping round the house all day in a tracksuits, hair un-brushed. He ended up making innuendoes like, 'Women in China just get on with it, do their work and give birth in the rice fields whilst they're working.' Joanne really didn't know what he was implying when he said it… Was he hinting he wanted her to give birth in the back garden or something?

Her hips expanded daily and she found it hard to maintain a chic appearance at times instead each morning she'd drag her body into a tracksuit bottoms and a baggy pullover when David left for work. Everything else made her look like she had unimaginative dress sense and now David was affectionately nicknaming her his Heffalump.

It was now December. The baby wasn't due until the beginning of February. Joanne's parents arrived on Christmas Eve loaded with present and food her mother had already prepared. Although it was Jess and Oliver's turn to go down to Bath, they'd decided to stay at home instead, much to Abby's delight.

'I just want to be on hand, dear, should you need me,' Jess said, not wanting to be left out in case anything happened whilst they were away. The usual Christmas schedule went ahead at their house, which included an invite for Christmas lunch along with the rest of the motley crew who usually turned up each year, except for Abby, Jonathan and the girls who Joanne missed dreadfully.

Helen and Jess got on relatively well, surprisingly enough, seeing they were two exceptionally strong characters. Helen had to be, coping as she had with Henry's illness all these years; Jess – well, she was the matriarch in David's family. Oliver was the boss, of course, but Jess controlled Oliver quite cleverly at times without him knowing, despite his indiscretions, which they seemed to have got over quite well! It was water under the bridge as far as she was concerned.

Both dads seemed OK in each other's company but that was more out of politeness than a 'let's go and have a pint down the pub' sort of friendship. Oliver and Henry were as different as chalk and cheese.

Oliver was an articulate, no-nonsense sort of chap who loved his golf and his golf-club buddies. The only thing Joanne's dad was good at was swinging was a pair of secateurs. Nothing pleased him more since retirement than to don his old brown cord pants, check shirt and cardi then potter for hours in the orchard or rose garden. As for indiscretions, Joanne didn't think he'd even looked at another woman in all the time he'd been married to her mum, let alone made a pass at one.

Joanne gave a long sigh of relief once Boxing Day was over. She welcomed the fact she could at last take things more in her stride. Helen insisted on staying until after the New Year to help out. 'You can hardly manage the stairs, love, let alone hoover, change beds and so on. No, it would be best if we stay,' she said, plumping cushions and picking up empty cups from the coffee table,

'It's been an exhausting time, Mum. Now I just need some respite from everyone and everything in my final weeks. We only have Peter and Claire's New Year's Eve bash. Suzy and Gill will be there too, so I can't miss that. Then I promise you I'll put my feet up until the baby decides to say hello. David can do the hoovering, shopping, and heavy stuff as he's not back at work until the New Year.'

David's face crumpled at the thought of doing all that housework! Helen went into the kitchen to make a pot of tea with a disgruntled look on her face.

'Don't worry, pet lamb, I'll make sure she leaves you in peace,' Joanne's dad said, giving her a wink. 'I know she can be a bit much sometimes but she means well. She's just worried about you, love.'

'I know, Dad.' Joanne grinned as she tried to prise herself out of the armchair and headed off towards the kitchen to make amends.

The following day, as they left, tears were shed as usual but at least they left on good terms.

Savouring the silence of an empty house that night was blissful. The TV was silenced; seasonal scented candles threw a romantic flicker of light as Joanne lay on the couch, her head against a plumped-up cushion, her feet resting on David's lap. Soft music drifted from the speakers at the far end of the room. God, how she wished right now she was slim again! She felt slightly awkward under David's gaze but his eyes told her nothing really mattered anymore, just them being as they were that moment.

***

'Christmas was exhausting, even with Mum's help,' Joanne thought as she heaved her cumbersome body out of bed a few days later. The baby had prevented her from getting much sleep.

She waddled clumsily past David's side of the bed, trying not to wake him en route to the loo. He was comatose. Not surprising: he'd enjoyed a whole bottle of Fleurie to himself whilst she'd watched enviously.

'Ooooooh …God!' she gasped and grabbed the edge of the washbasin to stop herself from falling. Her lower back had gone into a spasm. Maybe the baby was lying on a nerve or something, she reassured herself.

It's Peter and Claire's New Year's Eve bash that night and all the gang would be there. She couldn't miss that one. She'd just have to take it easy! But the backache didn't subside; instead it began to creep slowly round to the front of her stomach and now felt like a vice.

'Probably one of those Braxton Hicks things everyone goes on about. Well, it's bloody uncomfortable,' she grimaced.

She decided not to let on to David; he would only have made a huge fuss, and it was a shame to wake him from his alcohol-infused sleep. But if the pain persisted, she would have no choice.

She managed to drag her way downstairs and flicked the switch on the kettle. A cup of tea might help – but as she reached for a cup from the cupboard the next pain gripped her and this time it raked its way through her body, taking her breath.

'Aargh Daaaaaavid!' she heard herself scream as the air was expelled from her lungs.

By the sound of him taking the stairs two at a time, she knew he'd heard her. He flew into the kitchen, a look of horror on his face when he saw her bent over in pain gripping the worktop. She was panting, 'Ambulance ambulance,' and gasped as the next pain gripped.

Within minutes the ambulance pulled up outside the house. David's face was pale. The baby wasn't due for another six weeks and, despite numerous attempts to stop labour, their beautiful daughter, Emily, was born three days later. A slippery slimy little body covered in mucus, weighing in at 4lb 4oz.

'Not bad, seeing she was so premature,' the midwife proclaimed as she handed her to Joanne for her first cuddle. She was perfect ... so tiny and what a fighter!

'What do you expect with parents like us?' David said wistfully, eyes glistening with tears as he was passed his daughter.

How like him she was: the same almond-shaped eyes, same nose and the way she pouted was just like David when he was having a strop. But before they had time to get to know her properly, she was whisked off to the premature baby unit.

'She's still not out of danger yet,' the nurse told them. 'The next couple of weeks are crucial.'

Emily was tiny as she fought for her life in the incubator. Joanne was able to provide milk so she could be tube fed, and the ritual of going back and forward to the hospital was a pilgrimage of love as far as they were concerned. They couldn't bear to be without her.

The morning Joanne left hospital without her daughter was the worst day imaginable.

It was three weeks before Emily was allowed to come home. Suzy and Gill were at hand and so were a host of others ready to celebrate with them.

Spring and summer came and went in a trice. Joanne and David brimmed with happiness. Every day, as they watched, Emily flourished and blossomed before their eyes. Helen and Henry cried each time they held her and nicknamed her 'Sunbeam'. Oliver and Jess were just as bad and generously threw a lavish christening at their house after a church service at The Lady of the Lords. Father Brannon, a friend of Jess and Oliver's, presided.

The christening was an elaborate affair – but wasn't everything Jess did elaborate? The sun shone the whole day, allowing guests to wear their summer clothes, drink champagne and eat canapés on the manicured lawns. As usual, guests came in droves and white-gloved waiters wandered between them with silver trays, replenishing their plates and drinks.

Octavia made a grand entrance halfway through, sporting an Armani outfit George had bought for her, trying to upstage everyone. She cooed over Emily in front of David, hoping she'd be back in favour with him after the wedding fiasco.

'She's the image of her father,' Octavia said with a smirk, knowing full well David was within earshot. 'Can't see any of you at all, Joanne,' she added with unmistakable sarcasm.

'Oh! By the way,' Octavia said in a low tone to Joanne once David wasn't around.' I must give you the number of my personal trainer. I'm sure you want get yourself back in shape as soon as possible. That mumsy look –well, it doesn't do anyone any justice. I'm sure David will agree but he's probably too polite to say. I have my own gym at the house to keep myself in shape.'

Abby overheard the acid-tongued remark and swivelled round. 'OCTAVIA!' she shot back. 'I heard that! Who the fuck do you think you are?'

The two woman's eyes locked in combat but Octavia remained calm. 'I don't know what you're talking about. You've obviously had too many glasses of bubbly, Abby. I'm only trying to give Joanne a bit of friendly advice. I mean, David has always been one for the ladies, you know that…' She stared wide-eyed at Abby. 'He's always been a man that likes a woman to look her best.' She flicked back her long hair. 'Nothing like Jonathan, who probably doesn't bother what size your hips are.'

Octavia knew full well that winding Abby up like this would make for an explosive scene with everyone watching. Joanne acted instinctively before Abby emptied the content of her glass over Octavia's face. 'Octavia, would your professional trainer be called Marco, by any chance?' she enquired.

'Why yes – do you know him?'

‘No, not personally… It’s just I’ve heard David and Philip mention him on a couple of occasions. Marco drinks in the Swan with Peter and a few others and he mentioned that you’re one of his clients. According to Peter, you hire him regularly as a male escort then at the end of the night you pay him extra to give you a good seeing-to! Fifty pounds an hour, I think he mentioned! And by the way, Octavia, the Winston boys do like a bit of flesh on their women! Not that it’s any business of yours, but seeing as you are so interested in their preferences, perhaps you’d like to know their nickname for you is “Bag of Bones.”’

Abby and Joanne grinned triumphantly as they watched her leave. ‘Strange, isn’t it, how Octavia always seems to gets a migraine at every family party she attends these days?’ Joanne sensed a grin behind Abby’s remark.

Chapter 14

Before David and Joanne knew it, winter was upon them. A heavy fall of snow made them aware it was probably going to be a harsh one this year:

Joanne was glad she made the decision to leave the heating on when they took Emily to see her first bonfire and firework display. She was a bit young at ten months, Jess commented abrasively, but they were doting, parents now and couldn't wait to show her everything life had to offer.

Emily was shattered when they got back: the excitement, bright lights, noise and crowds all got a bit too much at some point so they left after just a brief spell and brought her back home. Then, whilst Joanne gave her a bottle and put her to bed, David cranked up the fire and opened a bottle of St Emilion they'd been saving.

Joanne joined him on the settee once Emily was asleep. As she held the glass of wine to her lips, the phone rang.' Who the hell's ringing at this time?' David grizzled.

'I'll get it…it's probably Suzy.'

Joanne picked up the receiver and found it was her mum. Her voice sounded strange.

'Joanne, Dad's not too good. I called the surgery. Dr Wyley came straight out and he's given him an injection and taken some blood. He said it doesn't look good, thinks it could be another stroke or hardening of the arteries. I've been trying to ring you for ages. Where've you been?' She gave an involuntary sob, making Joanne's heart plummet.

'I'm sorry, Mum, we took Emily to the fireworks display.' Joanne's voice was starting to fail and her eyes were full of tears.' I'll throw some clothes in a bag. I can be with you within the hour.'

'No, love, best leave it. If you turn up tonight, he'll know something's wrong. Dr Wyley said not to get him agitated. Come tomorrow instead, it's Saturday so he won't think anything's amiss. He'll just think you've come over for a visit as normal .Dr Wyley will probably have his test results by then.'

David sprang up from the couch and took the phone from Joanne when he saw how upset she'd become.' What's the matter Helen? Is Dad ill?' His face turned ashen as Helen relayed the news.' Helen, we'll come over tonight. You can't go through all this on your own. Are you sure? Well, we'll be there first thing then. I'll put Jo back on.' He squeezed Joanne's shoulder reassuringly and handed her the phone.

'Mum, stay strong. We'll see you in the morning. Ring me if anything changes. I'm just at the end of the line should you need me.'

'I will, love. Dad will probably sleep for a while with the injection he's had. Try not to worry, love. He'll more than likely rally round. He always does.'

'I know, Mum.' Joanne blew a kiss down the phone before replacing the receiver.

She threw some clothes into an overnight bag and loaded everything she thought Emily would need. They were up at the crack of dawn the following day and arrived at her parents just after nine.

It was a massive shock to see her father's frailness. The six-foot gentle giant, as she always saw him, now seemed so small and vulnerable as he lay in his bed.

Emily got excited as soon as she saw him. 'Gamp Gamp,' she squealed, clenching and unclenching her hands. David placed her on the bed beside him and Henry's crumpled face lit up when he saw her. She instantly grasped his finger.

'What have you been up to, Henry, landing yourself in bed like this? I thought you and I would have been able to go for a pint this weekend whilst we're here,' David jested.

Her father looked up and managed a weak smile back. 'Think it must be a flu bug or something, lad. It's knocked me for six, that's for sure.'

Joanne became tearful so, before her dad could see, she made the excuse that she was parched and was going to see if the kettle was on, leaving Emily and David to entertain her dad.

Joanne caught her mother standing by the sink, staring aimlessly out of the window. As she ventured into the kitchen, she clung to her. No words were said; it was just great comfort knowing they were there for one another.

Later that morning Dr Wyley rang. 'The news isn't good Helen,' he said quietly. 'It's basically the beginning of the end, I'm afraid. Hardening of the arteries has reduced the flow of blood to his heart and another stroke looks imminent. He could linger on for a couple of weeks or he could have one relatively soon. It's all in the lap of the gods … I just want you to be prepared. No good taking him into hospital, I know that's not what he would want. The district nurse and I will call in at regular intervals to keep an eye on things and you have the emergency number should you need it. I'm so sorry, Helen.'

Helen nodded mutely and her hand went to her mouth as she replaced the receiver. She sank into her armchair, ashen and tearful. Each word he'd said was now painfully lodged in her mind.

The next two days, they took turns in keeping vigil. It was now quite noticeable that the movement in Henry's arms and legs was much weaker, but his sense of humour was still intact and he joked about how much of a fusspot Joanne was becoming – far worse than her mum.

David, as always, became everyone's rock throughout that insane time. He sat with Henry, made him laugh, fed him and emptied his catheter, whilst Helen and Joanne got some respite by entertaining Emily and consoling one another.

'Look love…' Helen said. 'I know you want to be here to give me a hand but Dr Wyley said Dad could linger for weeks like this. David's got his business to see to and it's not a healthy place at the moment for Emily. I think it's best if you go home, even if it's only for a couple of days or so. I can manage. Dr Wyley's arranged for the district nurse to call in twice a day.' Sadness distorted her lovely smiley face.

With that in mind, Joanne and David said goodbye and hugged Henry the following morning then joined Helen by the car. Joanne looked at her mother's red-rimmed eyes and pale, gaunt face. She held her tight and took a sharp intake of breath. Her mother reassuringly said that she'd be OK but Joanne very much doubted that.

Joanne was just about to step into the car then decided she needed the loo; too many cups of coffee and a long journey ahead were not a good combination. She went back in and climbed the stairs. At the top, her dad's door faced her. Something compelled her to go back in and see him one more time.

The door creaked opened as she turned the handle.

Her father was propped up against a pile of neatly plumped pillows, listening to his favourite Radio Four programme, and shot her a quizzical look. 'Hello, love – thought you'd already left.'

'We were just about to, but you know me and my bladder.'

He gave her a knowing look and smiled.

'I love you, Daddy. Please hurry up and get better soon– I hate seeing you ill like this,' she said tearfully, going over to the bed and reaching out to give his hand a squeeze.

'Oh, don't worry about me, pet lamb. I'll soon be up and about again. You just make sure you look after that little one for me …and your Mum… She's not as strong as we all take her to be, love.'

At that moment, Joanne felt her dad, in his infinite wisdom knew this would probably be the last moments they would spend together. She saw a tear trickle down his cheek. Sixth sense told her the same.

'I love you, pet lamb,' he said, his voice now almost a whisper.

'I love you too, Daddy. Anyway,' Joanne said, sniffing loudly, 'we'll see you at the weekend.'

He didn't answer just nodded. Reluctantly she left him to finish listening to the rest of his programme.

Her mum was giving Emily a last-minute cuddle and grimaced when she saw her daughter's tear-stained face. David took Emily from her and secured her into the car seat, whilst Joanne gave her mum one last hug.

'Don't get upset, love. He could quite easily surprise us all and be right as rain by next week. You know your dad!'

Joanne gave a forced smile, knowing all too well that that wasn't going to happen. 'Let me stay a while longer with Emily, please. David can go back on his own.'

'No, love, you get off. I'll be OK. Come over at the weekend again.'

The drive home was made mostly in silence. 'How are you feeling?' David asked at some point, his hand on top of hers, the other firmly on the steering wheel.

She was grateful for his concern but she knew that she wasn't in the right frame of mind to give a logical answer.' I feel horrible …terrible …angry…and totally, totally lost,' she yelled, then burst into floods of tears and buried her face in a handful of paper hankies. 'How do you expect me to feel?' she squeaked, blowing her nose noisily.

There was pity on his face as he looked at her. Emily was oblivious to all that was happening and slept contentedly throughout the whole journey, only waking tight-lipped and tearful when a police siren rushed in the opposite direction.

The next morning they all woke earlier than normal. Emily was enjoying her bottle in her high-chair and Joanne was trying to digest some toast when the phone rang, making them all jump anxiously. Dread filled Joanne and her mouth tightened as she let David answer it.

She knew by the pained expression on his face that it was bad news. She heard her own voice shriek out a pitiful cry as she sank into the chair. David handed her the phone then snaked his arm supportively around her shoulders as she placed the receiver to her ear. Sobs stopped her from saying anything so she just listened to her mum's voice as she relayed the news she did not want to hear.

'Joanne, Daddy has left us, love… He died about ten minutes ago.' Helen paused to take control. Her voice wavered.' It was very peaceful when he went. I'd just taken him his morning cup of tea, he'd had a restful night and we were talking about you coming at the weekend.' She stopped, there was an involuntary sob. 'He just smiled... Squeezed my hand and closed his eyes.' She broke down at that point – they both did.

It was Joanne who spoke first. 'Mum, have you rung Dr Wyley?'

'Yes, just before I rang you. I'm waiting for him to come Joanne,' she sobbed. 'What am I going to do without him?' The sound of the doorbell chimed in the background. 'I'll have to go... sounds like Dr Wyley's here.'

'We'll be there as soon as we can,' Joanne managed to say before the line went dead.

David held her in his arms as she howled. No one should ever feel as she felt at that moment. It consumed her.

David got in touch with Steven, his business partner, and told him what had happened. Joanne packed a case and sorted out Emily's things in readiness for a long stay. She was semi-delirious and felt like she was walking that fine line between the real and the unreal.

Joanne stayed with her mother to help sort out all the arrangements, whilst David made his way back home on the train, leaving Joanne the car as it had Emily's seat in it. He would use hers when he got back. There was nothing he could do and he had work to attend to. Joanne just needed him back when all the arrangements were made.

It was a week in which Helen and Joanne were swaddled in everyone's sympathy and condolences. As they sat and watched the embers flicker each night whilst Emily slept, they reminisced about the good times, which brought them comfort.

The day of the funeral seemed to pass in a fog. A huge number of people turned up to pay their respects. Jess and Oliver came over, which Joanne thought was pretty decent of them; they'd only met her father a handful of times.

Jess saw to Emily's needs and kept her occupied, which was a blessing All Joanne could really remember of that day was the piece of music which her mum and her had chosen, 'Cavalier Rusticano', a piece her father had played on the piano since he was quite young. They though it fitting.

Holly Lodge was chosen for the wake; it was a stone's throw from her parents' home and the food was first class, so they were told – not that Joanne and her mum could face eating that day. Thank goodness David felt detached enough to take control of everything and everyone.

Joanne stayed on long after the funeral. There was so much that still needed to be sorted out: probate, insurance policies, changing everything into her mum's name. Ten days of constant crying left Joanne's face wrinkled and puckered. What would her dad have made of it all?, she wondered, as she surveyed herself in the mirror one morning.

'I miss Dad so much, Mum,' she said tearfully.

'I know, love, we both do. But life goes on, Joanne, and we have both got to be strong.' Helen said placing her arms supportively around her daughter's shoulders in an emotional hug.

Her mother was the one who walked out each day with the buggy to feed the ducks and take Emily to the swings; her mum turned out to be the more dignified of the two in the aftermath of the funeral. Joanne felt wilted most of the time and disappeared under the duvet whenever she got the chance.

Then one night, after checking Emily was fast asleep, her mother perched on Joanne's bed. Her tone was gentle.' Joanne, I think it's time you went back home to David. We've done everything that needs doing. I'm really grateful but I'm going to have to be on my own at some point.' Her face looked serious.' You need to get your life back on track and it's not good for Emily to be around all these glum faces. She needs her daddy and children her own age to play with. I'll be OK.' She smiled that motherly smile.' Dad put some money to one side for you –its £10,000.We thought it would come in handy with the little one and all.'

'Mum, you need that money.'

'I'm OK, love. We sorted out all our finances a long time ago. He left me nicely provided for. Always knew he'd go first, him being so much older…You never think it will happen…' Her eyes misted over as she said it.

And so mid-morning the next day, with no prolonged goodbyes just one great big tearful hug, Joanne and Emily started their journey home in the car. Surprisingly enough the drive was pleasingly uplifting. Emily chuckled and giggled as she pointed to sheep and cows in the fields they passed along the way. Joanne slotted in a cassette of nursery rhymes, one she kept permanently in the car, to amuse her for the rest of the journey.

Her mum was right; Joanne had become dysfunctional and slightly depressed. Her father would have been furious had he seen her like that, knowing he'd been the cause.

The car at last glided onto the driveway. She turned off the engine and lifted Emily from her car seat. Trying to juggle keys, handbag and a small wriggly child was a task in itself. Once inside the house, she scanned the room and stood rigid.

Joanne hadn't mentioned to David that she was coming home; she wanted to surprise him. Newspapers were on the floor where he'd discarded them; half-empty coffee mugs were on the mantelpiece with empty beer cans; his jacket was thrown over the back of the dining-room chair; read and unread mail covered the dining table. The whole place was swaddled in dust and, by the look of the overflowing bin in the kitchen and the sink full of pots, he'd virtually lived off take-aways since she'd left.

She glanced in the fridge to see if there was anything remotely edible but all she spied were two eggs, some mould-covered tomatoes, bacon that resembled chewing tobacco and some green cheese. Thank goodness her mother had packed enough food for the evening meal and Emily's lunch, which Joanne proceeded to give her, as by now the baby was becoming tired and hungry and protesting loudly.

Joanne put her down for her afternoon nap then started beavering her way through the mess. She opened their bedroom door and saw chaos prevailed in there too. A heap of discarded clothes lay in the corner next to the unmade bed; three pairs of shoes lay on the floor, including the ones he'd worn for her dad's funeral. Flinging open the window, she let in an icy blast from the November wind as she got stuck into stripping the bed.

Any other time, the mess would have instigated a massive row but the man responsible had captured her heart a long time ago. She heard his key turn in the lock at seven on the dot and his head appeared round the lounge door, looking sheepish and ashamed. Then he gave a heart-stopping smile and, before he could say anything, Joanne ran into his outstretched arms and kissed him. Emily laughed with delight as David swooped her up with both hands and swung her round at head level.

'Jo…I am so sorry about the mess. If I'd known you were coming home I'd have cleaned up, but I've been working every hour God sends and I'm whacked,' he said anxiously, raking his hands through his hair, as he joined her in the kitchen once he'd bathed Emily and put her to bed.

Joanne continued scraping the Jersey Royals her mum had given her and grinned. 'You're forgiven. One thing's for sure –you were never going to bring any wayward women back here whilst it was like this.'

'Fat chance.'

She cuffed him mockingly

As they ate, she blushed under his gaze. It was nearly three weeks since her father had died and so much had happened in that time. He held out his hand across the table and held onto hers as they continued to talk. But she couldn't respond to his advances even after half a bottle of Châteauneuf was consumed; she was still too fragile.

She climbed into bed next to him that night and could smell the unmistakable smell of his freshly scrubbed skin as he gently took her into his arms. She could tell he didn't know how to be with her. For the last few weeks, she'd been like some unhinged, grief-stricken stranger at the other end of the phone.

He caressed her shoulder, kissed her neck then leant over and kissed her on the lips with a feathery lightness, which seemed to unlock feelings, She started to resent every moment she'd not been with him. His mouth closed on hers and consumed her; as they made love, she felt more like an adulteress than a wife and he told her she was beautiful as they lay afterwards under the cool clean sheets.

Chapter 15

Helen coped incredibly well after Henry's death; far better than Joanne had anticipated she would. There were the odd days she sounded low, others where she embraced her new life with gusto. She even joined the WI again, something she vowed she would never do but Joanne felt it was done more for the company.

Helen adored spending time with Emily and drove over see them whenever she could. 'Where has the time gone?' she always muttered when she was about to leave.

Joanne often wondered that too. Suzy and Gill were married women now with families of their own. They had all moved on to the next chapters of their lives.

Gill moved in with Brian shortly after Joanne's dad died and gave birth to Oliver nine months later. Theirs was a registry office wedding followed by a rowdy piss-up at the George and Dragon. They were "as happy as pigs in shit" even though they struggled at times with finances.

Harry and Suzy's life was very different. They had a very grand wedding and were well-paid occupational therapists. Both having OCD issues, they lived an immaculately tidy life; everything had to have a master plan. Even their daughter Lilli was planned around a schedule and born ten months to the day after they married. Even so, Suzy still retained her wacky sense of humour, which Joanne adored her for, and they all socialised together whenever they could.

Joanne admitted to the girls that she still missed the buzz and banter of being in a salon.

'You still have that money your dad left you if you want to open a shop,' David jested across the table when they had the girls and their spouses round for dinner one night.

Joanne gave him a hard stare. 'Where did that old chestnut come from?' she asked. Her eyebrows rose and the atmosphere thickened with interest. Maybe it was the fact she'd voiced openly that she missed working but their guests wouldn't let it go. Gill and Suzy stared at her as she finished carrying loaded plates to the table.

'You want to go back to work!' Gill said looking at Joanne like she'd grown two heads.

'Wouldn't you like to have any more Emilys instead?' Suzy grinned over in David's direction.

'Well, we would,' Joanne said with a poised fork. 'Only no more Emilys seem to be coming along. The fact is I have endometriosis, as you all know. Apparently it's quite difficult to get pregnant with it. We must have just been extremely lucky with Emily.' David gave her a supportive smile.

'But you've never mentioned it,' Sue said, lifting her glass to lips.

'No …well, we just thought I would get pregnant again. Obviously not.'

Joanne sensed there had been a dramatic change in atmosphere; as everyone picked ravenously at their food, others started to knock back the wine to compensate for the glances that were being exchanged.

Joanne had to think rapidly in order to get off this subject. 'So, I've been thinking of starting up my own business when Emily starts pre-school after Christmas.'

David nearly swallowed his glass but went along with everything she was saying. 'Yes. Her dad left her a small inheritance and it's been sitting in the bank doing fuck all for a couple of years, so if we can find a decently priced bit of property… Well who knows.' He grinned, sitting back in his chair, legs outstretched in front of him, arms folded, having finished his meal. He had picked up on what she was doing and, when Joanne disappeared into the kitchen, he even elaborated on the story.

Joanne threw him a grin as she carried in the cheeseboard and placed it centre table.

'Well,' Harry said holding his glass of wine in the air. 'A toast to David and Joanne and their new business venture.'

Everyone chorused this and glasses were chinked.

Joanne hoped that would be the end of that, but what had started as a bit of a story to lift everyone's mood now catapulted into a full-blown web of lies about this fictitious business. The way this was going, before the night was over they'd have a chain of shops in the offing.

Joanne beckoned David to follow her into the kitchen. 'I'll help,' Gill said getting up.

'No, you stay there,' Joanne said, smiling at her.

'This is all snowballing out of control,' David said when they were out of earshot.

'What are we going to do?' she whispered, still laughing. 'They really think we're going to open a shop.'

'We'll just have to go ahead with it then,' he said in response.

It had been a while since they'd done something so juvenile; they had become a little complacent in the last few months and all this felt good.

She handed him the tray loaded with the best china cups, sugar and cream and as he picked it up she gently brushed her hand against the hardness in his trousers

In this brief, cordial moment David's eyes went soft and he gave a throaty groan. 'Oh, go home you lot – I want to make love to my wife,' he muttered in a low voice, as his lips brushed gently against hers.

'Later,' she whispered as she followed him through to the dining room holding a cafetière.

Good humour was fuelled by the wine they'd consumed and now they were well into the port and brandy, whilst devouring Stilton, Stinking Bishop and Roquefort as if they'd not eaten a morsel all night, still talking about the new shop.

'What sort of property are you looking for?' Brian said. Gill threw him a glare.

'An inexpensive one,' David said, taking a puff from his cigar and blowing the smoke heavenward then grinning at Brian.

'Well,' Brian continued, as his eyebrows rose, 'I don't know whether you'd be interested but my granddad had a butcher shop many years ago on Ash Street. It's been closed since he died and that's fifteen years ago. Nan still owns it... It's quite neglected, as you can imagine after being left for that length of time, but Ash Street is a busy street, lots of surrounding houses, an ideal spot for a hairdresser's. I know it's not in a posh area but at the same time you wouldn't have the hefty rates the town-centre shops have.'

'BRIAN!' Gill gave him a caustic glare. 'They don't want to buy that old wreck of your granddad's.' She looked at Joanne apologetically.

'No, that's where you're wrong, Gill,' David said, sitting bolt upright in his seat, bright eyed and bushy tailed. There was something about his expression that told Joanne his mind was going into overdrive; cogs were being put into motion and it was frightening to watch.' Yes, if you can get me the keys, I'd be very interested in having a butcher's.'

Everyone laughed loudly at the pun.

'Sure.' The two men locked eyes as they puffed contentedly on their cigars like they'd just pulled off the deal of the century, whilst the rest of them were left a little perplexed by what had just happened.

It was gone three by the time David and Joanne had cleared the debris in the dining room once their friends had left. As she lay beside her alcohol-infused husband, she began to wonder what was actually going on in his head. 'Were you serious about looking at Brian's granddad's shop,' she asked.

'Of course,' he said in an upbeat tone. 'Look, you have ten grand in the bank doing fuck all. If we can get that shop for a song, do it up, you open it up and then work in it for a while, we can sell it as a going concern. Your dad's money will triple in the space of two years.'

His words filled Joanne with enthusiasm.

Chapter 16

It took a couple of weeks for Brian to get round to letting David and Joanne view the property – and what a grim sight it was! The shop was a small, antiquated wreck at the end of a long line of semis on a busy main road. To add to Joanne's disappointment, the interior looked much gloomier than the outside.

'How long since your granddad worked here, Brian?' Joanne asked, as she wandered aimlessly through each murky room. It resembled a setting from 10 Rillington Place: grey, eerie and covered in cobwebs, and the air was thick with dust.

'Well now, let me see.' His eyes narrowed thoughtfully and he pulled a sort of constipated expression.' He's been dead twelve years and he was ill for a couple of years before that. So I'd say around fifteen years since it's been in use. We dismantled the cold room and all the counters and sold them off, but Nan never seemed to want to get rid of the shop until now.'

In Joanne's eyes the place was beyond redemption but the look on David's face told her he thought differently. 'It's perfect!' he proclaimed, raking his hands through his hair.

Both Brian and Joanne's jaws slackened. Was he talking about the same building that they were standing in?

'Yes… can't you just see it?' he enthused, emitting an impatient sigh, when he saw the negative looks on Joanne and Brian's faces.' If we knock this wall down between the shop and the back room, it would open the whole place up, making the salon huge. We can have the staff room at the back where the cold room was and beyond that a kitchen, utility room and a loo. The place is like a bloody Tardis! It goes on forever.'

Brian and Joanne still didn't share his enthusiasm. David turned on his heels and took the stairs two at a time. 'Wow! It's massive,' he shouted as he reached the summit.' How much did your gran say she wants for it?'

'Well… she was thinking around twelve grand,' Brian said sheepishly.

'Tell her we'll give her eleven – cash.'

'Ha!' Joanne mused, then realised he was deadly serious. Her face metamorphosed into Victor Meldrew. 'DAVID!' she bellowed, her face reddening. 'I think we should talk about it first, don't you, before we make any hasty decisions?'

Brian saw that his friends were on course for a major row, so wisely decided to leave them to thrash out their grievances.' Look you two, here's the key. I'm going to head off home. You obviously need time to talk things through.' With that, he threw David the keys and left.

'Are you bloody insane? This place is horrendous,' Joanne fumed, surveying the dusty, dilapidated room they were standing in after Brian left.

David shoved his hands deep in his Wranglers and faced her squarely. 'Jo, just listen to yourself! It might look like the back end of nowhere but can't you see the potential? The roof, at a glance, looks pretty sound. I know the rooms are grubby but it's superficial. It's on a busy main road – there's enough room on the front for five cars.'

She had to think rapidly to try to catch up with his enthusiasm but she couldn't get beyond the butcher's chopping block and hanging carcasses that were once there.

'Upstairs,' David continued, 'there are three huge bedrooms and a decent-sized bathroom. Just have butcher's.' That bloody pun again brought a huge grin to his face. Joanne didn't see the humour.

'Look… before you make any concrete decisions, let me give Dad a ring, see if he will give it the once over. If he says it's OK, we'll go ahead. It's your shout, Jo.'

His face was deadly serious but his eyes couldn't hide the excitement he felt as adrenaline surged through his veins. He wanted the shop; his mind was already made up and it was a done deal, no matter how much Joanne protested.

After a long chat on the phone, Oliver drove over the following day with his box of architectural gadgets to do an assessment of the whole place.

David had been spot-on with his brief summary. The place seemed structurally sound, even though it had been left empty for such a long time. It had been well-maintained; the fact it was blanketed in November gloom didn't help with its presentation. The price of eleven grand was agreed and work began before the ink was even dry on the contracts.

Joanne's life from that moment was like someone had thrown a huge firecracker into the centre of it, creating chaos, mayhem and uncertainty.

Her mother was delighted that at last Joanne was putting her dad's money to good use. She also had news for them too.' I've decided to sell my house. I've been thinking about it for a while now. Under the circumstances, with what you've just told me, it looks like I'll be more use to you over there than sitting in this rambling old house doing precisely nothing,' she said generously.

They both embraced her decision. It would be a blessing having her around, especially knowing what tasks laid ahead.

David spent each waking moment planning, costing and knocking down walls. His aim was to finish the shop by the end of March at the very latest. That gave him just over four months to complete the project! He squared it with Steven to take any holidays that were owing and asked if he could work part time for a couple of weeks after that if needed, so he could make headway with the place.

For the whole of January and February the blitzing took place. Helen held the fort on the home front, keeping Emily entertained, ferrying her to pre-school, cooking meals and doing household chores. That enabled Joanne to organise and purchase building materials and sort out her salon equipment.

One particular Sunday in February there had been sleet through the night but the skies were now clear and the sun's feeble rays had started to melt what sleet had fallen. David climbed reluctantly out of his side of the bed at the crack of dawn. He threw on his work clothes and left Joanne to sleep in. His dedication held no bounds, even on days like these. Walls were now down, windows were replaced and plumbing and wiring were in full progress.

Joanne joined him around ten o'clock, armed with some docker-sized bacon butties and a flask of tea.

'It's going to be great.' he said with a grin, as she handed him a mug of tea. Both perched awkwardly on upturned wooden boxes in the middle of mayhem.

'When it's all up and running it'll be a little gold mine.' A dollop of sauce escaped his sandwich and landed on his chin. He wiped it with his sleeve before Joanne could reach for the kitchen paper. 'Another thing I've thought of,' he said mid-chomp. 'If we put the house on the market, once it's sold we can move into the flat above.'

Joanne threw him a look of horror, 'I mean just while we look for another house. Obviously it wouldn't be a permanent situation. I mean, we never intended to stay in that house, did we? It'll be just a stepping stone until we find a house we really like.' He was fumbling with his words, knowing full well he was digging a great hole for himself.

Joanne could see she had no viable option; David's mind was made up once again. The flippant comment he'd just made was his way of telling her the 'For Sale' sign was already hammered into the lawn. All these plans, all this chaos, which had stemmed from one glib comment at a dinner party some months back!

At one stage Joanne had been miserable about the whole thing but now she was caught up in the spiral of unpredictability, she too embraced the changes. And for some unknown reason, she was becoming excited by everything that was happening.

David took another mug of tea from her, grinned and gave her a kiss. 'Thank you, Mrs Winston,' he said with some tenderness.

'For what?'

'For being you ...for mucking in, for taking on whatever challenge I throw at you, for giving me such a lovely daughter, for not complaining... for looking sexy even in that bobble hat.'

Salty tears sprang up into her eyes.

'Hey, that was supposed to be a compliment, not make you cry!'

Their life together had always felt like a journey, and up to now an exciting one at that, although over the last year their relationship seemed to have lapsed into complacency. David's mind was always elsewhere at times when they were together. The last five months of craziness had injected some stimulation, excitement – even unpredictable sex – back into their life again.

The salon looked huge now the wall was gone. The flooring was down; backwashes, work stations, mirrored walls and mood lights were all in the process of being fitted, as were the state-of-the-art dryers hanging from angle-poised brackets above each station.

Joanne kept the colours neutral throughout, just injected great splashes of reds, browns and black by way of paintings, towels and accessories. A huge hardwood bow window had been fitted to the front of the shop in front of which York-stoned flags were laid and an old lamp-post from which hung the sign: 'JOANNE DAVID', as simple as that. The chosen name for a joint effort.

An official opening party was held in the salon and everyone involved was invited. Jess and Oliver brought Philip and Kristy. Steven, David's partner, brought his wife, Tess, both healthily bronzed from their holiday.

David and his father had orchestrated each job they took on; both were hotheads, both perfectionists, so there were moments where tempers flared and heated words were exchanged. But now Oliver brimmed with pride at David's achievements and told him so as they shared a private moment at the party. Oliver generously donated a couple of cases of champagne and Jess managed to put her broomstick to one side for a short while to plate up some canapés.

Christine Belshaw, Lily Shaw and Sally Winters, Joanne's newly appointed staff, mingled and chatted to people and got acquainted with the place.

Joanne and David exchanged smiles at some point and both acknowledged the chemistry that was still there, which filled her with excitement and gave her hope.

***

It was a cold, wet Monday morning at the end of April when Joanne and David eagerly unlocked the salon door, flipped on the lighting and announced proudly to one another, 'This shop is now open for business.'

She clung to him excitedly. 'Thank you for all your hard work.'

'My pleasure. It's your job now to make lots of cash.' He grinned back.

The girls arrived looking very professional in their white tunics, anxious to tackle the onslaught. 'Morning,' Joanne sang excitedly as they all piled in through the door. The girls laughed nervously as they went through to the staff room where David was making a fresh pot of coffee. Chris gave Joanne a hug of reassurance,

'All will go well, you'll see …don't look so worried.'

Joanne was glad the girls had been there to help prepare things the last few days now they had been able to familiarise themselves with everything and achieve some team bonding in the process.

She hadn't anticipated just how exhausting the first day would be. Clients, old and new, started to pour through the door due to the cleverly engineered advertising campaign Suzy and Gill had helped her with.

Once again Joanne was back in the saddle, she realised just how much she'd missed the work. It was the kick-off-her-shoes and count-the-takings moments at the end of the day, though, that made it all worthwhile.

Helen was able to take the reins at home thankfully where Emily was concerned. She gave her breakfast, took her to pre-school in her clapped-out old Mini, then went back to take care of the chores

It was all going to plan, better than Joanna had anticipated it would. But then, out of the blue, a buyer made an offer they couldn't refuse for the house and wanted to move as soon as possible.

As luck had it Helen was in the throes of finalising her contract on a smart, two-bedroom apartment on the promenade, with a balcony that overlooked the sea. 'There's plenty of room for us all,' she insisted brightly. 'Just put your furniture in storage and take your time with the flat above the shop.'

'It's alright, Helen. Joanne and I have decided to rough it in the flat above the shop whilst it's being done up.'

Joanne threw him a look of disbelief. 'Have we?'

'Yes, we discussed it. Don't you remember? You said we can get on with jobs if we're on site once everyone's gone home.'

'Yes… Oh yes, lots of finicky stuff to do when the workmen have gone home,' she flushed.

‘Well, at least let Emily stay with me then,’ Helen said, traipsing off to bring the washing off the line.

‘What was all that about?’ Joanne whispered.

‘Don’t you think we’ve had our privacy encroached on long enough? We need some us time. I love your mother to bits but our sex life since she’s been with us has been limited.’

David gave instructions down the phone for his team to get a whistle on with the flat and to work round the clock round if need be: a bonus was offered for speedy results. New floorboards, bathroom suite, a fireplace, wardrobes – all had to be fitted before the move. The kitchen was already finished downstairs behind the shop, which simplified matters. At least they’d be able to eat, use the shop loo and even get washed in the kitchen if they had to.

Emily took it all in her stride. She was so adaptable, just as long as she had her colouring book and her parents close by; nothing seemed to faze her.

Chapter 17

It was a time of political unrest. Headlines stated steel prices had gone into a decline, so to even think of selling what steel stock David already had would be ludicrous until prices started to recover again – however, it was a good time to stockpile even though that meant borrowing from the bank to do it.

Colin, their accountant, came to do a yearly audit and stated that they needed to develop the import-export side much more than they already had. 'Higher profit margins would be achieved overseas, especially in second-hand industrial machinery,' he reminded them sternly.

Then he mentioned a chap, a retired liquidator, who might be able to help. 'Gerard Dunn, a self-made multimillionaire by all accounts, made his money through buying run-down businesses, bringing them back up to scratch, then selling them on for profit. He does mostly consultancy work these days to keep a hand in.' Colin reached into his briefcase to root out his address book. 'He helped Radford's get back on their feet when they were more or less going under. Ah! Here it is. If you like, I could give him a ring to see if we can set up a meeting.'

Steven and David glanced at one another. The thought of someone else, a stranger at that, coming into the business didn't bode well. But the realisation of what might happen if they continued to go on as they were didn't bear thinking about, so they finally agreed.

That meeting turned out to be fruitful as luck had it. Gerard Dunn had only just arrived back from the Far East and had nothing pencilled in his diary for the foreseeable future. He was only too pleased to help out with a business plan, stipulating a set fee and expecting a percentage from any deals he set up for them.

'A bit steep!' David said to him. But knowing their hands were tied, they finally agreed.

Contracts were drawn up and wheels were set in motion almost immediately. Gerard started the ball rolling by jetting David and Steven off to Germany and Japan, leaving Oliver to oversee the business in their absence. Whilst they were there, Gerard instructed major companies he'd dealt with before, who were interested in buying what was on offer, to set up a meeting. He left David and Steven somewhat impressed.

In the meantime, Joanne's business seemed to be flourishing. An introductory offer promoting the salon, which Gill set up as she now worked for the local paper, brought in clients by the droves.

Helen popped in most morning, after dropping Emily off at school, to help launder towels, make drinks and be a general dogsbody. Then, at three thirty, she would scurry off in her battered old Mini to pick up Emily from school and take her home for tea, leaving Joanne to work on long after her staff had left.

She thought it was a time that David and she should have been enjoying each other's company much more than they were: going for dinner, dancing, overnight stays at grand hotels! They'd talked about it often enough some months back, when they were up to their eyeballs in cement and plaster. But now that time had arrived and money was plentiful, sadly though they were like ships in the night–too busy, too tired, too distant to make social plans.

David threw her the odd invite when he entertained clients, but all she wanted to do was curl up in front of the fire with a large glass of wine and have some Emily time instead. In the end David gave up asking.

In the weeks that followed, she saw less and less of her husband as the life of a lucrative businessman claimed him.

Joanne had only spoken to this Gerard chap a handful of times over the phone but each time she did, it left her with this jabbing feeling in the pit of her stomach. There was something about him she didn't like.

Steven was a family man at heart and wasn't really interested in the social side of things or flying off to foreign shores to clinch a deal. He preferred to be a nine-till-five chap, then home and slippers and a meal with the family. He asked David if it would be OK for him to be just the front man in the office instead. David jumped at the chance; he loved the vibrancy and excitement of his new life and came to realise that there were benefits to being in this world after all.

New cars were ordered on Gerard's instructions and the firm's building was given a facelift. They also took on extra staff to accommodate the workload from the new contracts that were coming in.

Steven wasn't comfortable with the speed at which things were moving. Cars were an expense they could ill-afford until the revenue from jobs was secured but Gerard argued, saying they had to move with the times. But it seemed it was now a case of big cars for big egos.

David's car turned out to be a silver 500 Mercedes, with cream-leather upholstery and a state-of-the-art sound system. Joanne was warned not to breathe near it, let alone try and drive the beast. But she was more than happy with Betty the Boneshaker, as she called her four-year-old Toyota. It ticked the boxes as far as she was concerned; there were no worries if Emily spilt her drink, dropped ice cream or even puked in it.

The flat was taking shape nicely. The sitting room looked impressive with its marble fireplace and living-flame fire and the interior designer Joanne had commissioned was doing a terrific job with the sofas and drapes. Wardrobes had been built and were ready for Joanne's clothes. The bathroom and loo just needed grouting. Not that David noticed any of this; he was far too busy being a high flyer these days. The week the carpets were fitted and the furniture arrived, David was somewhere on the other side of the world.

Emily loved her new home, loved the attention from the girls in the salon, loved staying with her gran. She oozed excitement when her friends came for tea and were allowed to play in the salon after the girls had gone home.

Summer arrived; with it came Sundays with the gang at the pub by the canal and barbeques in friends' back gardens. Joanne hinted to David that it would be nice to have some time away –a short break or maybe even take Emily abroad.

'Sorry, love, I've got wall-to-wall appointments for god knows how long Why don't you organise something, take your mum with you? I'm sure she'd love that. My treat.' His eyes flashed irritably as he continued to scan the stocks and shares pages in the *Telegraph*.

‘I’ve got a hefty workload too, you know! You’re not the only one working,’ Joanne snapped irritably. ‘I’m thinking more of Emily than you and I; she needs a holiday with both her parents.’ She didn’t know why she bothered; he wasn’t even listening.

Luckily, Jess and Oliver came to the rescue by taking Emily down to Bath with them to see her cousins. It was nice for her to see them all again and spend time with David’s family who Joanne knew would spoil her.

Chapter 18

Joanne realised there was now this giant hole in their relationship and it seemed there wasn't a damn thing she could do about it. The more she tried to talk to David, the more he flew off the handle. They shared the same lives, the same daughter, but Joanne was forced to face facts that there was no longer an 'us'.

David's schedule was usually manic; even so, quality time with Emily always took precedence. He adored her; his sole purpose in life was coming home to her! Joanne watched as they giggled and played most nights .She'd become a voyeur though in her own life, no longer allowed to participate, emotionally redundant, an outsider.

She tried to hide her feelings from her mother, afraid Helen would think of her as failure yet again with another marriage down the swanny. But Joanne knew by her mother's furrowed brow that she'd guessed things weren't as they should be.

On rare occasions still when David wasn't away, they would donned their Wranglers and met up with the crowd for the Sunday piss-up at the pub by the canal. It was there she got a glimpse of the David she once knew. For a brief time, he no longer looked guarded and was charming as he showed off his daughter to everyone there. A couple of times, he even threw a few warm glances her way when the alcohol clouded his judgment. To everyone, they were still Mr and Mrs In Love – but she knew differently.

Joanne's sixth sense now told her other women were on the horizon. There was no hard evidence but they rarely made love. She missed being woken by his early-morning kisses, missed him leaving her with the pleasure they'd just shared. She missed the smell of his skin, missed his touch and, most of all, she missed him.

She was lucky if they made love once a month and even then sadly it had turned into the roll-on, roll-off, kind. Most night she lay alone and hugged her pillow; it was better than hugging nothing at all, she told herself!

The one glass of wine she enjoyed at the end of the day had now accelerated to a whole bottle. David had been telling her to get a hobby when she grumbled that she was lonely. Well, now she had one – it was called drinking!

The nights, when he wasn't away on business, her slumber would be interrupted by him coming back from wherever he'd been, a cold, prickly tension creep down her spine when she heard him undress on the landing then slide in quietly beside her. No more did they spoon or nuzzle into one another as they fell asleep. Instead tears fell silently onto her pillow and she bit her lip to muffle her sobs.

The next morning, she'd wait until she heard his car tear from the forecourt before she threw back the duvet, wrapped her robe tightly around her and made her way to Emily's room, eyes still swollen from crying and the booze she'd consumed. How familiar all this felt but this time around there'd been no violence, plus she had Emily's love now to console her.

A hay fever attack was the answer she gave when clients enquired sympathetically about her eyes; they seemed to accept this, even offered advice on remedies.

She was now at the stage where she didn't even care about the women in David's life anymore. She was happy for him to leave her alone and, whilst he was having non-committal sex with other woman, he seemed to be doing just that.

The only person she could divulge her innermost thoughts to was Chris at the salon. They were working a late night as a bride wanted a rehearsal for her wedding the following week. Emily was staying at Helen's for the night and Joanne prepared lamb Kleftico for dinner, in the hope that David and she would be able to sit like two civilised human beings, enjoy the meal and a good bottle of wine and thrash out their grievances. But it wasn't to be.

Another phone call saying that he was seeing a client. 'Yeah, right!' she shouted frostily down the phone, realising that once again her plans were squashed.

When Chris saw how upset Joanne was, she told her she was in no rush to get home and would be more than delighted to share her meal. After the second bottle of wine was opened, Joanne blurted out everything that had been happening. 'What the fuck am I going to do?' Joanne wailed ruefully. 'Do I really want to know if my suspicions are justified? .Can I cope with a head-on confrontation at the moment? I'm fucked whichever way you look at it,' she said with an alcohol-infused hiccup.

'It might just be a seven-year itch – maybe once he's scratched it, he'll come back to you! Ride the storm, say nothing. That's what I'd do,' Chris said, replenishing her glass with the last dregs from the bottle. She took hold of Joanne's hand across the table and stared wide-eyed at her. 'If you really feel you have to know for sure whether your suspicions are justified or not, there's one way of finding out without confronting him. Start playing detective, pick up on things he says, follow him. Do anything, Jo! But don't just sit there and take it. You've already gone down that road once with James.'

She was right; this was history repeating itself. In their drunken stupor, they came up with ways in which Joanne could trip him up over the next few nights,

From then on, Joanne decided to give little cause for him to criticise her.

Emily's jovial chattering always lifted David's mood and brought laughter to the table, where normally he'd have a glum face. Emily always had his undivided attention. When he was reading her a story after tucking her into bed, Joanne searched his pockets and briefcase, took his keys from his jacket and searched his car. Sure enough there were scraps of paper with scribbled telephone numbers, hankies tinged with lipstick, a diary with dates that were question marked! Where did she go from there, though?

Seven o'clock on the dot the following evening, David's meal was almost ready as he walked through the salon door. Emily was having tea at Gill's. Joanne had it all planned –tonight she'd confront him.

He shouted, 'Hi,' but there was no kiss, no 'how was your day?' His attention was immediately fixed on the seven o'clock news on the kitchen TV. She sensed his agitation.

Suddenly he got up from his chair. 'Just popping to the garage to fill up the car with juice. Won't be long.' Scooping his keys from the table where he'd thrown them seconds before, he headed for the door.

'OK, but don't be long. Dinner's nearly ready.' He'd driven past several garages on the way home! Why didn't he fill his car up then? A question mark hung in the air. She had to follow him.

At a snail's pace she drove behind him in her bone-shaker, hoping he wouldn't notice her in his rear-view mirror. He came to a halt by the phone box a couple of blocks down the road. Who the hell would he be ringing from there? And why couldn't he use the home phone to make his call?

'For Christ's sake, Joanne, wake up and smell the coffee.' Angrily she banged her hands down on the steering wheel. It took a minute to regain control then her lips pursed together in a line of misery.

Quickly, she turned the car round and drove back to the shop just in time to get to the kitchen before he walked through the door. His mood had changed greatly when he came in.

'Mmmm, smells good,' he said, sitting down in front of his loaded plate. Whoever he'd been speaking with had certainly said something agreeable. 'Just seen John Harper at the garage. You remember him? He plays golf with Dad and he's asked me to go for a pint later. You don't mind, do you?' His eyes never left his plate as he spoke. He couldn't even look at her as the lies spilled from his mouth.

Her heart plummeted. If he no longer loved her, why didn't he just come out with it and say it? She watched him closely as he ate and listened to him gabbling on about deals at work. Inwardly, she fumed.

The cavalry came to her rescue in the form of Gill, who burst noisily through the shop door with Emily and Oliver in tow, all brandishing a Tupperware box full of newly picked blackberries.

'The weather being nice after school, we'd thought we'd pop and collect the last of the blackberries,' Gill boomed enthusiastically. 'Oh and Emily wanted to collect some rosehips for her play kitchen too. Hope you don't mind but I told her not to cut them up as they have little hairs inside that will itch like buggery if you get them on your skin… Oh hi, David,' she said brightly, spotting him at the table. She pecked him affectionately on his cheek. He kissed her back and turned on the charm.

'They've had sausages and mash with brown sauce for tea, plates scraped clean,' Gill told them in her kindergarten lingo.

'Gill you're an angel. Was Emily good for you?'

Emily gave a sigh of annoyance that her mother been as bold as to challenge her behaviour.

'She was – always is. Not like Oliver Twist there,' Gill's eyes settled on her own offspring.

'Thank Auntie Gill for having you for tea,' Joanne whispered softly in Emily's ear as she took her satchel, anorak and the box of berries from her daughter.

Gill bent, scooped Emily into her arms and gave her a huge hug.

'Thanks, Auntie Gill, for having me.' Emily giggled and squeezed Gill's neck tightly whilst planting a wet kiss on her cheek. David took her from Gill and proceeded to blow raspberries on his daughter's neck.

Oliver belted up snugly in the car. Gill gave Joanne a quizzical look before climbing in beside him. 'You OK? You haven't been yourself lately. Nothing wrong, I hope? Buggerlugs in there giving you grief?' she joked. She hadn't got a clue what a Jekyll and Hyde David had become these last few months but Joanne didn't feel like enlightening her just yet.

'No, I'm a bit tired, that's all. The shop's been mad busy.'

'That reminds me, whenever you can fit me in for highlights and a trim, I'd be grateful.'

Joanne nodded then waved her friend off and made her way back through the shop to the kitchen. The sound of laughter from her daughter induced her to smile. Why wasn't it always like this? Was it so bad sitting in front of the TV, being nice to one another at the end of a busy day, then climbing in beside one another, arms and legs entwined, and slipping into a contented slumber like they used to?

She soaked up the silence as she lay alone in bed much later that night. Emily was tucked up tight; David was off drinking with his fictitious friend.

Her mind began to swim with negativity. Was this all her fault? She'd been a mother, a businesswoman but she'd probably forgotten somewhere along the line to be a mistress to her husband.

She threw back the covers, grabbed her robe and made her way to the loo. The sight of herself in the mirror made her recoil slightly. Was she really only thirty-five? She didn't look or feel that at this moment; neglect oozed from the mirror. There were dark circles under her eyes, roots betrayed her true colour and her complexion was shallow. All work and no play had turned her into an extremely dull girl it seemed.

She trod softly down the stairs and walked barefoot into the kitchen, opened the glass leaded door and lifted down a crystal glass. The fridge light illuminated her silhouette as she lifted the chilled chardonnay and poured herself a nightcap. Tomorrow she was having a well-deserved day off; the girls could cope on their own, she decided.

She was dropping Emily off at Jess and Oliver's first thing and they were motoring down to Abby and Jonathan's for the last of the summer holidays. Emily had been talking about nothing else for weeks. It had been unusually warm for the time of year and Joanne had bought her lots of new, brightly coloured clothing for the trip plus presents for her cousins. Normally, Joanne would have gone too but time away from the business was still limited, especially with it being summer.

After she dropped Emily off, she'd have a long overdue day out with her mother, she decided. Some retail therapy and lunch somewhere chic. She'd neglected her mum for too long, she thought sadly.

She drained her glass, gave it a quick rinse under the tap then placed it upturned on the draining board. She didn't hear David come in that night, just felt his presence as he climbed into bed.

Next thing she knew, the alarm clock was spooking her awake. She cranked her body quickly into morning mode, visited the loo and woke Emily. David had already eaten breakfast, showered and was scanning the *Telegraph* while he drank his coffee. He threw her a look of disdain, as she dropped two Alka-Seltzers into a glass of water and popped some bread into the toaster.

'Self-inflicted,' he sneered from behind his paper. 'I'll drop Emily off at my parents on my way to work –it'll save you doing it. Looks like you're still over the limit anyway,' he said sarcastically.

'Mmm,' she muttered, ignoring his snide remark. 'That would be a huge help.' She didn't want to get into an argument. Him taking Emily though would give her a chance to get her roots done and have a trim before meeting her mother.

Emily was too excited to eat her Coco Pops, she exclaimed noisily as she chattered her way into the kitchen. Joanne warned her, 'If you don't eat them, you don't go!' prompting more protests as Emily spooned the cereal reluctantly into her mouth.

David jumped on the bandwagon too by protesting loudly when he saw the huge amount of things Emily was taking with her. 'My parents won't be pleased,' he said sharply. Joanne rolled her eyes and smothered her daughter's face in kisses before waving her off. Then she rushed to shower and dress before her staff arrived.

Christine gave her a new hairdo that took years off her. The shops were a blaze of colour as Joanne and Helen meandered. All the new season's must-buys were in the windows. Both armed with an obscene number of carriers bags, they entered Chez Moi, a decadent place packed with smart people. There they were fussed over, fed and pampered by the handsome waiters. As Joanne ate her antipasti, she tried to dismiss exactly how much she'd actually spent that day. The midnight-blue Garbachio dress, which clung to her in all the right places, the six-inch heeled patent shoes and matching bag that she'd picked up in the Russell & Bromley's half-price sale, makeup, costume jewellery – you name it, Joanne seemed to have bought it.

She'd even indulged in some La Perla underwear which turned out to be more expensive than the dress, and she'd bought a large bottle of Chanel since David no longer bought perfume for her. Tonight she was on a mission, she told her mother.

'Oh? Why is that, dear?' Helen asked, before placing an overloaded forkful of lobster thermador in her mouth.

'Things haven't been so good lately between David and me.'

'I had noticed, love. I'm not exactly blind, and Emily tells me the odd thing or two. I guessed you'd tell me when you were ready.' She smiled across the table.

Joanne didn't elaborate further, as she didn't want to spoil this mum-and-daughter moment and the delicious food they were cramming into their mouths.

It was gone six by the time she returned to the shop after dropping her mother off at home. The place was swathed in silence as Joanne let herself in – the staff had already left. Two messages flashed on the answer-phone on the desk. She dumped her bags on the salon floor and pressed the play button. One was from Emily; she'd arrived safely at Abby's and sounded beside herself with excitement. The other message was from David.

'Joanne. Going to dinner with Gerard after work. Won't be home until late, don't wait up.'

Shit, fuck, bollocks – of all nights! She was sure nothing had been pencilled into his diary when she'd looked. She had to find out where he was going – and there was one person who would probably tell her without raising suspicion.

She punched Steven's home number into the phone and made the excuse that David had left a message on the answer phone for her to join him for dinner, but she couldn't make out where he said he was eating.

'I think he and Gerard said they were going to the Atlantic for dinner,' he said vaguely. 'But I got the impression it was a boys' night out and they were going out on the town afterwards.'

'That was the *original* plan,' Joanne replied brightly. 'But apparently Gerard had a call from home. Something cropped up that needed his immediate attention. I got the invite as an afterthought,' she laughed.

'Nice one, Jo. We must get together sometime. Tess was only saying the other day that we haven't seen you for ages. Shop doing OK?'

'Brilliant thanks, Steven. I'll get David to sort out dinner one night. Now I must dash.'

The Atlantic, eh? Night on the town, she thought irritably.

The hotel's receptionist confirmed their booking. When she rang them the table was booked for half eight – that meant David had probably had a flutter first at the casino.

She caught sight of herself in the salon mirror, and admired Chris's handiwork. She'd been a bit dubious when Chris insisted on using her as a guinea pig to test out the new colour the rep had left, but now her blonde shoulder-length locks looked stunning –knocked years off her. Tonight she just needed to somersault herself into a more flamboyant mood if she wanted to make more of an impact on David.

The Atlantic was one of Liverpool's busiest and most renowned hotels. She managed to get a spec in the car park and then took the lift to foyer. Giant double glass doors automatically opened into an oak-panelled lobby where large crystal chandeliers covered nearly the whole ceiling. She noticed that the ladies loo was close at hand so disappeared quickly into it and stared at her own reflection in the mirror. 'God, what a difference,' she beamed. Her dress, makeup, hair – and wondered why she hadn't made this effort before now.

Lipstick and perfume renewed, she ventured back into the lobby and headed towards two more glass-panelled doors, which led into the bar. The same navy carpet; chandeliered ceiling, as before plus a highly polished mahogany bar which ran the length of the room. The back of it was walled with neatly placed bottles and glasses.

Apprehensively she glanced round. An ivory-jacketed gentleman was playing 'Strangers in the Night' on a grand piano at the far end. How appropriate!

David's eyes bulged in disbelief as he spotted her. Before Joanne could reach his table he'd rushed over to intervene.' What the fuck are you doing here?' His voice was tense and his fingers gripped her arm like a vice.

'Now don't go all grumpy on me?' she said. 'You left a message saying you were having dinner here with Gerard – I thought I'd join you.'

'No I didn't.'

She broke free from his grip and walked past him in the direction of the portly, stone-faced chap at his table. David followed silently, spitting bile yet fearful of a confrontation in front of Gerard. 'Gerard. This is my wife Joanne,' he said uneasily.

Gerard glared at David, a vein pulsing in his neck, and then offered a toothy grin. Joanne extended a hand; his fat sausage-like fingers grasped it and gave her hand a squeeze. Yuck! How she wished she hadn't bothered.

'Nice to meet you at long last,' he said watching as she lowered herself into the chair opposite and seductively crossed her legs, knowing full well he was enjoying the view.

'Yes, nice to put a face to the voice at long last. It's not a problem me joining you both for dinner, is it?' she said, glancing at the two men with raised eyebrows. 'David did mention it was a business meeting, but I'm sure you won't be talking business all night,' she said flippantly.

Gerard stared back unblinking; his cheek twitched as he turned to gaze at David, who was standing, hands in pockets, shuffling nervously.

'I'll get the drinks, shall I? Same again, Gerard? And what do you want?' he hissed through clenched teeth at her.

'Mmm,' she murmured, looking at the cocktail list in front of her. 'I think I'll have a Singapore Sling. The last time I had one of those was on our honeymoon. Maybe it will have the same reaction it did then.' She giggled mischievously.

'Right then – two G and Ts and a Singapore Sling it is,' David said, with forced brightness, leaving Gerard and Joanne to get acquainted.

It was obvious by the disappointed look on Gerard's face that she'd kyboshed their plans. This was her taking control. She wanted her life back and Porky the Pot-Bellied Pig sitting opposite her was probably the reason it had all gone pear-shaped in the first place.

Stone-faced and silent, Gerard sat in his slightly crumpled grey pin-striped business suit –predictable white shirt –red tie; annoyingly, he drummed his little fat fingers on the arm of his chair.

'Do you and David eat here often?' she asked with a slight edge.

'Yes,' he said hesitantly. 'The food's pretty good and the people here are quite accommodating when David and I need a corner to ourselves to entertain associates, but I'm sure he's told you all that.'

'Yes…' she said scanning the room to see how David was getting on with the drinks. There was no sign of him anywhere but the cavalry arrived in the shape of the waiter with their drinks instead. Joanne picked up her glass and sucked furiously at the black straw sticking out of the top of the glass.

'God I needed that,' she muttered gratefully under her breath. It looked like being a long night and Gerard was proving to be extremely hard work.

David returned with not a trace of a smile. She'd thwarted his plans, she could tell.

The maître d' then came over and told them politely that their table was ready in the restaurant and would they like to follow him through. He scooped their drinks onto a tray and led them to a table that had been lavishly laid for three people! She felt dubious; there had been no time for David to inform them that she was joining them, so who had this place been set for?

The penny dropped why David had disappeared so quickly after ordering the drinks. It was to make a brief call to tell whoever was joining them that their plans had to be aborted; normally she was on the end of a call like that.

A middle-aged, straight-laced waiter stood close, notebook in hand, ready to take their order as they scanned leather-bound menus. Although she'd already eaten a lavish lunch, she decided she'd make David pay dearly for tonight.

'The langoustine starter sounds wonderful and I fancy the Mediterranean sea bream for the main course. Thank you.' She threw David an enigmatic smile as she snapped her menu closed.

Gerard's meal was as predictable as his dress sense: duck pâté to start, and a medium-rare rib-eye steak with all the trimmings. David's order mirrored Joanne's; at least they still shared similar tastes in food.

The clatter of cutlery from fellow diners who were talking at full volume made it difficult to make small talk, so she concentrated on eating. She could see that David was starting to relax a little as the evening sailed on; he even shared a few jokes he'd heard from the guys at work, looking at Joanne, encouraging her to blush. It had been a while since his charm had captured her like this.

Gerard wasn't exactly the Don Juan she'd envisaged. 'Pot-bellied pig eating from a trough' confirmed her initial impression as she watched him consume his meal. Knocking back the last dregs of his wine, he wiped his mouth with his napkin then clicked his fingers impatiently to the passing waiter and pointed to his glass for a refill. The waiter picked up the bottle on the table and replenished everyone's glass. Gerard's expression was smug and pompous. No humble thank you, or even an acknowledgment as the waiter asked was there anything else.

'No, thank you,' Joanne chipped in, which encouraged a smile from David.

There was a time when David would have jumped down someone's throat for behaving so badly in front of her but Gerard was his new-found buddy and something of an icon in his eyes.

Gerard continued to prattle on throughout the meal, mostly about himself, spitting particles of food as he spoke. A sliver of cabbage hung from the corner of his mouth at some point on which Joanne's eyes were transfixed. David willed her not to say a word with a look she knew well.

Gerard droned on, making her feel like she wanted to push his face into his Pavlova just to shut him up! How does David cope with this on a daily basis, she thought. How she wished for a Scottie to beam him up, leaving David and her alone.

Joanne lapsed into silence as she finished her meal. David and Gerard continue to talk shop. The waiter brought coffee and Joanne decided to end her mute state. 'Does your wife mind you spending so much time working?'

Gerard looked startled at her directness. David's eyes widened.

'Err… no, not really. She knew when she married me that I was a workaholic.' His face was sweaty through over-stuffing his mouth and his eyes were bloodshot and like golf balls from the wine he'd gulped down.

'Amanda has lots to keep her occupied. She plays a lot of golf and has committee meetings, which take up most of her time. I just keep her happy financially.' Both men roared with laughter. Joanne didn't see the humour.

At least with Gerard being there, David had dropped the cold tone he always used at home. The last couple of hours, it was as if the clock was turned back and civility between them was intact.

She got a slight whiff of David's cologne, causing memories to race through her mind of how it used to be. She wanted to reach for his hand, laugh into his eyes and kiss his face as she sat and sipped her coffee. She felt contented just being near him.

Knowing a night on the town with a couple of floozies was not now going to happen – not that night anyway – Gerard rose ungraciously from the table, gave a huge burp and bade them both farewell, leaving David to pay the bill, as she guessed he did on most occasions. Joanne was thankful Gerard hadn't lunged over to kiss her before he left.

There was an uncomfortable silence once he'd left. David leaned back in his chair, folded his arms, stretched out his legs and stared at her defiantly. She blushed beneath his gaze.

'You look nice…new dress?' he said, feasting his eyes on her cleavage then raised his brows and grinned mischievously.

'I thought I'd treat myself …no one else seems to these days.'

He moved closer. 'Your hair's nice too. Want to go on somewhere?'

'Why not? It's early,' she smiled back challengingly.

Was that an actual smile he gave? She never knew these days if it was just wind!

They moved on to a long line of themed wine bars and ended up at The Aruba Rooms, a chic Caribbean nightclub on the Albert Dock. The walls seemed to vibrate with the sound of the music that made everyone's hips gyrate as they made their way through the crowd.

'Are you dancing?' David asked.

'Are you asking?' she grinned and he guided her across to the packed dance floor, which was a melting pot of cultures. It was like the clock was turned back as they danced together and partied the night away. At the end of the night, he crushed her to him, lowered his lips and kissed her in a way that made her heart beat faster.

'Let's get a room…' His voice was almost a whisper and his lips brushed against her ear. 'We've both had far too much to drink to drive home.'

'Is that the only reason you want to get a room?' She looked into his eyes as she knew his eyes wouldn't lie.

'That isn't the only reason.'

His innuendoes and kisses filled her with hope and her heart almost skipped a beat.

It was gone one but they managed to secure a room at the Atlantic. She felt juvenile, light-headed and almost sluttish as the guy on reception handed him the key. In the lift, they both erupted into a fit of hysterics and then once inside the room, they hurriedly discarded their clothes.

David took pleasure in her new underwear as she slipped out of her dress. She had bought it in a desperate gamble to inject some sexual passion into their marriage. It was more daring than sensible and his eyes feasted on her. 'I've neglected you for far too long,' he said, taking her into his arms.

His eyes fell from her face and gazed at her nakedness as his hands expertly explore her uncherished body. She closed her eyes and let him dictate the pace as he playfully caressed her. It had been so long since they were entwined and wanting. Then they made love in an all-consuming, reckless and daring way which left them both exhausted and speechless. They collapsed into each other's arms on top of the crumpled sheets and fell asleep.

It was eight thirty the following morning before they fumbled into consciousness. A rancid taste filled Joanne's mouth and the room appeared to be spinning but she'd woken feeling optimistic. The familiar feeling of him nuzzling her neck and his arm around her waist felt good. 'What time is it?' she asked.

He glanced at his watch. 'Bloody hell! Eight thirty! We're both late for work.'

What should have been a memorable morning, waking up slowly, maybe making love again, showering and having a leisurely breakfast together was replaced by them jumping out of bed, throwing on their previous night's clothes then hurriedly heading for the car park. Strangers glared as they made their way to the cars. But she didn't care. As they reached the cars, Joanne gazed at David with the realisation of what the previous night's antics now meant.

She fumbled through her bag for her keys. David intervened by turning her around, cupping her face and kissing her. 'I love you, Mrs Winston! Last night was wonderful.'

She gave an unsure smile. Were they really back on track? Was it that simple? Had the last few months really been washed away for good?

Through his open car window, he said that he'd ring her later. Her face broke into a smile and she realised that this was the nearest she'd been to happiness for quite a while. She gleefully sang along with a guy on the radio on her journey home. A weight had been lifted; she felt as if she hadn't a care in the world.

She drew onto the forecourt of the shop and saw her mother's car already there. Bollocks! She'd forgotten she'd promised her a hairdo. Sheepishly she walked through the salon and spotted her first client, already gowned. Everyone's jaws seemed to drop as she scurried through into the staff room, hair askew, no makeup, low-cut dress, which her mum recognised as the one she'd bought the previous day.

Chris grinned, half guessing what Joanne had been up to, but her mother wasn't amused by the state of her daughter. 'Joanne, we've been worried about you. I rang several times last night and again this morning and got no reply.'

'Sorry! Sorry! Sorry! I'll get Lillie to shampoo you when I've done Mrs Palmer,' she apologised, giving Helen a quick hug. 'David and I went to dinner with Gerard last night at the Atlantic, then went on to a couple of clubs and by the end of the night we'd had too much to drink to drive home so we got a room instead.'

Chris's eyes widened. Joanne couldn't hide her huge grin.

Chapter 19

Joanne took the stairs two at a time, quickly disrobed, showered, blasted herself with deodorant then threw on her uniform. The morning went relatively well, seeing she could hardly stop herself grinning the entire time. At lunchtime the shop had nearly emptied.

Chris called over from the desk, 'David's on the phone, he wants a word.'

Joanne felt her face brighten as she took hold of the receiver. 'Hello you,' she said in an upbeat tone.

'Jo, I'm so sorry, love. Looks like I won't be home tonight. Gerard's set up a meeting with the Fallow brothers down in Solihull. It's an important account and one we can't afford to lose so it looks like I won't be back until tomorrow at the earliest. I've got clean clothes in my overnight case back at the office so I won't need to come home to get changed.'

She felt like a knife had been thrust deep into her heart. He was lying, of course he was lying – she could tell by the feeble way he was fumbling with his words. Last night it all seemed so perfect, at the end of which her body had responded so spontaneously to him as he made her feel so complete.

'That's OK,' she said with forced joviality. 'I'll probably take Mum out for tea in that case.' Her voice began to falter. She was close to tears, and swallowed hard to regain control. 'Mum loves going out for tea,' she croaked, then coughed to cover her emotions. 'David, I have to go, I'm in the middle of a perm,' she lied. Chris caught the end of the conversation and threw her a puzzled look.

'I'll see you tomorrow then, babe…love you,' David replied.

Babe! When had he taken to calling her babe? Was this so he wouldn't get confused when someone else was in his arms? She replaced the receiver and stood rigid as she looked onto the forecourt. It was as if the pause button had been pressed on a remote control; time stood still.

Last night, his words had ignited hope and at one point she even she saw remorse in his eyes, knowing the hurt he'd caused – but today it was as if last night never really happened.

She could remember a time not so long ago when all she had to do to drive him mad was to let him know she was wearing stockings and suspenders when they were out! Life was simple back then. All the gang were newly married, all starting out on life's journey, throwing dinner parties, fancy-dress parties, parties for the hell of it, drinks with the gang every Sunday at the pub by the canal. Happy times, sad times, boring times – but looking back they were the best times of her life.

Sally tapped her shoulder, bringing her promptly back into the world of reality. 'Chris wants to know if you've eaten lunch yet. If not, do you want some of hers?' she asked, handing Joanne a mug of freshly brewed tea.

'Tell her no thanks, love. I'm just going to go pop upstairs for a spell; I've got heaps of paperwork to organise. Give me a shout when my perm comes in, will you?' Keeping a smiley face would have been a massive strain now, plus she was in no mood for idle chat about her antics last night.

She climbed the stairs, flopped onto her bed and pulled the duvet loosely over her, feeling the need to think and adjust. His words had changed everything! She would now have to somehow navigate herself through these rough times the best she could, hoping she'd come out unscathed.

David wasn't going to Birmingham; he was seeing whoever he'd let down the previous night, probably using the same room at the same hotel. Was it any wonder the receptionist smiled when he passed him the key? No doubt he was a regular. She'd been just another notch on the old bedpost, she seethed.

She looked up at the cracks in the ceiling, the same ceiling she'd scanned most nights when she lived in hope he'd be home early for once and climb in beside her, hold her for the sake of holding her and not just to instigate sex.

Why was she not crying? Why was she not playing the wronged, anguished wife, wailing and thrashing all over the place? Any other woman would be, knowing her husband was screwing around.

Their life hadn't been perfect but it had been meaningful. They had a beautiful, funny, delightful daughter. Did that not count for something?

She could cope on her own if she had to but knew if she threw him out Emily would be the one to suffer. The one thing David was a pretty amazing father; his world rocked purely because Emily was in it. So what did her future hold without him, she wondered.

Joanne didn't mention the phone call to Chris when she ventured back into the shop. She couldn't stand the thought of anyone thinking she was throwing herself a pity party. Instead, she continued to let everyone think all was OK in the Winston matrimonial household once more.

The following Sunday Joanne dropped her mother off at her flat after treating her to a meal at the pub as Emily was still in Bath, .As she unlocked the salon door, she noticed the answer phone flashing, so she pressed the playback button.

Beep… 'Hi David, it's Steven. I forgot to tell you I won't be in in the morning. I've got a dental appointment, but could you tell Octavia not to file the Germany account just yet? I need to finalise a couple of things… See you around lunchtime.'

Joanne stood rigid, not able to believe what she was hearing. Octavia was working in David's office! Why had it not been mentioned? No wonder he'd been so insistent that she never ring the office. 'Don't clog the office line up with personal calls,' he'd grizzled more than once, plus, 'I'm never there these days anyway.' And silly fucking me believed every word he said, she fumed.

Blood surged up into her face. Jess and Oliver must have known, along with the rest of David's bloody family. Octavia would be positively gloating. How long had the bitch worked there, she wondered. There was one person who would tell her the truth without it causing a fuss… Abby!

Joanne went upstairs and, after changing into something more comfortable, she punched Abby's number into the phone by her bed.

Amber answered almost immediately. 'Hi, Auntie Jo. Emily loves being with us. Do you want to speak to her?' she said brightly.

Emily's voice came on almost immediately 'Guess what… Amber and Lily are getting a pony each. Can we have one, too, Mummy?' Emily said excitedly.

'No, love, we haven't got anywhere to keep it, darling. But I'm sure they'll let you ride theirs when you go down in future.' Joanne's eyes welled up, hearing how happy she sounded. 'I miss you, darling.'

'I miss you, too, Mummy. I'm going to play now.' With that, she was gone.

'Hello, stranger, how are you?' Abby's voice sounded comforting. 'I'm going to kidnap your daughter, she is a delight.'

'Thanks. I know that already. How's the Brady Bunch down there? Are his parents behaving?'

'Fair to middling.'

'Take the phone out of earshot, will you? There's something I need to ask you,' Joanne said.

'Why …what's up?'

'Abby, I want to ask you something and I want a straight answer.'

'Sure, what's the question?'

'Did you know Octavia was working for David?'

'Yes, why?'

'Well, I bloody-well didn't! I only found out a few moments ago.'

'Oh no! Jo, I'm so sorry – I thought you knew. If I'd known you had no knowledge of the fact, I would have rung you straight away. When Jonathan told me, he said you were alright with it. I thought at the time that didn't sound like you, but we all have to bow down to Jess's demands in the end, don't we?'

'Jess…what's she got to do with it?'

'It was Jess who suggested it to David in the first place. Octavia's been staying with Jess and Oliver on and off for a while, whilst her parents were at their house in Barbados. Did you know that?'

'Yes, David mentioned that part. I've been so busy with the shop, I haven't had time to see Jess lately or even phone her for a chat. To be quite honest, I felt a bit guilty when it was David who dropped Emily off before they came to yours. But she never rings me or drives over. David's dad pops in on the odd occasion on his way home from the golf course then relays what's been happening in their world but I'm not really bloody interested. They don't live in the same world as us, do they?'

'Well…' Abby continued.' Octavia had been whining onto Jess that she needed a part-time job as her life was getting far too boring, as she put it! She hasn't got a clue, has she? George gives her an allowance and buys all her clothes. Christ! Wish someone would give me an allowance and buy all my clothes! I did think at one time that's what husbands did! Apparently not.' She paused for a second, remembering where she was up to with her story. 'Oh yes…When David's secretary left to have her baby, Jess more or less insisted David take Octavia on.'

'The fucking bitch!' Joanne spat out. 'She knows how I feel about Octavia. Why would she do such a despicable thing? No wonder David hasn't said anything. He knew I'd erupt if I found out.'

'Like I said, if I'd known the situation, I would have rung you straight away.' The loyalty in Abby's voice was quite touching.

'Abby, don't beat yourself up about it. You are the only one in the family I *can* trust.'

'Anyway, apart from Octavia working for David, how are things between you and my brother-in–law?' Abby said brightly, changing the subject.

'How long have you got?'

'That bad, eh?'

Joanne decided to refrain from mentioning the night before, knowing it had been a huge mistake. ''Fraid so – I think he's going through some sort of mid-life crisis at the moment. He's out on the town, tom-catting most nights… Has Jonathan spoken to him lately?'

'Actually they met up about a week ago. Jonathan was in Liverpool at the pharmaceutical AGM at the St George so he stayed at his parents'. David called in to say hi and Jess invited him to stay for dinner – didn't he tell you?'

'Noooo! Was she there?' There was a long silence at the other end of the line. 'She fucking was there,' Joanne spat out venomously.

'Octavia is definitely flavour of the month in Jess and Oliver's eyes,' Abby said irritably. 'She can do no bloody wrong. It's a no-win situation, love. If you say anything detrimental about her, you'll be classed as being childish or even jealous. Even Kristy's becoming a turn-coat. She's doing this personal-training programme thing for

Octavia and Jess in return for presents, money, you name it! What does your mum say about all this?'

'She doesn't know much. She just thinks we're having a few problems with David being away so much. I try to put on this blissfully happily married face when she's around. I can't face up to the fact of her knowing I'm in another fucked-up relationship. Don't mention it to Jonathan – or anyone else for that matter – that we've had this chat. I have to figure out what I'm going to do. If I start to erupt, I'll be classed as a woman possessed. I have to be cleverer than that.'

'I can hear the cogs turning in your brain from here,' Abby said, laughing. 'Ring me, let me know what's happening. If you feel it's all getting too much, you and Emily get in that bloody car of yours and come and stay for a few days. Any time you like –it might help to clear your head. I'm sure Emily will benefit from the break. She can ride this bloody pony we're getting – another sodding present from his parents which I wasn't consulted about. But I bet I'm the one who will have to clear up the mess and muck the bugger out. I really wanted that far field as an orchard, but no one takes a blind bit of notice what I want these days… You will be claiming your daughter back next weekend, by the way?'

'Thanks for having her, you're a gem,' Joanne said, and blew a kiss down the phone,

Joanne felt grateful; Abby was her ally in all this. She classed her and Jonathan as rock-solid as couples go. Jonathan's whole world revolved around Abby and the girls – but when it came to Jess and Oliver, he seemed to let them take the reins at times.

Joanne placed the phone in its cradle and suddenly felt peckish so she went down to the kitchen to see what she could find in the fridge. The light came on as she opened the door and she spied Emily's Tupperware box, still with half a dozen rose hips she'd collected .She remembered Gill warning her that should some hairs touched her skin they'd itch like buggery.

'Better chuck them out before Emily gets back.' As she lifted them from the fridge, a menacing thought rushed into her head. She took the rosehips from the box, placed them on the chopping board and carefully dissected them. Sure enough, they were filled with thousands of tiny soft hairs. She placed a couple carefully on the back of her hand and it wasn't pleasant to the skin. She rooted out an empty jar lurking at the back of the cupboard and filled it with the hairs from each bud.

Her plan was to place some in David's favourite underpants each time she did his laundry, right in the vicinity of his nether regions. Then she came up with the idea that she would add laxatives to his favourite food and replace his athlete's foot powder with the rooting powder from the garden shed.

'Don't get angry, get even,' her mum always used to say when she'd had a barney with her dad.

Joanne slept incredibly well that night considering what a disturbing day she'd had. She woke early, eager to get started with this new regime, knowing full well it would disrupt David's plans.

Chapter 20

Joanne started her day with a pot of tea and a phone call to her mother. 'Hi Mum, the shop is a bit quiet today so I've decided to have some me time. I'm going to rustle up a few things for the freezer. Fancy popping in for a coffee at some point?'

'That would be lovely, love. I've just got to nip to the chemist first to pick up my prescription. Do you need anything?'

'Yes…' she returned gleefully. 'Do you remember that chocolate Ex-lax stuff you got me when I had that bout of constipation? If they still sell it, you couldn't get me a couple of packets, could you?'

'You won't need a couple of packets, love, one will do – it's quite strong stuff.'

'One's for Chris,' she lied.

Joanne spent the rest of the morning beavering away in the kitchen, knocking up the most decadent chocolate torte cakes she'd made in a long time. They were David's all-time favourite but this was a chocolate torte with a difference. When they had all cooled she plated two, cling-filmed the rest and placed them in the freezer for use at a later date. She covered one half of the one she plated with melted chocolate, the other half with chocolate and Ex-lax.

She dotted the half that was OK with Smarties and Hundreds and Thousands. Emily loved them but for some unknown reason David hated Smarties, so she knew he'd plump for the other side should he sneak a sly slice when she wasn't there in the cake tin it went and on the shelf in the cupboard A cup of tea and a slice of cake – David never could resist at any time of the day! The other cake she gave the girls to have in their break.

Joanne climbed the stairs and started to rifle through David's underwear drawer. In the crotch of every pair of his Hugo Boss and Calvin Kleins, she placed a couple of hairs from the rosehips and neatly placed them back in his drawer. She went into bathroom, took down his athlete's foot powder then emptied the contents into the bin and replaced it with rooting powder, which was similar in colour and texture. Everything's fair in love and war, she grinned, and this would be far more effective than any amount of arguing.

David came in that night, after collecting Emily from his parents on their return from Bath. Brandishing a huge bunch of flowers, elaborately cellophane wrapped, he was half expecting her to be wielding a rolling pin because of the message Steven had left on the answer phone the previous day.

'Did you have a good trip? Where was it, Leeds?' she said, kissing him gently on the lips. She went on to tend to her daughter's needs; Emily was now chattering about all the comings and goings down in Bath.

'I'll pour you a gin and tonic, shall I? Bet you're jiggered.' David shot her a look of disbelief. 'The flowers are lovely, by the way. Thanks,' she said, sniffing them as she took them from him.

'Just a small thank you,' he said smiling, thinking he could play her once again like a finely tuned fiddle.

'Oh, by the way,' Joanne said, giving him a hard stare. His eyes widened and he braced himself for a full attack. 'I think the answer phone's knackered. A couple of clients said they'd left messages but it wasn't flashing and there was nothing on the tape. Damn thing must be faulty. I'll get Mum to take it back to Argos tomorrow – I've got the receipt somewhere.'

A relieved grin settled on David's face. As Joanne continued to busy herself putting the flowers into a vase, she watched him from the corner of her eye as he listened to Emily chatter about the meal at Pizza Hut she'd had with her cousins. Relief oozed from him as he sat and sipped his drink.

'I bet you're feeling pretty smug. Well, let me tell you, your gallivanting days are numbered,' she muttered under her breath.

When Joanne had David's full attention, she reminded him about the dinner party Gill and Brian were giving the following night. Joanne was looking forward to it and told him so. It was a rare occasion these days to have any sort of social life with David's busy schedule. Everyone had stopped ringing, even to see if they were going to the Sunday pub get-togethers. David had told them at some point that Sundays were now classed as a family day, dedicated to Emily exclusively with him being away so much.

Gill and Brian's dinner party had been earmarked on the calendar for weeks; it was their fifth-wedding anniversary. All the gang were invited and David had been warned weeks earlier to keep that date free. But a phone call came through just before he was about to have a shower and get ready, which brought about a sudden change of plan.

Jo could tell it was a woman's voice on the other end of the line, even though David pretended it was Gerard he was talking to.

'Sorry, Jo – you'll have to go to Gill and Brian's on your own. I'll try and get back as soon as I can and join you. Gerard needs these papers ASAP. He has a meeting at 8.30 tomorrow. Sorry, love.'

'But tomorrow's Sunday,' Joanne shot back.

'I know, love, but it's for one of our German clients and he's flying home Monday.'

She could have gone off into one of her screeching rages but what was the point? It wouldn't have changed anything. She'd got used to playing gooseberry at dinner-parties these days, she thought sadly.

Joanne insisted he have a cup of tea and some cake before going out as he'd not eaten. Not wanting to antagonise her, he complied. Joanne sat and watched him eat every morsel of the large slice she placed in front of him. She could see from the look on his face that he'd enjoyed it.

'God, that was delicious,' he said, wiping his mouth on a paper napkin.

She managed a smile as she took his plate then sloshed it about in the soapy washing-up water.

Whilst he showered, she laid out his clothes on the bed, which included a pair of the sabotaged boxers. The disappointment she'd felt previously was now overturned. Her mission had been accomplished.

Emily was staying at her mother's; Helen had taken her home for tea and a sleepover, giving Joanne chance get ready in peace. It was Sunday the next day and a lie-in would be welcome, she thought, knowing full well she'd probably have a throbbing head.

David wouldn't even try to get back for the party. He'd probably ring to say he was staying over wherever he was as he'd have a skinful. With that in mind, she decided to enjoy the night anyway. Wide-eyed and legless, around two o'clock, she staggered through the salon door. She hadn't even noticed David's car was on the forecourt. Joanne caught her breath as she noticed the silhouette of a man in the kitchen doorway. Through alcohol-impaired vision, she just about made out it was David standing there and let out a throaty giggle, realising he was home.

'Hello, ocifer, I'm not as drunk as thinkle peep I am.'

'You're drunk!' he spat out in annoyance.

'Noooooooooo! Whatever gives you that impression?' she slurred back at him in a vain attempt to make light of things. 'You're a bit late for the party, it's finished,' she asserted firmly then started to laugh as she walked unsteadily past him into the kitchen. She dumped her bag on the chair and wriggled out of her coat.

'I've been home since ten o'clock. I'm ill – my stomach's giving me gyp. Think I've got a bug or something. You don't know where the Milk of Magnesia is?' he said, gripping his stomach with one hand, scouring the medicine cupboard with the other.

A feeble 'no' escaped her mouth. She was starting to enjoy this turn of events; it was usually her that was straight-faced and sober and David the intoxicated one.

Joanne was unfazed by the acid remarks he started to throw at her. She left him alone to nurse his aching stomach and lick his wounds. She fumbled her way up the stairs, discarded her clothes in a heap on the bedroom floor then disappeared under the duvet, naked as the day she was born.

She woke the following morning, her eyes like pee-holes in the snow. Her tongue had doubled in size. 'God, was it bloody worth it?' she asked herself, surveying her bedroom.

She had no recollection if David had got into bed last night. All she knew was that he wasn't in bed now; the covers were ruffled on his side so he must been there at some point.

She remembered going to Gill's and the meal, and remembered spilling some wine down her dress when she missed her mouth, but beyond that it was just a blur. She glanced at the bedside clock; her head felt like it was full of lead. Then heaved herself gingerly off the bed and made her way to the bathroom.

In the shower she let the steaming water do its best to bring her round, then went to the kitchen for a full-bodied Kenco. As she drank it slowly, the memories of the previous night start to filter through. She recalled the mucky jokes she'd told and the barrage of laughter that followed, then remembered the wonderful food Gill had prepared and Brian refilling her glass for the umpteenth time.

Oh God, now she remembered! David…he was angry. She was drunk, he was complaining bitterly he had gut ache or some such thing –it was all coming back. The laxatives – they had actually worked!

She felt herself brightened; her plan had succeeded. It had thwarted his evening, at least. This was going to be the first of many!

Chapter 21

Work was a welcome distraction from David's harsh words and criticism each time they were close to one other in the weeks that followed. Jabbing, jabbing, jabbing– he just wouldn't stop! He had become someone she no longer recognised.

The atmosphere became so toxic she couldn't even think straight, so would retaliate by turning on him, hitting out with her words. It could be anything from the basketful of dirty laundry she hadn't yet got round to doing or that his meal wasn't ready on time that ignited harsh criticism. The fact she was still randomly sabotaging his nights out was the only thing that kept her sane.

Joanne couldn't sleep one night so went downstairs, tidied up ,emptied the tumble dryer then made her way up the stairs with a loaded washing basket and placed more rose-hip hairs into the gussets of his newly washed-underwear. 'Hell hath no fury,' she grinned, calculating that just around now David would probably be making a move on whoever he was with.

Flatulence would be building up, so would the constant bollock scratching he'd started to do. She doubted whoever he was with would be very impressed by all this.

It had been all so easy these last weeks to watch him greedily devour the dishes she'd rustled up, but only on the occasions it looked like he was going out would she lace them with laxatives.

'One thing about you,' David said, as he mopped the last of the sauce from his plate with some crusty bread, 'you have always been an amazing cook.'

'He'll never know just how amazing,' she thought, as she sloshed his dish around in the washing-up water.

***

Emily fell fast asleep almost the instant her head touched the pillow, so Joanne used the time to catch up on some stocktaking and general tidying up in the salon. The last batch of towels from the dryer were folded and neatly placed in the pigeon holes. She flicked on the kettle to make a coffee and caught the last of the ten o'clock news. The place felt peaceful, orderly, but she knew that before very long David's car would sail onto the forecourt and mayhem would start all over again.

She wasn't wrong. Before she'd even finished her coffee, the salon door burst open. In rushed David, complaining bitterly about the stomach cramps and constant itching that were driving him insane! Joanne fought hard not to laugh.

'Have you changed your washing powder? I can't seem to stop scratching down below,' he said anxiously.

'No, same one I always use,' Joanne replied, eyes still glued to the news.

She tackled his demands for a binding remedy and gave him a bottle of camomile lotion for his neither region, knowing full well they'd be less than useless. His complaints came as music to her ears.

In the kitchen he dragged his buttoned shirt over his head and begged her to inspect his torso, his imagination running riot, fearing his whole body was becoming rash-ridden.

'You've probably picked up something like scabies or a parasite!' Joanne said flippantly. 'Have you been unusually close to someone who wasn't particularly bothered about their personal hygiene?' she asked, keeping a straight face. 'Where did you say the itching was?'

'Mostly between my legs, but I'm sure it's spreading,' he said, firing a loud burst of wind from his rear end and fleeing to the loo like a bat out of hell.

It never struck him that there was a pattern amongst all this. The onslaught of stomach cramps and excessive itching only seemed to materialise when he was being unfaithful. He even sought advice, fearing something sinister was going on. But the doctors ended up scratching their heads in confusion, after putting him through numerous tests to rule out likely illnesses.

The Big C, the Clap, all ran riot in his imagination. At times there was even sadness in his eyes as he told her what the doctors had said and done to him. A question mark surely must have filtered through his testosterone-filled brain by now that whoever he'd been sleeping with might just be the cause!

The only thing the doctors could come up with was anal fissure; they explained it was cracking and tearing of the back-passage walls but to diagnose it accurately would mean an intrusive investigation under anaesthetic. David felt he'd been through enough; he needed respite from all these tests and time to think, maybe even get a second opinion.

Up until then, Joanne felt it had been a clever plan on her behalf to curb his wayward ways but the ramifications were now starting to weigh heavily on her. It had to stop!

The next day she purchased some sterile jars from the wholesalers and filled them with Sudacrem, widely used for nappy rash. That night, when David walked in from work, she greeted him brightly. 'I called in at a holistic clinic today and mentioned all you've been going through. After a long search through this huge manual, they gave me these of pots of cream, explaining they were crammed with essential oils and herbs. It just might help … worth a try,' she said with false sympathy.

David was at the stage where he'd try anything. He smiled, something she'd not seen in a while.

'They mentioned that you will have to plaster it on quite thickly over your feet as well, where your athlete's foot has broken out, and around your whats-its before bed and not to worry about how it looks,' she proclaimed. She knew full well there would be no way he would miss applying this miracle cure for two whole weeks, the length of time Joanne said it was prescribed – so he couldn't go out.

Sure enough, each night he breezed in from work, scooped Emily up into his arms and nuzzled her neck. And she would giggle, loving the attention. He seemed genuinely happy to be home. There were even times when they shared the odd glass of wine over dinner and talked about the day's happenings. As she cleared away the dishes, David would bathe Emily, tucked her into bed and read her a story.

Seeing him dressed in track suit bottoms and flip-flops seemed strange –they were items he always swore he wouldn't be seen dead in. But now it seemed they were his favourite items– loose fitting when he'd applied his cream.

His attitude and moods were changing daily. He got into the habit of picking up a DVD en route home some nights. And for a short time his acid tongue and Heathcliff attitude were dropped.

There were no frantic phone calls from Gerard or Steven, or anyone else for that matter, to interrupt their evenings. She watched him as he made himself comfy on the couch opposite her, legs outstretched, ankles crossed, hand folded behind his head, and saw the look of contentment on his face .She remembered that this was how things were oh-so-many-moons ago; maybe it had been the male menopause after all! Or even a seven-year itch. Maybe their relationship might survive after all; she was prepared to work at it if it was.

All hopes of that disappeared rapidly once the cream miraculously cured him. Stomach cramps, itchy what nots, athlete's foot all disappeared without a trace and instead of their life continuing to flourish, he returned to the lifestyle he'd led before.

Once again there were phone calls, saying he wouldn't be home. Or 'had his laundry been done?' as he was going away on business so needed clean clothes. Joanne stood outside herself to observe and ended up seeking refuge in a glass of wine once more.

She'd been deluded to ever think he could be contented with the simplicity of family life, or could be monogamous – or even that she could come through all this unscathed. She was made to feel that her back was continuously against the wall – unsure, raw and unconfident. Until in the end she felt she'd had enough!

It puzzled her why he still hadn't told her about Octavia. In the weeks they'd been civil, she thought the subject would have been broached over dinner or when they were having a cosy chat in front of the fire when his guard was down. She'd given him ample opportunity but probably he hadn't wanted to antagonise the situation, knowing Octavia wasn't her favourite person.

Doing all she had turned out to be a pretty senseless exercise at the end of the day but she had done it purely out of frustration, desperate to find again the husband she once knew. She was sick of the loneliness. It irritated her beyond reason that the brainless bag of bones who was working in his office probably felt quite smug because she was spending far more time with David than Joanne was.

So Joanne decided to do something about it.

Mondays, the salon was usually closed so, after dropping Emily off at school, Joanne called back home, showered and stepped into her black business suit and heeled shoes, and picked up her Chanel bag.

The drive to David's office was long and tense; road works caused havoc and the traffic was congested. How would she tackle Octavia's icy glare when she confronted her?, she wondered. Her hands were clammy as she turned into the firm's car park and headed for the office.

Steven threw her a friendly wave from the far end of the courtyard and Joanne waved back. She pushed open the office door and walked in boldly. Octavia looked up from her desk and, when she saw who it was, flashed her teeth in a nervous, pretend smile as their eyes locked.

'Joanne! What are you doing here?'

'S'cuse me ...I'm the boss's wife. Or is that something you seem to have forgotten these days? More to the point, what are *you* doing here?'

Steven must have tipped David off about Joanne's arrival, as the next thing she knew the door burst open and David walked in, a mixture of anxiety and nervousness on his face. 'Joanne. What are you doing here?'

'Your new secretary's just asked me the very same question.'

As he glanced at Octavia, his face was engulfed in guilt.

'I'm on my way to meet Gill. We're having some retail therapy...' Joanne said, throwing Octavia a benign smile. 'I've forgotten to call in at the bank. Would you be a love and give me some money?' she said, using a sugary tone purely for Octavia's benefit.

'Yes... of course...' Fumbling in the inside pocket of his jacket for his wallet.

Octavia pretended to get on with some filing but Joanne could tell she was picking up every word. Joanne stood rigid, arms folded, as she watched him count it out in twenty and fifty pound notes. 'Three hundred enough?' he said, handing her the cash.

'Make it four hundred, would you? We're having lunch.'

It was the way his head turned and the way Octavia's and David's eyes met that made the penny drop. Of course! Octavia working here made sense – she'd been the one he'd been screwing all along She was the person who had put Joanne through all this hell, not Gerard Dunn. He'd been the scapegoat.

Joanne felt out-manoeuvred and slightly light-headed as she faced them both squarely. 'I know what's been going on between the two of you! I'm not bloody stupid, I've known for a while,' she lied. 'I just needed to have some fun, David, before I confronted the pair of you. Did you honestly think all those symptoms you had were due to a bug or a parasite? Hah! You're more stupid than I took you for! You were so pathetic, whingeing and wallowing in self-pity and making all those embarrassing examinations. That miracle cream was nothing more than nappy-rash cream but it gave me a laugh!'

David's face paled; his eyes were now blazing as they bore into hers. 'You ruthless, venomous bitch! How could you do such a vindictive thing? You could have killed me.'

'Oh it was so so easy. You were like a worm wriggling on a hook,' she sneered.

Octavia flashed Joanne a look of defiance. This confrontation was just what she'd been waiting for; she knew once her and David's affair was out in the open, David's marriage would be over. She was right! David stood mute, red faced, shaking his head in disbelief.

'Don't bother coming home, David. Not that you were going to, probably. Your father can pick up your things up.'

Joanne could feel herself teetering on the edge of deranged, neurotic, wronged-wife mode and clenched her fists tightly by her sides to regain control. All she wanted to do was kill the pair of them with her bare hands.

David's eyes began to mist over as he realised he'd been found out… his game was up. He'd made his bed, now he must lie in it with the bag of bones he'd been bedding for some time.

Joanne doubted that Octavia could ever be the soul mate she'd been to him, or could dig holes, fill skips or listen to the words of a song and cry. What was the old cliché? Better to have loved and lost… Bollocks!

Joanne was empty of words now, too shocked at what she'd uncovered. Angry that she hadn't seen the writing on the wall before now. She had to get out of that place while her dignity was still intact. 'Have a nice time in hell! You two deserve one another other,' were her parting words before she turned stone-faced and ran from the room, nearly taking the door off its hinges as she left.

The sheepish look on Steven's face as she passed him at the gate told her he'd heard every word. She fumbled in her bag for her keys as a large tear tumbled down her cheek. She swallowed hard then tried to breathe deeply through her nose. All she wanted to do was get away from this place as fast as she could.

Her hysteria heightened even further as she turned the key in the ignition and revved the engine loudly. There was one more person she had to see before she could achieve closure to this awful day – and that person was Jess. Joanne had to look into her in the eyes and confront her head on. Had she been a part of all this or was she just a pawn in Octavia's plan to get David?

Joanne drove recklessly to their house, not noticing her speed, screeching around corners, accelerating on the straights, until she came to an abrupt halt on the gravel path outside her in-laws' house, just missing Jess's brand-new Jag by a fraction of an inch. She grabbed the keys from the ignition, jumped out of the car and headed towards their front door, where her finger rested heavily on the bell until someone opened it.

'Joanne!' Jess said, slightly flushed. 'What's wrong? You look upset.'

Joanne didn't wait to be invited in, just stormed past her and headed for the kitchen. Jess followed subserviently behind.

'I'll tell you what's bloody-well wrong,' Joanne said, facing her squarely, arms folded. 'Have you had any part in David and Octavia's affair?'

Her mother-in-law's eyes widened. She looked shocked then angry, and gazed confrontationally at Joanne. 'Joanne, I think you've got your wires crossed somewhere along the line. Octavia has been working in David's office in a professional capacity. There's nothing going on between them, I can assure you.'

Her naivety made Joanne break into a sarcastic grin. 'Jess, wake up and smell the bloody coffee! THEY'VE BEEN HAVING AN AFFAIR! I've just confronted them in the office and they were as guilty as hell. David was rigid, realising he'd been found out. And

Octavia… well, the bitch positively glowed. It was a confrontation she welcomed, I assure you.'

'Joanne, I'm so sorry…I…I had no idea.' Jess's hand went to her mouth, as if she were making a calculation before she spoke. 'Oliver will be furious.' Jess lowered herself slowly onto a kitchen chair and stared with disbelief into space. How ruthlessly Octavia had been, using them both for her own means. 'She wanted David. Always did! And now, she's got him,' Jess continued to rant.

'I've told David not to bother coming home again. Oliver can collect his things, if that's OK with Oliver,' Joanne said sternly, looking down at her fumbling hands, avoiding eye contact with Jess. 'You'll just have to be prepared for him to turn up here tonight, looking sheepish and wanting to stay. That'll be cosy, with Octavia still living here as well.'

'Oh, Octavia doesn't live here anymore, Joanne. She rents a swanky new apartment on Albert Dock in Liverpool. She's been there roughly eight weeks now – I thought David would have told—' Mid-sentence Jess stopped short, realising what she was saying. 'Of course he hasn't told you!'

'David is probably the one renting the flat – probably puts it through the books too, if I know him. It's been their love nest, Jess, a place they spend their nights when he isn't with me,' Joanne said, embellishing their web of lies. 'All these untruths – meetings with clients in Birmingham, London, Bristol, when all the time he's been with Octavia here in Liverpool.' She felt totally betrayed.

Jess got up from her seat, opened the glass-panelled cupboard and took down Oliver's treasured bottle of Remy and two brandy glasses then silently poured them both a drink. Joanne downed hers in one go, desperate for the alcohol to numb how she felt.

She went on to confide about David's countless acts of thoughtlessness, his anger and him not coming home for days on end.

'David has definitely changed.' Jess admitted and then roared with laughter when Joanne confessed all she'd done to him in retaliation.' I should get a few tips from you next time I have trouble with Oliver … seems I've been doing it all wrong.'

This was the first time in a long time Joanne had felt at ease in Jess's company, though the brandy had probably helped loosen both their tongues.

Jess confessed that she thought David had always been Oliver's favourite; they'd been as thick as thieves ever since she could remember. She was well aware Oliver had used David as an alibi more than once when he'd been seeing other women.

'He's a chip off the old block, by the sounds of things,' Joanne said, rolling her eyes.

'Yes, I fear flirting seems to be a way of life to them both. I'm so sorry for misjudging you as I have, Joanne. I was led to believe you were unsupportive when David's business went global and unfortunately I was the one who encouraged David to take Octavia on at the office, thinking she would be an asset.' Jess sighed. 'But I promise you I'll do everything in my power to ensure Oliver and I help you in any way we can, financial or otherwise. And I can assure you that once the rest of the family find out how despicably Octavia's behaved, she and her parents will be ostracised. If David wants to visit us, then he must come alone.'

Joanne felt grateful for her support and assured her Emily could visit and stay with them whenever they wanted her to.

She left her in-laws' house with some degree of uncertainty, facing the dilemma of what she'd do next. She'd just found out that David had leased a love nest, a home for Octavia to live in. How could he be so stupid? It was one thing finding out he was bonking his sectary but the shock that he'd paid out hard cash to live a secret life hit like a hammer.

Today had been earth shattering – but at least Jess and Oliver were as shocked as her and were supportive.

The answer phone on the desk was flashing as Joanne unlocked the shop door. There were three messages; reluctantly, she pressed the button.

'Beep…Abby here… Jess just called me. I'm so sorry, Joanne. I'm here for you, ring me… Love ya.'

'Beep…Hello darling, Mum here. Emily and I are going to the pictures after we've had our tea to see Walt Disney's *Dalmatians* – I think she said that's what's showing. She wants to know if she can stay the night too. I'll take her to school in the morning. You'll probably be tired after your shopping expedition with Gill. If I don't hear from you, I'll know it's alright for her to stay.'

'Beep…Hi, Gill here. Were we supposed to go shopping today or something? I've got the oddest message on my answer phone from your mum saying if you're here after our retail therapy, they're going to the pictures. Tell her to give me a call.'

Joanne suddenly felt nauseated so made a hasty dash to the loo where she threw up the contents of her stomach. 'Shouldn't have had that brandy on an empty stomach,' she muttered breathlessly, wiping her mouth on some loo paper.

Reminders of David were everywhere; in the loo his cologne sat squarely on the window ledge. She picked it up and sprayed some on her wrist then inhaled deeply. Her eyes blurred with tears, a vision of the two of them making plans clearly visible in her mind.

She went into the kitchen and flicked on the kettle. She resented David and Octavia's happiness, their time together … their entwined bodies. She was weary of being at war with him. She blotted her tears and aborted plans for tea. Instead, she opened the fridge and lifted out the bottle of chilled wine. The place was swathed in silence as she filled her glass to the brim, hoping that the wine would make everything that was going through her head go away. She sat back in her chair and looked down at her wedding ring; it was a reminder of how much he'd once loved her.

'Get a grip, girl – not the end of the world –no one's died.'

Suddenly, she felt quite hostile. What exactly was she mourning?

Their relationship had gone toxic a while ago. Their sex life had come to a halt about the same time he'd deemed her surplus to requirements and replaced her with a high-maintenance whore. So much for white lace and promises!

EMILY! Oh God, what was she going to tell her? Suddenly Joanne's hand flew to her mouth. She closed her eyes in horror and raked her hands through her hair, desperate for a solution. One good thing – at least David hadn't left them homeless and needy.

Tap. Tap. Tap. The knock on the shop door jolted her quickly back to reality. Gingerly she heaved herself out of the chair and peered round the door. It was Gill. Joanne's eyes were still tearful as she let her in.

Gill gasped. 'Oh, Joanne! What's happened?' she asked, placing a reassuring hand on her arm.

'David and I…' She couldn't get the words out.

Gill guided her through to the kitchen, sat her down and handed her some kitchen roll. Through broken sobs and noisy nose blows, Joanne poured out everything that had happened. Endearingly, her friend listened and gave her a hug. Joanne soaked up her sympathy.

'Why didn't you tell me what you were going through? I could have helped,' Gill said sombrely. 'I knew things weren't as they should be but I thought David was just bogged down with work pressure. I mean, you hid it so well from us all… I would have been in a heap if it had been me.'

'I *was* in a heap! But I was too ashamed to tell anyone – not even Mum.'

That poignant moment made Joanne realise she had more support than she knew, not only from Gill but a whole bunch of people that cared.

Reassured she'd be OK, Gill trundled off home. The first thing on Joanne's agenda was to pack all David's things while Emily wasn't there. Oliver would probably be on the doorstep by nine the next day to collect them.

She made her way upstairs, dragged two suitcases from the landing cupboard and placed them on the bed. She quickly pulled each item from its hanger and threw it in a heap into the cases. She screwed up his best YSL shirt between his shoes then continued to empty his drawers, wardrobes and cupboards.

She continued in a rampage after that, searching the house for his belongings, cramming them into the cases which were now bursting at the seams. The colognes she'd bought him, along with his toiletries, she bagged for the charity shop and grinned at the thought of some vagrant walking round the streets wearing Hugo Boss.

Once everything was bagged up, she carried the cases to the foot of the stairs, walked into the lounge and flopped, exhausted onto the settee.

The telephone rang and she picked it up eagerly, thinking it was him wanting forgiveness,

'Hello, darling. Emily wants to say night-night and God bless,' her mother sang brightly down the phone.

Joanne's heart plummeted as she heard her mother's voice.

'Hi, Mummy. We've had a lovely time. We've seen *One Hundred and One Dalmatians–* Nanny was crying when they took the puppies. I'm going to bed now. Is Daddy there?'

Joanne grimaced at Emily's question. 'No, darling, he's away on business. He might be away for a while but you and I can look after ourselves, can't we?'

'Nanny can look after us, Mummy .She's good at looking after people.'

Joanne wiped her tears on her sleeve.

'Night, night. God bless, Mummy – see you tomorrow after school.'

'Goodnight, poppet. I love you. See you tomorrow.'

Helen's voice echoed down the phone again. 'How did your day go, love? Buy anything nice?'

It took Joanne a moment to gather momentum. 'I haven't been shopping, Mum. David and I have split up. He's been having an affair with Octavia – George's stepdaughter. I went to the office to confront them today.'

Her mum's silence said it all. She was probably too shocked to speak.

'I'm still trying to get my head round it. I've managed to pack all his things whilst Emily's at yours. I'm too upset to talk now, Mum, but we'll speak tomorrow.'

'Joanne…'

'Don't, Mum. Don't say anything. Not in front of Emily. I'll ring you tomorrow.'

Joanne replaced the receiver and stared blankly out of the lounge window, down at the empty space where David's car usually sat. She couldn't contemplate life without him; she knew that even her sleep would be contaminated with thoughts of him.

The phone ringing on her bedside table woke her the following morning. She glanced at the clock. It was 7.30 a.m.

'Hello.' Oliver's voice echoed from the earpiece.

'Oh. Hello, Oliver,' she yawned.

'Sorry to ring you so early, love. Did I wake you?'

'No – I was just contemplating getting into the shower. What can I do for you?'

‘Firstly, let me say how sorry I am, Joanne. David’s a bloody fool and the girl’s a brainless trollop. Always thought so. I just don’t know what he’s thinking – or what to say to you to compensate for his despicable actions. We haven’t heard from him … too ashamed I suppose. I’ll be up at yours before the shop opens to collect his things, then I’ll drop them off at his office. There’ll be a few harsh words to the pair of them from me, I’m telling you! Have you mentioned anything to Emily?’

‘No, she stayed at Mum’s last night. They went to the pictures. She phoned to say goodnight and I just told her David was away on business. I thought it would give me time to think.’

‘Yes – we’ve got to handle this with kid gloves, love. I know Jess has told you that you have our support.’

‘I know and thanks for that, Oliver… I’ll get through it.’

‘I know you will, you’ve always been plucky Lancashire lass. I’ve liked you for that!’

Joanne smiled at his comment; she had always thought Oliver looked down on her for not being one of the Cheshire set. Now it seemed she was being praised for it!

Chapter 22

It would have been all too easy to stay in bed, to tell her staff she had the flu and shy away from the world, seek solitude and lick her wounds – but why should she? She had to start as she meant to go on, had to earn a crust to keep a roof over their heads.

She threw back the duvet, swished open the curtains and took in the blue haze of the morning above the rooftops. She felt light-headed, almost dizzy, and flopped back onto the bed again. She knew she had to embrace her new life but perhaps she shouldn't do it with so much gusto!

The next thing was a mad dash to the loo to throw up then she flopped down onto the bathroom floor, totally drained, clammy and tearful. Was she having a panic attack? Or was she really sickening for something? She couldn't tell?

She showered, dressed and decided a morning off wouldn't do any harm. If the doctor could fit her in then maybe a tonic might help with her tiredness.

Oliver arrived brandishing a huge bunch of flowers, looking embarrassed by the whole affair. He didn't say much as he quickly loaded the car, just took everything she'd stacked at the bottom of the stairs and got off before her staff started to arrive.

Chris and the girls agreed after she confessed all that had happened, that a tonic might be a good idea and she told them she'd be back in a trice should they need her.

But she wasn't prepared for what transpired at the doctor's. Missed periods, tiredness, full bosom; there wasn't a shadow of a doubt that she was pregnant. It looked like it had happened the night she and David took a room at the Atlantic. The last time – the only time in a long time – they'd made love. In that case she was roughly three months pregnant, it seemed.

The endometriosis had led her to believe she couldn't have any more children. Once again, she'd proved the medical profession wrong. She was having David's baby, their baby, after all this time. Great timing, eh?

The miracle for which she'd prayed for such a long time had now come to fruition. A mixture of feelings overwhelmed her. The fact that David had gone was now of no consequence. A new life had started to grow inside her!

From the doctor's office she drove to the park and walked in the autumn sunshine, thinking it might help put things into perspective. She passed dog walkers, women with prams, pensioners ambling and children playing noisily on swings. She came to a decision: she wasn't going to say anything to David for the time being, or anyone else for that matter.

This was her moment, a moment that was precious to her and her alone. Not a single thing was going to rain on this parade – not just yet anyway. She could imagine the long pitiful looks people would give her, thinking that this baby was wrongly timed! That was far from the truth; this baby was conceived through love. There was no doubt that David was tender, committed and head over heels that night; he told her so after they made love. If it hadn't been for Octavia's intervention, he would have been there now, sharing this news with her… but he wasn't.

***

The salon forecourt overflowed with parked cars when Joanne arrived back. She'd forgotten that today was pensioners' day! What was she thinking, taking time out to walk round the park on a whim? She'd told the girls she was doing a quick sprint to the doc's and wouldn't be long. Her mother's eyes went as wide as dinner plates when she walked in.

'The cavalry has arrived,' Joanne sang out brightly. On her way to the staff room, she apologised to clients she'd kept waiting.

'Someone's double-booked some of the appointments too,' Sally said, flustered. Joanne had a feeling she might have done that herself – she'd taken to having a crafty glass of wine with lunch when she was feeling slightly under par and ended up having a muddle for the rest of the day.

Joanne ran up the stairs to put on her overall. Once she was back in the salon, she started delegating who should be shampooed, who should be neutralised, and who should be gowned, and took over winding Chris's perm while Chris attended to her two waiting trims.

Her mother brought the sherry bottle down from the flat and gave disgruntled clients a complimentary tipple, which seemed to pacify and delight a couple of old trouts. By mid-afternoon, they were more or less back on track.

'Don't know what we would have done without you today, Mum,' Joanne smiled, handing her a full-bodied Kenco and a digestive biscuit.

'I second that, Helen,' Chris muttered, as she sailed past her with a pile of used towels.

'Just leave them by the washing machine, love, I'll sort them out when I've finished my drink,' Helen asserted firmly.

'No, you won't! You've done enough, Mum. I'm sorry I left you all in the lurch! What was I thinking of –buggering off without checking the book first! I always check the book,' Joanne said, cradling her mug thoughtfully.

'I think you've been a bit preoccupied lately!'

Sally put her head round the door. 'Your perm's ready to be neutralised – the timer's just gone off'.

'Thanks, Sal. I was going to do it myself but if you're free?'

'Sure,' she smiled back and disappeared back into the salon.

'Chris mentioned that you've been to the doctor's. Nothing wrong, is there, love?' Helen said, eyeing her daughter tentatively.

'Nothing to bother yourself about. I just needed a tonic, that's all.'

'Tonic, my eye. What's really wrong with you?'

Joanne swirled her coffee around her mug with a spoon, still calculating what to say.

'Look, whatever's happened between you and David is your own business, but if you're ill, Joanne, I need to know about it.'

'I'm pregnant, Mum,' she said. She waited for an onslaught of "Oh my God" or "What bloody awful timing." Instead, her mother gently placed both hands on top of her daughter's hand and gave the loveliest of smiles.

'Darling, that's wonderful news. But judging by your expression, I sense it's come as a bit of a shock.'

Joanne nodded wordlessly.

'David's been a very stupid man but he's made his bed – now let him lie on it! You, on the other hand, have a great deal to look forward to, husband or no husband. You're not on your own –I'm here to help and support you. Plus you have great friends and loyal staff. What more do you want?'

'Try a loving, loyal husband!' Joanne's throat tightened. 'For the time being, this news is just between you and me. I need time to adjust,' she said in a whisper.

'Fine by me ... mum's the word,' Helen giggled impishly.

'Your lady's ready, Jo,' Sally's voice echoed from the salon.

'Thanks. I'll be right out.' Joanne levered herself from her seat. 'Be lost without you, Mum.'

'Works both ways, ducky,' Helen smiled. 'I'll pick Emily up from school when I've sorted that batch of towels and she can stay at mine again.'

'Thanks, Mum …if it's not too much trouble. If Emily sees I'm upset, she'll wonder what's wrong and I need to make a few phone calls, put friends in the picture, before David throws his tuppence in.'

Once again her mother had managed to pick her up from the great height to which she'd fallen. She'd brushed her down and placed her back on her feet. There'd been no interrogation about David's affair. No "oh my goodness." No grimacing when Joanne told her about the baby. Instead, her mother had put things into perspective, reminding her to count her blessings. She had a beautiful daughter and another miracle was growing inside her; the fact that David was no longer around was of no consequence. It was going to be his loss.

Joanne sat in the kitchen alone once everyone had left, legs outstretched, arms crossed after yet another busy day. It was strange being the master of her own vessel; she was on a mission to reclaim her life back. She didn't need David to explain the council tax, MOT, standing orders, and it wouldn't take rocket science for her to pay a few bills. She just had to root everything out and put together a budget; she'd show him she wasn't the airhead he'd always made her out to be.

She'd mourned losing her best friend some months back; even the sex when it did happen seemed such a lot of trouble with not much to show for it anymore.

Nothing and no one was going to overturn the happiness she was feeling now, knowing another Emily or Herbert was growing inside her. It inspired her to spend the next couple of hours cleaning cupboards, sorting drawers, and making good use of the now empty cupboard space. She hoovered under beds, loaded the washer and dusted every square inch of the place, desperate to rid herself of his presence. In the end she fell into the armchair exhausted and clammy but with a feeling of exhilaration.

The next morning, Joanne woke to the same routine as always – it was just that David was no longer around to throw a spanner in the works. Emily didn't enquire where her father was or when he would be home; she just took it for granted that he would be at some point.

Jess rang daily, Abby rang daily, Gill and Suzy rang daily, every bloody person on planet Earth rang daily, except the one person who should have rung daily to speak to his daughter!

Abby relayed to her she'd heard that David had been bombarded with abuse from literally everyone for what he'd done. 'Just desserts,' Joanne replied smugly.

***

Joanne kicked off her shoes, lit the lamps and drew the curtains in the lounge. After a gruelling Friday in the salon, her tiredness was making it all so much harder to cope. A glass of chilled Chardonnay would have been nice, she thought wearily, but alcohol was off limits for the foreseeable future.

Joanne secured the salon door, turned out all the lights downstairs and promised herself a hot bath and an early night. However, instead she made herself comfy on the feather-cushioned couch in front of the TV and drifted off into a well-deserved nap – only to be woken by the phone ringing an hour or so later. She threw her arm in the direction of the coffee table and lifted the receiver, expecting it to be Emily going on about leaving her Barbie doll at home and could

Mummy drop it off at Granny's – but it was David at the other end of the line.

'Joanne!' She shot bolt upright. 'Joanne, please don't put the phone down. We have to talk…' He sounded strained

'*Talk? Talk?* Don't think so. In fact, I'm out of words right now, as far as you're concerned.'

'I'm so sorry, Jo. I didn't mean to hurt you like I have, but you were always tired and you never wanted to share the excitement I felt with the business doing so well. Octavia was there for me. She understood the thirst I have for life. She seems to yearn for the same excitement too... things just happened.'

'And while you were both doing all that yearning and thirsting, I was looking after our daughter and working my tits off in the shop you insisted I buy. David, I no longer care what you and your trollop get up to. What I do find totally unacceptable is that you haven't spoken to your daughter in a whole week.'

'I couldn't.' His voice trailed off.

Joanne found herself shaking. Anger was building up inside her. 'Have you seen your solicitor yet?' she asked bluntly.

'I'd hoped it wouldn't come to that, Joanne.'

'Oh did you? So how do you want to play it, then? Have a cosy little *ménage à trois* every Saturday night in front of the telly?' Her voice spiralled. 'Let me spell it out for you! You've made your bed with Frosty the Snow Bitch. Go and lie in it. I want nothing more to do with you and I want prior notice when you want to see Emily. And Octavia must never be within a ten-mile radius when Emily is with you. *Comprenez?*'

'Bit unreasonable—'

'NO! What you've done to me is unreasonable. If you can't abide by my rules we'll have to do it the legal way through our solicitors– and believe me, my way will be a hell of a sight more lenient.'

'Fair enough, point taken,' David replied coldly. 'Can I see her tomorrow?'

'You can pick her up from my mum's around twelve and I suggest you take her to your parents' house, not your flat! That way, I'll know Octavia won't be around. And while you're with Emily, explain the reason we're living apart. Why should I have to be the one that breaks her heart?' She felt her demands were justified. With that, she abruptly ended the call.

Joanne caught sight of herself in the bathroom mirror as she undressed to take a bath; her waistline had started to disappear, not surprisingly. She'd sought refuge in the fridge so many times in the last few weeks. The bath water dulled her aching limbs as she submerged herself. Although her breasts were slightly fuller, her brain still hadn't registered any of it yet. She climbed into bed and found she couldn't sleep because David was always at the forefront of her dreams.

The following morning, she wore a navy dress instead of her uniform then blow-dried some volume into her hair and carefully applied her make- up. She knew full well that David might appear at the salon door at any moment with Emily. She saw him now as a challenge and needed him to know exactly what he'd let slip through his fingers.

The girls admired the way she looked and asked what the occasion was. 'Nothing … tunic needs a wash, that's all,' she replied briskly.

The phone rang in the salon at midday. 'David's taken Emily to his parents,' Helen said cagily.

'At least he was playing by the rules, Mum,' Joanne said as her heart plummeted.

'He'll be dropping her back off at the salon around six. Do you want me to be there with you?'

'No, it's alright thanks, Mum. Emily's presence will keep things civil.'

'Will you ring me when he's gone?'

'I will. Stop worrying. Speak to you later.'

The thought of seeing him again was a massive strain but she had to keep buoyant, not act like the wronged tearful wife she was. This time last year, the news of her being pregnant would have sent shockwaves of happiness through them both. Now she couldn't even bring herself to tell him because she couldn't bear the thought of him coming back purely for that reason alone.

Once the girls had left, she made a mad dash to tidy herself up then busied herself with the evening meal, mashing potatoes, pricking sausages and laying the table for Emily and herself. At last the salon door opened and her daughter's feet ran noisily across the salon floor. Excitedly she came into the kitchen, arms outstretched; ready to give her mother a huge hug.

David's silhouette appeared in the doorway, which disarmed Joanne as she turned.

'Daddy took me to Granny and Gramps, and Gramps gave me ten whole pounds to spend on whatever I want and Granny made roast chicken. She said to say "hi." Daddy, are you staying for tea? Daddy's been telling me all about the new flat he lives in because he has to be on call all the time in case the alarms go off.' Emily was talking at speed, not pausing once for breath.

It seemed David had covered the facts nicely, Joanne thought in annoyance as she continued to fluff potatoes, drain peas and avoid looking his way. She sensed his eyes were on her continuously.

Emily dumped her coat on the chair then raced upstairs to switch on her TV in the lounge, naively unaware of the hostile situation between her parents. At last Joanne turned to look at David. His handsome face was wracked with tiredness or fucked-up-ness, she wasn't sure which.

'So... you managed to explain about our situation to Emily, I see?' Joanne said, lowering herself onto the chair opposite him and staring at him squarely.

'Well, I thought it was less complicated than telling her what had really happened.'

'You gave her the bedtime story version, eh, not the adult one?'

'Jo ... don't.'

'Don't? Don't what? Don't blame you for ruining our lives? Don't blame you for humiliating me with the whore, because that's what everyone knows she is. She's had a game plan for years and you couldn't see it. When she saw how vulnerable you were, she played you like a bloody fiddle.'

'It was my fault as well, don't just blame her. Everything seemed to be moving so fast. The business was expanding and I was going places I'd only ever dreamt of. You didn't seem to want to be part of it.'

'Why is that, David, I wonder? Mmmmm? Maybe it's because you came up with this bright idea to invest my dad's money in this bloody salon. And maybe it didn't enter your thick skull that I was trying to make you proud of me by making a success of it.'

At that point it all got too much– having him close, his fragrance, not being able to touch him or tell him she was pregnant. Her hands covered her face and she erupted into floods of tears. His reaction was to envelope her in his arms but that made matters worse. He'd become someone she no longer recognised.

'Jo, I didn't mean it to be like this, honestly.'

Emily came bounding down the stairs, on hearing her mother's cry. 'Mummy, what's the matter?'

David was quick to respond. 'Mummy's sad because I have to go back to work.'

'Don't cry, Mummy. Daddy's going to make lots of pennies to buy us all nice things, so don't be sad. I'll look after you,' Emily said, opening her arm in order to give him a hug

He scooped up his daughter and tried to hide the fact he too had been reduced to tears. Joanne could see what a wrench it was for him to leave her.

'Daddy, will you read me a story and tuck me in?'

His eyes met Joanne's and she shook her head dismissively. This was all too much, too soon. 'No …I have to go darling, but I'll read you a story next time.'

Emily accepted that, gave him a kiss, and scampered back to watch her programme.

David had become a key jangler when he was anxious and, whilst he jangled, his eyes were focused on her.

'I think it's time you went,' Joanne asserted, getting up from her chair and flicking the kettle on.

'Not pouring a glass of wine?' he asked sarcastically.

'No, I'm a single parent now – got to keep my wits about me.'

His face stiffened. 'Right I'll be off then. Can I come in the week to see her?'

'Make it Wednesday. Pick her up from school and take her for a pizza.'

'I've got work,' he snapped back.'

'Get your secretary to reschedule. Tell her to put in your diary: a meeting with my daughter.'

'Don't be bloody sarcastic.'

'Oh, it's alright for me to reschedule *my* appointments when she's ill or if I have to take her to the dentist, but not for you? You're a part-time father now – sacrifices have to be made. It's not as easy a ride as you think, is it, David? You should have used your brains more, instead of your penis.'

His face contorted with guilt as he realised how dramatically their lives had changed. Their parting words were hostile and in the end he agreed to pick Emily up mid-week after school.

And so a new regime got underway: Sundays, David took Emily to his parents' for lunch; Wednesday he had dinner with them at the shop, read his daughter a story, tucked her into bed, and went back to Octavia.

Joanne felt blessed that she was the one who shared Emily's life, heard her chatter on a daily basis, kissed her better when she was hurt, held her each night as she fell asleep. She was the one who listened to her fears. David would miss all that, she thought gravely.

Jess and Oliver were immensely supportive; they even paid for Joanne, Helen and Emily stay at one of their friend's apartment in Majorca. How blissful those ten days were. Ileitis was a small uncommercial resort with rustic beaches around which were peppered with smart villas and apartments just a stone's throw from Palma. It was a hop, skip and a jump from Portals Nous, where the stylish and rich moored their yachts, ate meals and drank cocktails in the classy restaurants and bars that lined the quayside.

The apartment was straight out of a magazine. Exquisitely furnished, it had a balcony that overlooked the olive-tree lined beach. When Emily took her nap in the afternoon, Joanne and Helen reclined there, listening to the gentle whoosh of the waves.

Joanne was healthily tanned and confident when they all arrived back. The girls couldn't get over how different she looked – relaxed, smiley-faced. She'd even put on a few pounds, according to Chris.

David rushed over to see his daughter the instant he knew they were back but his eyes never left Joanne the whole time he was there. He couldn't get over how radiant she looked and kept telling her so.

Everything was going swimmingly, Joanne conceded. Her bump hardly showed and still no one knew. Then, after two weeks, her worst nightmare unfolded.

David brought Emily back from his parents' one Sunday. The salon door nearly flew off its hinges as David stormed in stone-faced, spitting bile. Joanne ran from the kitchen, thinking something had happening to Emily.

'Who the fuck is he? And how long have you been seeing him?' he barked unceremoniously.

'I don't know what you're talking about, David.' She glanced down at Emily, who by now was staring up at her with innocent wide eyes.

'You're pregnant, aren't you?' he said, staring at her stomach. 'I want to know who it is you've been seeing while you've been accusing me of being unfaithful.'

Joanne's face reddened.

'Emily heard you telling your mother how you'll soon have to start buying baby clothes and asked if we are having a baby. And now, looking at you, I can see why. I don't know why I didn't notice it before.'

He was scratching the surface; she knew her bump hardly showed, even without her cleverly cut clothes and scarves. Her horoscope that morning had read challenging times ahead; it seemed they were right.

'David…I haven't been seeing anyone.'

'Don't fucking lie!'

'The baby's yours! That night … the Atlantic… The night I turned up uninvited.'

His face turned ashen, his forehead furrowed, his eyes narrowed.

'Emily must have picked up on our conversations when Mum and I were talking about the baby while we were away,' Jo surmised.

David looked down at his daughter and gave a faint smile. 'Go upstairs and play, Emily. Mummy and Daddy need to talk,' he soothed.

Joanne walked through to the kitchen. David followed and sat down heavily on a chair and covered his face with his hands. 'How long have you known?' he asked, his voice now calm.

'About eight weeks.' She swallowed hard, trying to avoid his eyes.

'And how far gone are you?'

'Twenty weeks now.'

'Oh come on! For fuck's sake!' he said glaring at her.

'It was just as much of a shock to me as it was to you!' she almost exploded.

'But I thought you couldn't have any more kids due to your endometriosis.'

'So did I! Missed periods are part and parcel of the disease. That's why I never suspected a thing. I was just incredibly tired, which didn't surprise me at the time. Thought I just needed a tonic. Obviously not. I found out the day after I confronted you and Octavia … great timing, eh? By then I was already twelve weeks gone.'

'Why didn't you tell me?' he asked softly.

'Why do you think?' She felt a cold, prickly tension creep through her body and gave a sharp intake of breath. 'Me being pregnant changes nothing. You've made your choice, with Octavia.'

His eyes clouded in confusion as he ran his hands through his hair. Joanne lowered herself into the chair opposite him and his hand automatically reached for hers across the table. She recoiled. 'Don't. You and I are over.'

He glared. 'This is my baby, too, Jo. Don't shut me out.'

'That's rich. You managed to shut me out for long enough.'

Joanne got to her feet and sought refuge at the kitchen sink, sloshing the cups that had been left in the soapy suds. His eyes never left her. His baby was growing inside her, which unlocked memories of when she was pregnant with Emily. She sensed by the look on his face how he was feeling. 'I think it's time you left. I'm tired,' she barked irritably.

He asked tentatively, 'Have you had a scan yet?'

Joanne's heart plummeted. She'd hoped he wouldn't want to be involved, but he *was* involved – it was his child. 'Next Monday, at ten thirty. Why?'

'I'm coming with you.'

'YOU ARE NOT!'

'IT'S MY BABY TOO, JOANNE! I intend to be there just as much as I was with Emily. Get used to it.'

Joanne declined to answer. Her bladder was reminding her she needed to pee so, without saying anything, she headed for the downstairs loo leaving him to wallow in his thoughts.

Joanne sat upright on the loo; the relief of emptying her bladder was gratifying. She imagined the look on Octavia's face when he told her

Joanne was pregnant and he was attending the scan; it was worth letting him come for that reason alone. She smiled smugly.

After she'd freshened up, she rejoined him. 'OK, you can come with me,' she said with a smile.

His face began to soften; his dark eyes lit up and he grinned.

'Ohhhh…!' Joanne's hands went to her stomach. It felt like a butterfly was trapped inside her and she was slightly light-headed so she sat heavily on the nearest chair and stared at David wide-eyed.

'You alright?' he asked, concerned.

'I felt the baby. It moved, David. I actually felt it move.' She took hold of his hand, placed it on her stomach and stared into his eyes. The intimacy between them at that moment brought excitement and hope. The baby that had been created through love was starting to move. Tears pricked David's eyes as he felt Joanne's stomach lurch one more time.

At that moment she ached for him to hold her. In his face, youth still prevailed; she, on the other hand, seemed to have aged a thousand years in these last months.

The phone rang repeatedly, bringing them both back to reality. Joanne got up and made her way to lift the receiver from the cradle on the kitchen wall. 'Hello,' she said brightly, thinking it was her mother.

'Is David there?' Octavia's voice sounded angry as she bellowed the words sarcastically down the phone.

'DAVID!' Joanne shouted with an edge, waving the phone at him.

'Who is it?' His eyes narrowed.

'I'll give you one guess.'

He lowered his eyes in disbelief as he took the phone from her. 'Are you fucking insane, Octavia, ringing me here?' he shouted.

There was a barrage of abuse between the two. Joanne could even hear it from across the room.

'I'll speak to you when I get back,' were his parting words, before almost throwing the phone back in its cradle. A muscle pulsed in his cheek, his jaw was set and his eyes had gone cold.

'Joanne …I don't know what to say.' He raked his fingers through his hair as he paced the kitchen. His anger seemed inconsolable – but there again, Octavia had interrupted a very poignant moment.

Chapter 23

Joanne saw disbelief in David's face as he witnessed their baby move on the monitor and heard its heartbeat for the very first time the following Monday. But the moment was blemished by the fact they no longer shared a life together.

The drive home was made in silence. She felt resentful that he had abandoned her at a time when they both should have been filled with joy.

His car drew onto the forecourt; he placed a reassuring hand on top of hers. Her reaction was to snatch it away and throw a hostile look at him. 'Joanne, let me come home… please. I miss you, I miss Emily and I miss us.'

She stared at him coldly; the pit of her stomach ached. It had only been a short space of time since he'd deemed her surplus to requirements, last year's model! Dull, uninteresting and now replaced by Miss Supersonic Yo-Yo Knickers. She very much doubted he'd be making this statement if she hadn't been pregnant.

Everything she needed she already had, so why revert to sharing her life with someone who constantly threw tantrums, had a testosterone-fuelled roving eye, plus was difficult to please. Tranquillity had been restored in her life since he'd left!

'You really are clueless, aren't you, about the chaos you caused? You think all you have to say is sorry and that wipes the slate clean. You've chosen a new life with Octavia – now get on with it. There's no way I want you back, David, ever – under any circumstances!' With that, she climbed from the car and headed swiftly towards the salon door before he could come after her with more feeble excuses. Why should she take him back?

That feeling she always seemed to have of being in a maze and not being able to find her way out had now left her completely. She wasn't even resentful of his happiness because the anguish in his eyes told her he was far from being happy.

She walked into the kitchen and sat down in the first chair she came to without giving him a second glance as he drove off. Emily was at school, the salon was closed for the day, and the place was swathed in an unfamiliar stillness. A hot cup of sweet tea and a couple of Jaffa cakes would probably help.

When they first met, David's dashing looks and constant quest for all life had to offer were two of the reasons she'd been so attracted to him. But somewhere down the line, he'd become over-impressed by too many ruthless people, especially where work was concerned. He was no longer that funny, caring person she'd fallen for. Now he was someone who constantly kept telling her to act appropriately whenever they were in company –in other words, do as I say not as I do! Speak when you're spoken too and don't kick up a fuss when my morally bankrupt behaviour begins to surface.

Joanne drained her cup, placed it in the dishwasher with the rest of the unwashed pots, dropped a tablet into the compartment, and pressed the wash switch. Then she picked up the phone and punched in Gill's number.

'Helloeee,' Gill answered with an upbeat tone.

'It's me.'

'Oh hi, you! How did the scan go …did Shitface turn up?'

Joanne giggled. 'Yes, Shitface turned up. He also asked me to take him back. How's that for a joke?'

'I hope you told him where he could shove his offer?'

'Yep, I certainly did!'

'How do you really feel?'

'Oooh…Just that I think I've turned a corner now and I feel like going out to a smart wine bar with you lot. I need to inject some fun into my life before it's too late.'

'Welcome back to the land of the living, kiddo. For a time we thought we'd lost you. What time do you want to go out?'

'Early doors. Half-price cocktail hour used to be fun.'

'OK, I'll give Suzy a ring and see if she can join us, shall I? That's if Harry will let her out; they seem to be joined at the hip these days.'

'And I'll ring Chris, too; she's been a bit down in the mouth of late. A night out might cheer her up. And don't worry about driving,' Joanne responded. 'I'll pick you all up. I'm not drinking, remember, but that doesn't mean I can't enjoy myself.'

Helen seemed delighted that Joanne had at last woken up to the fact that she couldn't change the situation but at least she could enhance things by enjoying life a bit more.

'Don't worry about Emily, I'll pick her up from school. I'll have Oliver over for tea, too, if that will help Gill. Brian can pick him up on his way home from work. I'll give her a ring, shall I?'

'Mum, you are a love.' Joanne beamed.

'I know… it's a gift.' She giggled. 'How did the scan go?'

'Oh! OK. David became a bit tearful then decided to ask me if I'd take him back and we'd all play happy families again like nothing has happened.'

'Oh dear…'

'Don't worry, I think he knows my view on that one. So I'm going out with the girls before I start to resemble a beached whale.'

***

The piano bar pulsed with chatter and was packed with after-work drinkers when they all piled in. Joanne spied some rather good-looking suited and booted men standing at the bar who grinned as they walked past. She'd lost the language of flirtation or being juvenile a few months back, so felt woefully unequipped to smile back.

But once they settled at a table and the drinks were served, her eyes kept being drawn to a guy at the bar with piercing blue eyes and full lips who held her gaze once or twice. She'd quite forgotten just how exhilarating it felt to establish a mutual attraction and, in a moment of weakness, grinned defiantly back at him Then after a few more drinks, the others encouragingly smiled over at the rest of the guys he was with which was followed by a bottle of Moet being carried over and eight flute glasses.

He said his name was Joe and he had the bluest of eyes and a playful grin. As he struck up conversation with her, she felt her face redden. If he only knew the curvaceous figure he kept feasting on when he thought she wasn't looking was curvaceous purely because she was pregnant, she doubted he'd have given her a second glance.

For a brief moment, Joanne was propelled back to a time when she shared a flat with these girls and she was footloose and fancy free. The others seemed to have gone back there too by the way they were flirting and gulping down the champagne that was poured for them. She listened to the banter from these random strangers and smiled at how openly they talked about their lives, where they worked, where they'd holidayed and where they lived. Gill and Suzy confessed they were married. Joanne glanced at her naked finger and explained to Joe she was separated. Joe said he was newly divorced and they both related to the rawness of it all. She chose her words carefully when he asked her what she did for a living, not wanting to give too much away. She told him she owned a hair salon but didn't say where.

Suzy and Gill were still life's eternal partygoers but Joanne could see they were becoming quite hammered so intervened before they reached the slurring, loud stage. 'Time to make tracks, girls,' she said. That got a flash of annoyance and some strong objections but then they remembered that Joanne usually started to flounder around ten most nights. Tonight was probably no different.

They started to get up from their seats and thank the guys for a great night but before Joanne had a chance to make a move, Joe's arms closed around her and his lips found hers in a kiss she didn't resist. His lips felt warm and wanting – and it was good to be wanted again.

'I've been dying to do that all night,' he said with a grin.

She found herself unable to stop herself smiling too.

'Can I see you again?' he whispered, out of earshot of the others. She looked at his face, realising her life was far too cluttered and complicated to let one kiss cloud her judgment.

'I can't… but thank you for asking, Joe.'

Joanne arrived home once she'd dropped off all the girls and made her way up to the bedroom, where she threw off her shoes and flopped down on the bed fully clothed. She couldn't believe a single kiss from a random stranger could leave her feeling this high on life!

But once she was in bed that kiss was forgotten as she missed her daughter desperately. Since David had left, she'd got used to Emily climbing into bed with her most nights to give cuddles, played tickly-tum, then spoon into her and fall asleep. It had been the one thing that had kept her buoyant: tonight, though, it was her mother's turn for cuddles, she thought warmly.

***

Word finally got out that Joanne was pregnant. Abby was the first to ring to congratulate her and, whilst she was on, she gave her the lowdown on what was happening in the family at war.

'Octavia is outraged by the news, by all account, so well done you. Jess and Oliver are thrilled about the baby but are riddled with guilt at their son's behaviour. If you need me any time, just ring. I'm here – but you already know that, Jo.'

'Sorry, Abby. I didn't let on until now. You can imagine what's going on in my mind. Just one night we spent together some months back. I really did think it was a night where we were rekindling everything. Seems not – but I really am thrilled about the baby.'

Joanne came off the phone to her sister-in-law feeling a tad embarrassed that she hadn't mentioned the pregnancy before now but she hadn't mentioned it to anyone.

Jess became a regular visitor and even lent a hand with Emily when Helen needed a break. That turned out to be quite frequently as Helen's blood pressure began to soar and she became prone to fainting bouts, which ended with her having a pacemaker fitted. Joanne banned her from all salon duties and ordered her to take things at a much slower pace once she came out of hospital, maybe have a few days out with Dorothy. Helen objected strongly, saying she didn't know what all the fuss was about.

Jess was only too glad to lend a hand and, off her own bat, started to collect Emily from school each night. She even got roped into helping out with salon duties when they were snowed under. Generosity had no bounds now where Jess was concerned; she furnished the baby's room and replenished Emily's wardrobe with some obscenely priced clothing for a six year old. She admitted openly to Joanne that being useful again amongst people who smiled and laughed for no other reason but to be friendly was exhilarating.

Joanne broached the subject of divorce once or twice when David arrived to see Emily. She felt the need to move on with her life. He was living with someone else so couldn't see why he'd object but, each time it was mentioned, David flew into a ferocious rage. Was she looking for someone else, he questioned. If so, he wanted sole custody of Emily… Bit rich, she thought, coming from someone who was shacked up with a deranged nymphomaniac, so she dismissed the subject for the time being before it got out of hand.

Determined not to give him any false hope, Joanne handed him separation papers instead then tried to stay out of his way by taking a nap or going out when he was around. She even used him as a baby sitter when she felt the need to meet up with the girls. If he imagined being pregnant would clip her wings, he was delusional.

Joanne eventually managed to navigate herself though this rough patch of unchartered waters, never once acting like a victim of circumstances. She found spending time in the garden at the back of the shop on those long warm summer days when she wasn't working was blissful. Nothing had been touched out there since they'd moved in, except for clearing away the rubble and laying some turf for Emily to play on. Not a flower or a bush had been planted; there was just heaped soil around the edges of the lawn, which had become over-run with weeds.

Oliver took matters in hand and jumped at the chance to turn it all into a cottage garden for her. Hollyhocks, lavender, ferns, lupines, dianthus, forget-me-knots, climbing roses, red-robin bushes, ornamental conifers – all were delivered by their gardener who got to work almost immediately. To add a blaze of colour to the brick walls at the far end, he hung colourful trailing hanging baskets from brackets.

When it was finished, Joanne cried with joy. Jess and Oliver turned up one afternoon with a state-of-the-art gas barbeque which appeared far too big for the postage-stamp back garden but that didn't matter – it was a lovely gesture. They'd also brought bottles of booze and more food than she knew what to do with and produced a splendid Sunday afternoon feast in the sunshine for Gill, Suzy, their spouses and off springs. Helen and Dorothy were allocated to salad duty and Emily acted very grown up by seeing to all her friends' needs.

Joanne stood outside herself that day to observe how she was doing and came to the conclusion she wasn't doing half bad. Her hips were widening rapidly now and her body was much more cumbersome, so she was desperately tired most of the time. She was too tired some days to see to the menial tasks, when the washing basket overflowed and a thin layer of dust had descended throughout the flat.

David continued his visits and took Emily to his parents' most Sundays for a roast dinner then a visit to the park. Jess would always ring the next day to give a running commentary on what had gone on. Not once was Octavia's name mentioned; it was obvious David was sticking to his side of the bargain by keeping her at arms' length where Emily was concerned.

Bonfire night came and went triggering the start of Jess's festive planning. 'You will be coming Christmas Day, won't you love?' she said over the phone.

'I don't think so, Jess. I still feel pretty uncomfortable being around the family with everyone knowing what's gone on, especially now I'm so huge. You do understand? David will be bringing Emily, though,' Joanne managed to throw in. 'She's so looking forward to seeing her cousins and you lot on Christmas Day,' she continued brightly.

'Sure we can't change your mind? George and his wife definitely won't be there.'

'Thanks for that, Jess, but the answer's still no, I'm afraid.'

David's solitary invitation would probably go down like a lead balloon and cause chaos with Octavia, but if David thought for one moment he was going to let Emily down, then he had another think coming.

December brought thick snow and hazardous conditions to the country. Everywhere more or less came to a standstill but, as always, no one was prepared! Emily loved the excitement and chaos of it all. David took her sledging on the hill and built her a snowman in the back garden that she named Eric.

This year she'd been chosen to play Mary in the school concert. They'd picked Michael Brown as Joseph, on whom she'd had a huge crush since kindergarten, so for her life was pretty magical. The gang took up a whole row of seats in the audience: Gill, Brian, Suzy,

Harry, Joanne, Helen, Jess and Oliver all turned up, and David recorded the whole event on his new camcorder. Offspring fluffing words, kids waving at their parents as they fidgeted and picked their noses – all were captured then it was back to the shop for hotpot supper and a few beers.

Emily's Christmas list seemed to grow daily. Most of the things on it were extremely popular so they were scooped up as soon as they hit the shelves. The present she wanted the most was the most talked about in the whole wide world, according to Emily.

Abby rang to say there were plenty down in Bath so she'd pick one up for her. That just left all the odds and sods that Helen said she'd do her best to find to save Joanne traipsing round in the snow. She'd wrap everything up and keep them at hers in the spare bedroom until Christmas morning. Then Helen dug out her WI cookbook and made a very boozy Christmas cake and numerous batches of mince pies and sausage rolls to give clients with a tipple of sherry when Christmas bookings were in full swing.

'I hope you know I fully intend to be here on Christmas morning when Emily opens her presents,' David said, nostrils in full flare, on one of his visits. 'I don't want her to feel like this year's different to any other.'

Joanne didn't see a problem with that,

'You still not coming to Mum and Dad's with Emily and me?'

'No. Mum and I are going to La Bouillabaisse instead for a six-course lunch with a string quartet playing as we eat. I felt we deserved it,' she said defiantly, rolling her eyes. 'I'll give Stuart your regards, shall I?' she muttered sarcastically.

His mouth tightened and eyes narrowed. 'Don't be funny.'

'Oh, I assure you, David, I stopped being funny a long time ago… around the time you started sleeping with Octavia.'

Chapter 23

David's car drove onto the forecourt around eight o'clock on Christmas morning. Emily, predictably, was still asleep. Helen let him in as she'd stayed the night and was already downstairs in the kitchen making a pot of tea.

On hearing his voice, Joanne quickly scurried into the bathroom, dragged a brush though her dishevelled hair, swilled her face, cleaned her teeth and emerged out onto the landing only to see David taking the stairs two at a time.

She was taken aback by how handsome he appeared with his festive jumper, Wranglers and dishevelled hair. Their eyes met briefly and Joanne blushed because she was still wearing nightclothes when she gave him a friendly peck on the cheek.

'Merry Christmas.'

'Merry Christmas,' he smiled back. 'Is Emily awake yet?'

'No, we were just about to wake her. It was late before she eventually nodded off, she was so excited. Then Mum and I had to get cracking putting all her presents out, hence the fact we're all still a bit bog-eyed. I'm glad you managed to get here in time though,' she said brightly.

'It's my daughter… I'll never not be here for her on Christmas morning,' he said, straight-faced. With that, he turned on his heels and headed towards Emily's room. Joanne disappeared into her own room and quickly threw on her maternity leggings and top.

'Emily…Emily! Father Christmas has been and he's left you some presents,' Joanne heard David tell their daughter, as she tugged the brush once again through her hair, smeared on some lipstick and covered herself in cologne.

'Daddy, you came!' Joanne then heard Emily scamper along the landing towards the lounge where she was already waiting for her.

Emily was even louder as she spied all her presents, which near enough filled the entire room.

Helen appeared at the door with a welcoming pot of tea, three mugs and a glass of juice for Emily. Then all hell was let loose as Emily tore at her presents and shrieked with laughter, bringing tears to everyone's eyes as they watched. It was everything you would expect from Christmas morning in a household with a young child and for a brief time they were no longer the family at war.

Helen was unusually quiet a midst the mayhem but David had committed a huge faux pas in her eyes. There was probably a whole host of things she would like to have said to him, so keeping quiet really was her way of upholding some dignity.

Joanne got up from the couch and tried unsuccessfully to tidy the discarded paper. David grinned at the cumbersome way she bent and shuffled, until in the end he sat her down on the settee and took over. She felt embarrassed as she was lowered onto the couch. The vision in her mind's eye was of how Octavia would look when he got back, scantily dressed no doubt. Then they'd probably make love until it was time for him to pick Emily up. Her hormones were obviously playing up, making her hypersensitive and she was racked with heartburn through all the bending.

David walked towards her, smiling broadly. 'How've you been feeling?'

'Fine just tired…' At that moment she felt a hefty kick; it was automatic to say, 'Here feel this,' and grab his hand to place it on her stomach.

Helen watched with non-judgemental eyes as she sipped her tea at the way David and her daughter beamed in unison as they shared that private moment.

David reached over to his overcoat, which was discarded on the chair, and took out a small, beautifully wrapped gift from the inside pocket.' This is for you,' he said handing it to Joanne. He also handed Helen a parcel too .There were blinks of confusion from both women. Joanne felt suddenly nauseous; the only gifts she'd bought him were labelled 'From Emily to Daddy'.

'David …I thought we weren't buying for each other this year,' she said, blushing as she ripped open the wrapping and glared at the small oblong velvet box. She flipped open the lid and gasped, admiring the gold bracelet inside which was an exact replica of the one she'd lost on holiday three years previously, the last holiday David and she had had together. Her parents had bought her the bracelet for her eighteenth and she'd cried for days at its loss. David always said he'd replace it but he never had … until now!

'You must have searched endlessly for this! It's identical to my old one. Thank you,' she said, her eyes starting to brim as she stared at it.

'Well, I did promise to replace it, didn't I?'

She passed it to her mother to admire. Helen took it and noticed the turmoil the gift had caused on her daughter's face.

'What time are you picking Emily up?' Joanne said, catching her breath.

'Oh, around one thirty, if that's OK.'

'I'll have her ready. Our table at the restaurant is booked for two o'clock,' she said, looking at the mother for confirmation. Helen was admiring the earrings David had bought for her.

Emily dragged her daddy down onto the floor at that point to show him her new play kitchen and proceeded to tip pretend peas onto the tiny plate and hand it to him. Helen loaded the tray with the dirty cups and took them down to the kitchen.

Joanne didn't bother to enquire what Octavia would be doing while David was at his parents. Quite frankly she didn't give a damn, to coin a phrase, just assumed David would have to pay dearly for being with his family and not with Octavia.

Emily's soft wispy curls had been pinned up into a chignon and she was dressed in the midnight-blue taffeta dress and patent-leather shoes, all bought by Jess. Helen couldn't speak when she saw her; she looked so adorable. Joanne took great pains too with her own hair and makeup before stepping into a red dress with bugle-beaded shoulders. The dress had been cleverly cut so she no longer looked as wide-hipped, fed up and frumpy as she felt. She'd had an idea today was going to be difficult, but didn't realise just *how* difficult and craved more than ever now for David's assurance she looked nice.

Helen stepped from Joanne's bedroom looking twenty years younger in the navy velvet suit Joanne had treated her to. Three generations stood side by side in the lounge and Joanne balanced the camera on the drinks trolley, set the timer then did a mad dash to get in the picture before the flash went. That would be the picture to replace the one of her and David in the silver frame, she thought firmly.

'Doesn't Mummy and Nanny look lovely, Daddy?' Emily commented as David walked through the shop and scooped his daughter up into his arms. His eyes warmed at Helen's attire and then his face lit up when he turned round and saw Joanne. 'Wow,' he expelled, stopping in his tracks. Joanne knew at that moment that the obscene amount she'd paid for the dress had been worth every penny and she grinned with pride.

'They certainly do look lovely – and so do you, my little princess,' he said, giving his daughter a squeeze.

Joanne pointed to the pile of gifts by the door.' They're for the family.' Once he'd put them in the boot of his car, Emily's coat was buttoned and they left.

She felt emptiness inside as she waved them off and tried her best not to let her mum see her tears by making her way back up the stairs to tidy some of Emily's toys away.

Stuart the maitre d' greeted Joanne and Helen warmly in the foyer of the now lavishly decorated restaurant but Joanne detected a slight awkwardness when he noticed she was hugely pregnant. His brothers had probably filled him in on the fact that David had left her for Octavia: David had probably omitted to tell them his wife was up the duff when he'd abandoned her.

Stuart smiled generously as he guided them to their table in the dining room. Apart from the string quartet playing, 'Somewhere in Time', a particular favourite of her mother's which reduced them both to tears, Christmas lunch was damn near perfect.

Helen decided, after having a few too many glasses of bubbly, that she was tired and slightly squiffy so preferred to go back to her own bed instead of sharing Joanne's. So Joanne dropped her home before heading home herself.

David had just arrived back and was opening the boot of his car as she pulled onto the forecourt. 'Hi, you two! Had a good time?' Joanne shouted as she tried to huff and puff her way out of the car.

'Mummy, looks at all the presents I've got!'

David pointed to the loaded boot.

'Oh my goodness! Where are we going to put them all?' Joanne laughed.

'Some are for Mummy, though, aren't they?' David said, carrying three loaded bin bags up into the shop.

'Where's your mum?' he asked Joanne with some concern, pressing the beeper on the key fob to lock his car after lifting the last of the bags from the boot.

'She had one too many and felt the need to go home to her own bed,' Joanne enlightened him. 'How did your lunch go?'

'Lovely as always and everyone sends their love. You were greatly missed. Abby said she'll drive over tomorrow to see you. They're going back the next day. They want me to take Emily down before the New Year. Is that alright by you? It's only for a couple of days.'

Joanne nodded and smiled but couldn't resist winding him up. 'And what's Octavia going to do in your absence? Bet she wasn't too pleased about today, was she?'

'Octavia's gone to stay with her parents in Barbados. She knew I had commitments with Emily and didn't want to get in the way.'

'That was big of her,' Joanne couldn't resist. So that was the reason he'd arrived so early that morning: he hadn't had the distraction of getting his leg over after all! 'Want a nightcap?'

'Oh Daddy please … you can tuck me into bed and I can show you my new Mr Men books,' Emily urged.

'Alright, anything to keep the peace,' he said, scooping up his daughter into his arms. Anyone watching would have thought it just another normal Christmas day in the Winston household and at that moment Joanne wished to God it was.

The bin bags of unopened presents from David's family were placed on the sofa in the lounge. Emily dragged in her own small sack crammed with stuff from his parents and dumped it onto the rug in front of the fire. She threw off her coat and left it in a heap on the floor. David instantly scolded her to take her coat into her room and get changed into her jimmies before playing with her toys. The gob-smacked youngster obeyed in an instant, proving one thing: he retained some influence. Plus it was nice having him take charge; it had been a long day and now Joanne was beginning to feel fatigued.

'Help yourself to a brandy. I'm just going to make a pot of coffee. Want one?'

He nodded and headed for the drinks trolley.

Jess, Abby, and Kristy all knew of Joanne's weakness for expensive perfume and this year everyone had been exceptionally generous with their presents.

'How were Philip and Kristy?' Joanne enquired as she tore open their gifts.

Kristy had been the only one who hadn't rung after they split up. Joanne put that down to the fact that they never seemed to bond in the same way Abby and she had.

David looked awkward as he answered. 'They're both fine …keeping busy, running in marathons.' There was an edge to his voice and his hands were shoved in his trouser pockets, a dead giveaway something wasn't kosher.

Joanne knew then Kristy and Octavia must still be friends. They'd been as thick as thieves in the early days when Kristy became Octavia's personal trainer and it sounded like they still were. She knew Abby would fill her in tomorrow when she came.

Emily became cranky and slightly overwhelmed: a classic case of too much in one day. David hoisted her up in his arms, gave her a cuddle then carried her off to bed, where sleep instantly claimed her.

While he was out of the room, Joanne pushed her cup of coffee to one side and poured herself a half glass of Chardonnay. Well, it was Christmas Day, she thought brightly. Half a glass wouldn't do any harm, she was sure.

David caught her in the act as he came back in and raised an eyebrow.

'Only the second one since I found out I was pregnant,' she said, amused by the challenging look.

He lowered himself onto the couch opposite, stretched out his legs and began to scrutinise her face. 'I'm so sorry…' he began to say, his voice cracked with emotion.

'Don't. Let's just sit here and enjoy the moment, shall we? No melancholy moments, no declarations, no remorseful comments. It's been a long day,' she said, holding up her glass.

Without thinking, David got up and slipped a George Benson CD into the stereo.' Sorry.' He stopped short. 'Force of habit. You OK with this?' he said, realising he no longer lived there.

'It's fine …it's one of my favourites anyway.'

He looked more relaxed than she'd seen him look in ages and she got a swift, sharp punch in the solar plexus at the realisation that she still loved him.

'Was Emily OK today at your parents'?'

'Yes. Everyone made a huge fuss of her, but kept asking where you were.'

'That's nice… Mum and I had an amazing lunch, too. I had lobster to start, then pheasant,' she said, making light of the situation.

David got up and came and sat next to her and placed his arm supportively round the back of her on the settee as they continued to talk. His closeness unsettled her slightly.

'We all do things on a whim, Joanne. Mine was a huge self-destructive whim, I'm afraid. Give me a second chance. For Emily and the baby's sake, at least. I still love you,' he said scrutinizing her face. She could tell each word was painfully lodged in his throat as he spoke.

But a tourniquet had been firmly placed around her heart the day he left. And she needed a damn sight more from him than a declaration as weak as that to untangle it.

It was obvious he missed his life with them but she hadn't really missed him that much. And wasn't he forgetting one other person in this bizarre farce – Octavia? Where did she come into the equation? Joanne suddenly felt desperately tired; she felt she really couldn't cope with this confrontational conversation he was starting to have with her

The phone rang, bringing great relief, she hoisted herself up and picked up the receiver, expecting it to be her mother. Instead it was Jess, her voice sounding agitated. 'Is David with you, love?'

'Yes I'll just get him, Jess…Oh, thanks for the presents, by the way – they're lovely!'

'You're welcome, love …you were very much missed today, you know.'

David looked perplexed as he put the phone to his ear. 'What's up, Mum?'

Joanne could hear a fragment of their conversation as she was still standing next to him. 'Octavia's rung several times since you left!' Jess said. 'She demanded to know why you hadn't rung her and where you were. Kristy took the call and I heard her tell her you were at Joanne's.'

'The bitch.' David's face was ashamed.

'I assumed you'd be coming back here when you dropped Emily off, but when you didn't arrive we got worried. Sorry to ring you there, but Kristy promised to ring Octavia back when she found out where you were.'

'I'll be back shortly.' He retorted sternly.

His words caused chaos inside Joanne's head. It made a mockery of what he'd just said. He was still hankering after the best of both worlds – well, he didn't need to bother on her behalf.

There was a highly charged silence between them when the receiver was replaced.

'Just go, David,' Joanne said furiously.

'I meant every word I said,' he pleaded. 'Let me explain.'

'No, you're talking bollocks,' she said, trying not to raise her voice in case she woke Emily. 'Get out of my house. From now on, I don't want you at any of the scans and I definitely don't want you there at the birth, so don't bother asking.'

Knowing anger was brewing unhealthily inside her, he lifted his coat and made a hasty retreat. Any repercussions didn't bear thinking about.

Abby and the two girls arrived the following morning and, whilst the girls played merrily in Emily's bedroom, Abby enlightened her about what had gone on the previous day.

'Kristy must still have divided loyalties. Octavia and she are still friends. Jess and Oliver were outraged, so Jess listened in on the extension yesterday when Octavia called and heard her asking Kristy to find out where David was and who he was with. Kristy told her that he was with you, which caused Octavia to blow a gasket and use some pretty choice language. Kristy said she intended to remain Octavia's friend, no matter what, which caused chaos when she came off the phone because Jess had heard every word. By now the other guests were all beginning to cringe with embarrassment at the arguing that had erupted so they started to filter out. Oliver was furious.' She paused for an intake of breath.

'I told Jonathan to go and check on the girls and to stay well out of it. Philip buggered off somewhere too when it all kicked off. Kristy's the boss it their relationship, so he knew he'd be in deep shit if he didn't take her side. This all happened just after David left to bring Emily home.'

'Blimey, I wish I'd been a fly on the wall,' Joanne laughed.

Abby asked if it would still be alright to take Emily back with them when they went home the following morning, with the promise Jonathan would drop her off on the second of January on his way up to a conference in Manchester.

'But I thought David was bringing her down?'
Abby's brow furrowed. 'He's flying off to Japan tomorrow, didn't he say? I'm so sorry, love,' Abby said, giving Joanne an affectionate hug. 'I hate the fact you're having to go through all this alone.'

'But I'm not, believe me,' Joanne said. 'I'm swathed with kisses and hugs from my daughter. I have oodles of support from you guys and financially I've never been as well off in my life.' The words rolled off her tongue.

Tears, which they'd both held back until now, came to the surface when it was time to say goodbye. Abby promised she'd ring to tell her what time they'd pick Emily up in the morning before Joanne and Emily waved them all off.

Chapter 24

Emily had been gone a matter of minutes and already Joanne missed her never-ending chatter in the stillness of the place. She switched on the radio with the hope it would help fill the void while she sat and drank her coffee, taking in the unwashed breakfast pots, un-swept floor and messy worktop. Things had got a little lackadaisical over the last few weeks, she had to admit, and she'd become more than a little careless about tidying up. But there again, multi-tasking had never been an option while the Christmas rush was at full steam in the salon.

Joanne felt it was time to roll up her sleeves, don her Marigolds and knock the place into shape whilst no one was around. The salon would be closed for the next couple of days.

She pulled up the blind in the kitchen; the winter sunshine instantly flooded the room, inspiring her to smile. 'Nothing's healthier than a good spring clean and it's so much healthier than lashing out at friends when resentment starts to gather,' she reminded herself.

When she started, by loading the washing machine with the mountain of washing, then whooshed back the curtains in the lounge and pushed the furniture to one side, enabling her to hoover corners that wouldn't normally have been touched. She carefully washed every ornament, piece of crystal and china then attacked Emily's bedroom with gusto. She worked up a sweat and had never known energy like it as she shuffled barefoot from room to room. Then she caught a glimpse of herself in the mirror while she was changing the bed. Wide-hipped, full-moon face, no makeup, hair messily scrunched up in a band; no wonder David preferred someone else.

Joanne could feel her bulky body spread as she lowered herself onto the kitchen chair and started to devour the piece of Christmas cake she'd plated up for herself. It seemed these days that a piece of something sweet was her only guilty pleasure!

As she slotted her dish into the dishwasher, she chose to ignore the continuous ringing of the phone. 'The salon's still bloody closed…it's the weekend, for God's sake,' she shouted crossly. If it wasn't a client, then it would only be her mum wondering where her morning call was. Right now, Joanne had no cause to feel cheery; she couldn't even muster up the initiative to get showered and dressed, let alone confess to her mother all she'd been doing. She would only get a ticking off for overdoing things.

She couldn't believe David had managed to wangle his way into her affections yet again! Just when she thought she'd conquered that mountain of disrupted feelings, now she had to conquer it all over again.

'Come on, you airhead, snap out of this,' she chastised herself sternly.

Could she, though? Was she really strong enough to cope as a single mum with a new baby, a seven year old, and keep her business ahead of its rivals? She sensed her mother had noticed her heart convulse on Christmas morning when David gave her the bracelet and at that private moment when the baby kicked, but Helen had said nothing.

***

Emily returned from her trip to Bath in a flurry of excitement and went on for days about the firework display on New Year's Eve and how she'd helped with mucking out Poppy and Daisy and why couldn't we have a pony, too? She was sure Gran and Gramps would buy her one, if she asked them nicely. Joanne reminded her once again that there was no room for a pony in the back garden; far better to have a new baby instead. Joanne said sagely, 'At least you'll be able to play with a baby when the weather's bad,' trying to compensate for her daughter's glum face.

The salon reopened in the New Year. Business was always quiet at this time of year so Joanne decided it was time to take some well-earned maternity leave. It was only roughly four weeks until the baby was due and her energy level was now at an all-time low.

Chris took over as manager; she also took on board another girl called Cathy to do the menial tasks of shampooing and reception to help Lily and Sally, who were now trained to blow dry, set, tint and trim.

Helen had started to occasionally go to the theatre, and took the odd coach trip with Dorothy, who'd been constantly badgering her to do so since she'd come to live in Southport. It was nice to see her enjoying life again.

Only a week into retirement, Joanne felt semi-delirious with the boredom of it all. Her options now were either to push a single-person's trolley round a supermarket or to go through the tedious task of cleaning the flat each day! As it was, every knob, nook and cranny sparkled and the laundry was done. Or she could just sit all day playing womb music to her stomach. Whichever she chose, they weren't exactly awe inspiring.

Once or twice she lifted the phone to punch in Gill's number to have a chinwag, then remembered Gill was now working full time for Brian. Dorothy had her mother trained to go off somewhere new each day and Joanne wasn't in the mood for Jess, who'd probably persuade her to dress up and go off fine dining, only to go on endlessly about people who impressed her.

Joanne and David were barely speaking after his return from Japan so Helen became the mediator when important issues needed addressing.

Jess and Oliver called in twice as they were worried they hadn't seen much of Joanne. They thought she looked tired, which she supposed she did. She'd been waking earlier and earlier each day, aimlessly waiting for the daylight to arrive.

One Saturday night, backache caused her to get very little sleep. Her due date wasn't for two weeks so she wasn't concerned. Even so, she asked David if he'd bring Emily home from his parents a little earlier than usual as she felt the need to get an early night. She didn't relish sitting up waiting for Emily to come home until nearly bedtime, which it always seemed to be now when Emily and David had lunch at his parents on a Sunday.

She didn't hear David's car pull onto the forecourt but heard the salon door open and Emily's feet pad across the salon floor. Joanne heaved herself up from the chair in the kitchen in readiness for a hug but it was David who walked in first. Joanne saw concern on his face as he looked at her. Did she look so bad?, she thought wearily.

Emily's loud chatter followed him in. 'Daddy and Gramps took me to the park this afternoon and Granny made goose for lunch and she bought me a dress.'

David grinned broadly and produced a red knitted dress and tights to match from a Marks and Spencer carrier bag.

'Oooo…nice,' Joanne smiled.

'Go and hang it up and take your coat off and hang that up too,' David ordered his daughter, handing her the bag with the dress. Obediently Emily took it from him and ran off to do what was asked. David lowered himself onto the chair opposite Joanne. 'You look tired,' he said softly.

'Wouldn't you be if you were my size?' she said, eyes flashing, embarrassed by her state. 'I'm sick of people telling me,' she said crossly.

'You should be putting your feet up a bit more.'

She was too tired to argue, too tired to ask him to go, too tired full stop. She avoided his eyes by looking down at her fidgety hands.

Emily ran back in. 'Can I show Daddy the baby's room…please?'

Joanne stared at David unblinkingly; she didn't want him to see the dishevelled state of the flat. She'd been so worn out, she hadn't even got dressed until about an hour ago, let alone moved the coffee cups from the table, tidied away the Sunday papers or sorted out the mayhem of the bathroom. The list of things she hadn't done was endless. But then she remembered how she'd frozen him out of her life since Christmas.

'Yes, of course… And while you're up there, David, get your daughter ready for bed, would you?' His face brightened in response.

She felt close to tears as she listened to Emily chatter on excitably and how they both laughed at some point. She'd missed all that. Was she such a bad person to have denied him all this? She plucked a Kleenex from its box on the worktop and blew her nose then heard them both come thundering back down the stairs.

'The room looks amazing,' David marvelled.

'All thanks to your parents,' she smiled back.

'Is there anything else you need?' he asked tentatively.

'How about a new body?'

‘The one you have doesn’t look too bad,’ he grinned back.

She ignored his weak attempt at flattery; the last time she was taken in by his flattery it caused severe mental bruising.

‘Get yourself off to bed. I’ll stay with Emily and read her a story until she goes to sleep, then I’ll see myself out.’

Joanne didn’t argue; she just smiled then dragged her way up the stairs. The backache was still causing huge discomfort. Two more days passed and it hadn’t subsided. Once again she tossed and turned until in the end she climbed out of bed around 3 a.m., edged her way downstairs and flipped on the kettle. She was reaching in the cupboard for a cup when pain ripped through her body so badly she dropped the cup, smashing it into pieces on the floor as she grabbed hold of the taps on the sink to support herself. A gush of water surged from her. Now there was a great puddle surrounding her feet.

‘No … it’s too soon!’ she gasped as panic gripped her.

She lifted the phone from its cradle on the wall, pressed her mother’s number on speed dial. It was gone 2 a.m. but she knew her mum was a light sleeper.

‘Hullo,’ Helen said sleepily.

‘Mum, it’s Joanne. I think the baby’s started! I’m getting pains and my waters have just broken.’

‘Goodness, love,’ her mother’s voice was strained. ‘Whatever you do, don’t panic. I’ll throw some clothes on and be with you in a heartbeat!’ She was telling her daughter not to panic, yet she sounded close to hysteria herself.

‘Mum! Mum!’ Helen had put the phone down before Joanne was able to tell her to take her time. It would probably be hours before anything happened.

Joanne dragged the mop-bucket from the cupboard and cleaned the floor, then carefully made her way back upstairs to get changed and lift her packed bag from the baby’s room.

Helen’s car screeched to a halt on the forecourt. Her face was grey with concern as she rushed through the salon door. ‘Joanne! Joanne, are you alright? What can I do to help?’

‘You can calm down for a start. The pains are only half an hour apart. At this rate, the baby won’t arrive for hours. You can start by making a pot of tea while I give the hospital a quick ring and tell them what’s happened.’ After calling the hospital, Joanne said, ‘The sister on the ward is sending an ambulance seeing I have no husband at hand, just to be on the safe side. No point in waking Emily. She'll only get upset if she knows what's happened.'

Helen agreed. 'Do you want me to ring David?'

'No! I can do this on my own. Ring him when it's all over.'

Another deluge of pain materialised from nowhere just as blue flashing lights arrived outside the shop. Two paramedics knocked then walked in as Joanne was still trying to pant away the pain.

'Or rite, lav …your carriage awaits,' said a chap with a broad Cockney accent.

Joanne was lowered into a wheelchair and they gathered up her bag. Helen tearfully wished her luck and waved as she was lifted into the ambulance.

The room she was wheeled into was sparsely furnished with an adjustable bed, monitoring machine, gas and air and a crib. No curtains covered the window. Even the walls were painted in a cold, unfriendly shade of blue.

Joanne was helped into a gown by an ashen-faced nurse who examined her, booked her in, and then gave her an enema which worked almost instantly.

'AARGGGGGGGG,' Joanne screamed, barely keeping control as another pain ripped through her. Her mouth felt dry as she listened to the reassuring beep of the baby's heartbeat on the monitor.

'Three centimetres,' the nurse recited as she examined her.

Joanne didn't know what that meant. All she knew was that she wanted this ordeal to come to an end.

Gas and air was handed to her and then the nurse rushed off to tend to the woman who was screaming in the next room. She remembered David's words that most Chinese women gave birth in the paddy fields whilst they were working, so it couldn't be that bad. Silly twat! What did he fucking know?

'AAAHHHHRGGGG!' Another pain travelled into her back. It felt like one of those awful bear hugs her friends used to give in the playground but a thousand times worse. She grabbed the mask and inhaled but it didn't seem to help. What was that bloody nursery rhyme they told her to recite at antenatal, she wondered frantically. If she'd only taken it all more seriously instead of acting like the class clown.

Too scary, too painful and too bloody awful for words and now she felt incredibly alone! The pethadine they'd given was beginning to space her out a little; she was drifting in and out of sleep between the pains. The beeping of the instrument tracing the baby's heart seemed a long way off now.

Once again she was woken by a deluge of raw pain and automatically started to pant, blow, and howl. The nurse rushed in and thrust a gloved hand inside her. 'Seven centimetres,' she told her.

What did it all mean? Tears travelled down Joanne's cheeks.

'Come on, love, you're doing really well. It won't be long now, I'm sure,' the nurse consoled her. 'Is there anyone we can ring to come and be with you?' she asked, patting her hand and stroking her brow.

'No…I'll get through this on my own,' Joanne insisted. Then the next wave of pain came and the midwife helped her work through it until it subsided. Through a haze of tears, Joanne saw the silhouette of a man approaching her bed. She wiped her eyes on her sleeve. It was David!

He snaked his arm around her shoulder and held her. She was too tired, too miserable and too full of self-pity to dismiss him. Instead, she clung to him and sobbed uncontrollably into his shoulder as he held her. 'Did you honestly think I'd let you go through all this on your own, you silly girl? Whether you like it or not, I'm here for the duration.'

She was grateful for his comfort and solace. 'How did you know I was here?'

'Your mum phoned. She's worried sick.'

Another contraction arrives and she wanted to push. 'AARRGGGG! For fuck's sake!' she seethed through clenched teeth. 'I can't take it any longer. I'm too tired, I can't do it, I can't.' She let out a pitiful cry.

David skilfully held the gas and air to her face and encouraged her to fill her lungs. 'You can do it… we can do it together. Take deep breaths.'

'I'm too weak now to push.' But the midwife gave her encouragement by telling her the head was starting to crown.

David wiped her brow with something cool and wet. 'Come on, Joanne, you're nearly there. Don't give up now,' he said, kissing her forehead.

Nurses and a doctor appeared from nowhere and David had a worried expression on his face. 'Right, Joanne.' The doctor levelled with her. 'It's all systems go, young lady. When the next pain arrives, I don't want you to push just yet!'

David squeezed her hand and told her to pant instead but she wanted to push. God, the pain! The doctor shouted at the top of his voice, 'RIGHT PUSH – PUSH – PUSH!' which she did with all her might for what seemed an eternity. But nothing seemed to be happening and she was sweating profusely.

Then, with one almighty push, the baby was out – a slippery, slimy little body covered in mucus, bawling its head off from the moment it entered the world.

'It's a girl,' David proclaimed tearfully.

'Yes, you have a little girl,' the midwife grinned. 'Congratulations!'

Everyone in the room was now smiling.

Joanne struggled to raise herself to watch a nurse wrap her baby in a shawl then lift her from the scales and place her in Joanne's arms.

'She's perfect! Hello, lovely girl, I'm your mummy.'

'Wha… wha… wha!' At least her lungs were healthy. Fingers, toes perfect too. She was so beautiful.

David touched her tiny hand. This poignant moment between all three continued as Joanne handed her over to him and he beamed from ear to ear. 'I love you both so much. You were amazing and so brave!'

The nurse proclaimed the baby was a whopping seven pounds six ounces. Much later she was wheeled into the ward and David rushed off to break the good news to everyone that they had another daughter. Lucy was her name, chosen some months back. 'Lucy Winston, it's got a nice ring to it,' David said.

The evening brought a whole host of visitors. David, Helen and Emily were the first to arrive. Emily was besotted the moment she set eyes on the baby.

Most evenings Joanne's bed was the noisiest and most crowded in the ward. Gill, Suzy, Jess, Oliver and even Abby and Jonathan drove up to see their new niece. Philip and Kristy sent a huge bouquet and sent their apologies. David made an appearance most evenings and acted like nothing had ever been amiss but when the visitors left and they were alone, emotions ran high at the realisation he was going back to Octavia … to his other life.

Joanne watched him as he held his daughter, the bond already apparent. The paediatrician had told her they could take Lucy home the following day. Joanna couldn't wait to get back to her own familiar surroundings.

She was just enjoying her last few moments before they took Lucy to the nursery for the night. How strange it was going to be – just her, Emily, and Lucy.

Chapter 25

David peered round the maternity ward door at ten o'clock the following morning, armed with a baby carrier and a huge grin on his face.

Lucy was dressed in a sleep suit and was still fast asleep in her cot. Joanne beckoned to him and asked him to sit with Lucy whilst she slipped into her dress. He pulled a face at first then put aside his paranoia of being alone with all these new mums as she slipped off to get ready.

It was pensioners' day and the salon was packed when David's car drew onto the hard standing. Chris, Sally and Lily rushed out the instant they saw his car and teetered on the edge of tears as David lifted the baby seat out. It took him and Joanne a good ten minutes to make their way through the salon – everyone wanted to congratulate them and get a first peep at Lucy!

Helen embraced her daughter as she reached the top of the stairs. 'Well done you!' she said. 'Now let me get a look at my new granddaughter.' She grinned and followed David into the lounge.

David's face lit up as he lifted his floppy little bundle from her baby seat and handed her to Helen. She was overwhelmed as she held Lucy. 'Oh Joanne, she's wonderful!'

Joanne agreed wholeheartedly as she wriggled out of her coat and lowered herself gingerly onto the settee. It felt strange being home and now she felt tired through lack of sleep; hospital beds weren't the comfiest.

Chris came in with three mugs of tea on a tray, grinning like a Cheshire cat as she placed them on the coffee table, then rushed over to give Joanne a bear hug. She pleaded with Helen to pass Lucy to her, then proceeded to speak in a different language to everyone else in the room. 'Goochy-goochy-goochy, aren't we woob-aly!'

Joanne noticed David had disappeared, so she went to the window to check if his car was still there – but it was gone! Gone back to his other life already, she thought sadly … he never even said goodbye.

Lily and Sally rushed in like two excited chipmunks once Chris went back down to the shop and began to coo and fuss over Lucy, using the same dialogue Chris had used.

David suddenly re-appeared at the door, brandishing an enormous bouquet tied up with a bow and a card that read, 'You were amazingly brave. Always yours, David xxx'.

She took the flowers from him, held his gaze then smiled. 'Thank you…They're beautiful.'

Lucy let out a piercing shriek! Everyone panicked and disappeared from the room, thinking Joanne was going bare her left breast in readiness.

'I have to go.' David smiled, getting up from his chair. 'But I'll pick Emily up from school and bring her home.' She detected some anxiety in his voice and noticed his face had paled. She wondered if Octavia was playing up now because of Lucy.

Emily laughed with delight when she walked in and saw her new sister lying in the wicker crib, kicking her legs and making mewing noises. There was roughly seven years between the two girls, so Emily saw Lucy as a real live doll: someone to play with, dress up, kiss and show off to all her friends.

The days rapidly merged into weeks and were a blur of feeding, burping, changing nappies, loading the washing machine then trying to catch up on sleep. It was touching how many people actually cared and wanted to help.

Lucy turned out to be an incredibly placid baby – a blessing, as most days Joanne ended up with brain fog. 'Quite normal for a new mum,' she was told but she'd always been that way first thing in the morning.

She was still struggling with the fact that her heart beat so much faster when David was in the room; his cologne, the way he made her laugh, his doleful eyes, even the tearful moments they shared together over the girls, moved her.

Some nights they even shared a glass of wine with a bowl of pasta or a Chinese he'd brought in when the girls were asleep. And there were times she found herself stroking the empty space in the bed where his body used to be.

The worst times were when David went off on a business trip and Joanne knew full well that Octavia would be with him, all teeth and tan. They probably made love in a four-poster bed, which left Joanne with a feeling of desolation.

She'd promised herself she wouldn't erupt when resentment began to gather because their lives were sailing along pretty smoothly since Lucy's arrival. Even Emily seemed contented with the situation as it was.

Gill invited her to dinner one night; a few of the old crowd had been invited too. 'You really need to think about getting back on the dating circuit again, Joanne,' Gill said flippantly over the dinner table.

'Oh, I don't know about that!' Joanne felt herself go red as all eyes were now on her.

'Of course you do,' Brian joined in. 'You're an attractive woman. I know a couple of guys I can set you up with, if you like.'

'Ooooh no,' she exhaled, envisaging some geek with glasses and no sense of humour. 'I'm happy on my own, thanks Brian.' The words gushed out defiantly.

Still feeling a little tipsy from the wine when she arrived home, her thoughts began to gather. Just say she did decide to start dating again, what kind of man would she be attracted to, she wondered? Pot-bellied men with grim faces perhaps? She remembered Joe– blue-eyed, full-lipped Jo – the one whose words had made her heart beat faster.

She started to make mental notes of the credentials her applicants would have to have:

Someone with whom she could share warmth and laughter.
Someone who wasn't afraid of showing his emotions.
Someone who would love her children.
Someone who was protective and spontaneous.
Someone she could trust.
Someone who would pleasure her in bed and be open to exploring each other's needs.
Someone not afraid to talk openly about how he felt.
Definitely someone who could dance.

But she already knew someone like that and sadly he no longer loved her. That person loved and shared his life with someone else instead. She dismissed her rancid thoughts as she heard Lucy stir, she threw on her robe and scurried along the landing to give her a comforting cuddle.

***

Abby always kept her updated with family gossip but not a word was muttered about David and Octavia, even when Joanne asked. Abby said she didn't know much herself, other than they'd been seen together at a party a few weeks back.

Joanne tried to suppress her feelings for David; it was all too hurtful, though, seeing him with the girls and not being able to touch, kiss or hold him!

Spring, then summer, brought new challenges and fresh hope. Doing only two days in the salon enabled her to take long walks with the pram in the park. She even thought about going down to Abby and Jonathan's with the girls for a short spell. Goodness knows, they'd asked her often enough.

Jess and Oliver dropped a few subtle hints about the christening. 'What could be more decadent than a marquee in the garden in the summer months?' Jess said over the phone.

The idea of Jess organising yet another lavish do summoned up images of having to face the family's gossipmongers again. Joanne really didn't relish those thoughts. She mentioned her reservations to David and he agreed there was no rush to get Lucy christened. 'I'll have a word …don't let it worry you.'

But Joanne did worry; she knew Jess would see it as her being difficult about the Catholic thing again, and began an exhaustive search for reasons to assure her it wasn't that at all.

David she'd noticed had been quite tense the last couple of visits and Joanne wondered if things were not going well in the love nest. Then one night, as they both shared a glass of wine when the girls were asleep, he asked if she'd like to go out for dinner sometime. 'A night out might do you good. Plus there's something important I need to discuss with you; kill two birds with one stone.' His tone was slightly abrasive.

What was so important that he couldn't share it with her there and then? She felt anxious; he must want a divorce. Was Octavia pregnant, was he getting married to the witch? Did he now need his freedom... that must be it.

'Yes, dinner would be lovely,' she said with forced brightness but she felt miserable about going.

David made the reservation at the restaurant they used to frequent when they first married, West Towers, a stone's throw from his parents' house.

Joanne treated herself to a new dress, seeing she'd now trimmed herself down to a size ten. Chris cut her hair and gave her roots some colour. If David was getting married to Octavia, this would probably be the last chance she'd have of showing him exactly what he was throwing away. She had to look her best.

Joanne arranged for Helen to stay the night with the girls and gave her the number of the restaurant should she need it. 'Don't be silly,' Helen said. 'I look after the girls most days! What can go wrong?'

But Joanne felt anxious; her stomach felt like it was crammed with giant moths as she put the final touches to her makeup. At least she was thrilled with the way her pale blue dress looked.

It felt like a first date but with someone she cared for profoundly. At some point during the night though, he'd tell her he and Octavia were getting married. What would she do when that happened?

Her heart skipped a beat when he arrived earlier than planned, explaining he wanted to spend time with his girls before they went out. She made him a cup of tea and sat beside him in the lounge as he cradled Lucy and listened to Emilys chatter.

He wore an open-neck shirt with turned-back cuffs and a cashmere jumper loosely placed over his shoulder. His hair was slightly longer than normal, but it suited him; the sun's rays through the window caught the flecks of grey that were now there.

'You look lovely,' he said, his voice soft.

'Thanks,' she grinned back.

It was a warm night and Joanne's hair wafted slightly in the breeze from the open car window as they sped along. David's mood seemed to have lifted greatly from the last few weeks and he was more or less back to his old self as they both engaged in cheerful banter.

Michael, the restaurant owner, greeted them as they walked through the entrance of West Towers. It had been a while since they were last there. Michael guided them to their table overlooking the lake. It had always been a favourite table in the early days and he must have remembered.

A cork was popped on a bottle of Crystal, which David had pre-ordered when he made the reservation. 'Cheers,' he said, lifting his glass.

Joanne looked slightly puzzled but went along with it all. What were they toasting exactly, she wondered? His pending marriage or the closure of theirs? She wasn't quite sure.

'Your hair looks nice,' David said, as he took some bread from the basket that was placed on the table by a waiter.

'Chris did it this afternoon. It's nice being a client for a change.'

Over dinner they chatted about family, work and the girls, then David mentioned that Abby and Jonathan would be coming up in the next couple of weeks. 'Be nice to have dinner with them, if you feel like it.'

'That would be nice,' she replied wistfully. Again she puzzled where this was all leading. The night seemed a little bizarre; it was like layers of time had been stripped away to before it all started to go so horribly wrong.

'Don't leave it this long again before coming back,' Michael said warmly when David paid the bill.

'We won't,' he promised.

There was renewed enthusiasm inside Joanne now; nothing had been mentioned about him and the witch getting spliced…Perhaps he'd just felt she needed a cheerful night out after all!

Spirits ran high on the drive home as the music from the stereo filled the car.

'Do you mind if we stop off somewhere first before I take you home? I've got to drop some papers off at a client's house. He needs some pricing for a meeting tomorrow first thing– it'll only take a mo!'

'Sure… but…' Joanne eyed her watch. 'It's gone eleven. Isn't it a bit late to call in on someone?'

'It's OK. He knows I'm coming.'

The car came to a halt outside a large house in an affluent part of Southport. She sat up in her seat, trying to see what the house was like, but the six-foot brick wall surrounding it obscured her view. 'Come in with me,' David beckoned as he climbed from the car and lifted his briefcase from the back seat. 'You want to see the house, don't you? Plus, I'd like you to meet him.'

Joanne didn't need asking twice. 'Who is it we're going to see?' she asked.

'His name's Phil,' David said, lifting the latch on the arched oak-studded gate. The security lights flooded the garden as they entered, and the view that met her eyes totally enchanted her.

It was a Tudor-style house, surrounded on all sides by manicured lawns and well-established gardens. They strolled up the path, leading to the arched double doors. The house was quite lovely, with its leaded windows and black-and-cream Tudor-beamed front.

David rang the bell and waited but no one seemed to be answering, so he peered through one of the windows. Joanne grew more curious by the minute. 'He must have gone out,' David said impatiently, looking at his watch. He tilted a terracotta plant pot under which was the key to the front door.

'David, you can't do that,' she whispered sharply.

'Yes I can,' he whispered, mocking her. 'He needs these papers ASAP and he already told me if he wasn't here to let myself in and leave them on the kitchen table. Want a butcher's while we're here?'

'No,' she replied, horrified by the ramifications of what would happen if they were found wandering round the house.

'It's OK, he won't mind.' David grabbed Joanne's hand and guided her through the front door into a stylish oak-panelled, galleried hallway, where an impressively large brass chandelier hung from the ceiling. A deep-pile royal-blue carpet ran through the hall and up the barley-twist oak staircase to the upper floor. Joanne's eyes darted everywhere as they walked in.

David began the guided tour of the high-ceilinged, oak-floored rooms on the ground floor, and Joanne passed mutely through each room, surprised at how sparsely furnished it was for such an outstanding house.

David told her they'd only just recently moved in, so the rest of their furniture still hadn't arrived. He shepherded her around all five bedrooms, three bathrooms, a dressing room and an en suite. Joanne's silence continued until at last he led her into a spacious limed-oak kitchen, where every modern appliance she'd ever dreamt of had been fitted. 'Oh my God, David, it's to die for,' she said, excited by it all. 'Who is it that lives here? Do I know them?'

'Yes, better than you think. This house actually belongs to me!'

She looked stunned. 'Your house? Don't you mean yours and Octavia's?' She felt her temper flare.

'No, this really is *my* house. There is no Octavia. There hasn't been for a long time.'

Joanne lowered herself onto the kitchen chair and her words fizzled into silence.

'You were right about Octavia. She was everything you said she was: selfish, an egotistical maniac, a money grabber, bone idle. I must have been out of my mind to have fallen under her spell in the first place when I had someone like you who loved me and was loyal! I'm disgusted with myself for such appalling behaviour. I can't understand what drove me to it. Can you ever forgive me?

'When I told Octavia you were pregnant she lost the plot completely, said you'd done it on purpose to win me back. At the time the thought had crossed my mind, but I knew by the look on your face when you told me that you were as shocked as I was by the news. Then there was a succession of blazing rows when Octavia realised just how much the children would disrupt our lives. I suppose she also sensed that I still love you.

'I told her to leave. Then seeing the family would have nothing to do with her, Philip and Kristy took her in. Kristy got her a job at the health spa where she worked, but that didn't work out, so she took herself off to Barbados and moved in with her parents, hence the phone call on Christmas day. Apparently she got extremely drunk and wanted to cause mayhem between you and me. That's what all that was about. I couldn't let her undo all the hard work I'd put in trying to regain your trust so I asked Kristy to say I was at the golf club when she rang her, otherwise I knew she'd ring you and then you'd realize we no longer lived together.

'Unfortunately, you overheard only part of the conversation and took it totally the wrong way and froze me out of your life completely. I can't blame you … but I still didn't give up on you. I just had to let you see the real me again!'

Joanne blinked in amazement. 'But Abby mentioned you were seen at a party together only a short while ago.'

'Ah, that would be Gerard Dunn's party – and we weren't together. He'd invited her purely because he fancies her. When I arrived at his house she was already there and I left instantly,' he said with raised eyebrows. 'She was staying with Kristy and Philip at the time, so she must have complained to them that I'd been at the party and probably embellished the truth a bit. Kristy must have relayed this to Abby.

'Your mum had me sussed long before Christmas and invited me round for a chat. I must admit she was pretty decent about the whole thing. When I explained what I was trying to do, she said she'd box my ears if I hurt you again.' They both laughed. 'Then she helped me choose your bracelet as she recalled what the old one looked like far better than I did. When you went into labour, she rang me straight away.'

'The sly old dog!' Joanne said incredulously.

'I saw how embarrassed you were when you waddled round the place and I wanted to tell you how beautiful you looked. I longed to spoon into you in bed, like we did when you were expecting Emily.'

'Who else knows about all this?' Joanne enquired.

'Just the immediate family – but they were all sworn to secrecy. The only one I wasn't sure about was Abby. I knew you were both as thick as thieves, but I promised her I was doing all this to regain your confidence in me. I needed her to stay impartial for as long as it took to regain your trust. Whilst you still imagined Octavia was on the scene, you would think I was trying to bed you for the children's sake. Then I saw this house. I couldn't believe it – it's a house just like the one you and I always dreamt about. Do you remember the one on the chocolate-box lid?' he said, trying to jog her memory.

'Oh yes,' she beamed.

'The owner of it *was* a guy called Phil, so I wasn't lying. He was emigrating and wanted a quick sale. I snapped it up because I thought of you and the girls in the huge garden and how you'd all love living here. It was a pretty tense time when it was all going through, but your mum adored it.'

'Mum's been here?'

'Yes, I wanted to see what she thought of it before I signed on the dotted line. She loved it and said you would too.'

'So she knows I'm here now.'

''Fraid so. I've never stopped loving you, not for a single second. And I'm frightened to ask a third time. Is there a chance we can start again, Jo? I promise I won't let you down ever again.'

She looked at him. He'd betrayed her trust once; was he capable of doing it again, she wondered. Her life was in the balance as she tried to digest everything in her head. Then she noticed a bottle of Bollinger sitting in an ice bucket with two champagne flutes on the worktop, and her eyes widened. 'Is the champagne for us?'

'It is …but only if the answer's yes!'

'Then you'd better crack it open, hadn't you? I don't think you'll be using the car again tonight. I'm sure Mum can cope until the morning. There are enough bottles made up in the fridge.'

'Shall I be the one to a ring and tell her?' he asked, with an enormous smile.

'I think she already knows I won't be back tonight,' Joanne said, drawing him to her.

You never really know
how strong you are
until being strong
is your only choice.

Printed in Great Britain
by Amazon